I0778138

KEEPING THE COUNTESS

DAMSELS IN DISGUISE

LILLE MOORE

Copyright © 2025 by Lille Moore

All rights reserved.

No part of this publication may be reproduced, distributed, or transmitted in any form or by any means, including photocopying, recording, or other electronic or mechanical methods, without the prior written permission of the publisher, except as permitted by U.S. copyright law. For permission requests, contact Wildflower Press, 2232 Dell Range Blvd, Suite 242 #5182, Cheyenne, WY 82009.

The story, all names, characters, and incidents portrayed in this production are fictitious. No identification with actual persons (living or deceased), places, buildings, and products is intended or should be inferred.

Any use of this publication to "train" generative artificial intelligence (AI) technologies to generate text is expressly prohibited. The author reserves all rights to license uses of this work for generative AI training and development of machine learning language models.

ISBN: 978-1-968031-00-8

Cover Design by Dar Albert

www.lillemoore.com.

Sign up for Lille Moore's newsletter

CONTENTS

Chapter One 1

Chapter Two 11

Chapter Three 16

Chapter Four 22

Chapter Five 27

Chapter Six 33

Chapter Seven 40

Chapter Eight 50

Chapter Nine 59

Chapter Ten 65

Chapter Eleven 72

Chapter Twelve 89

Chapter Thirteen 98

Chapter Fourteen 111

Chapter Fifteen 119

Chapter Sixteen 131

Chapter Seventeen 144

Chapter Eighteen 160

Chapter Nineteen   168

Chapter Twenty   181

Chapter Twenty-One   191

Chapter Twenty-Two   199

Chapter Twenty-Three   209

Chapter Twenty-Four   217

Chapter Twenty-Five   223

Chapter Twenty-Six   232

Chapter Twenty-Seven   244

Chapter Twenty-Eight   253

Chapter Twenty-Nine   262

Chapter Thirty   269

Author's Note   285

Acknowledgements   287

About the author   288

Runaway Rogue   289

For my spouse. This is all your fault.

Chapter One

Somewhere in Cumbria, 1878

It had not occurred to Reverend Jonah Sinclair that traveling in the dark on a rain-soaked country road might lead him to his death.

Rather an oversight on his part. His formative years in Southwark's alleyways had cultivated a healthy fear of the dangers that could greet him in the shadows. And presently, he was far from the relative safety of the known unknowns of South London.

Eleven hours of travel—nine by train, two by stifling coach, all amidst a downpour—had landed him in a place deserted by human civilization.

Somewhere in the rain and the dark and mists surrounding him was the Earl of Rochford's estate, and his assignment for the next month. It had been no small feat to position himself for it. His hopes and expectations of what lay ahead were unfairly high.

First, he had to find the bloody place. An endeavor that would have been simple if the aristocrats who had engaged his services had remembered to send their carriage.

With his temper flaring, he trudged his way up the hill from the coaching stop to the lone public house in the village, identifiable by a withering wooden sign bearing the name *The Saltcoat.* As he strode inside, he avoided thinking about the damage the mud was inflicting upon his best suit.

Mustering the swagger that had helped him survive a host of awkward circumstances, Jonah walked past the sparse collection of patrons cataloguing his every movement and approached the narrow wooden bar.

"Good evening," he began.

No one acknowledged the sound of his voice.

His simmering ire prevented him from softening his accent and his posture. "Would any of you be kind enough to point me in the direction of Ravenglass Hall?"

The men standing by him, along with the barman and barmaid, all turned away in an eerily synchronous movement. As cold dismissals went, it was one of the frostiest he could recollect. But he'd grown accustomed to setbacks and fending for himself. Twenty years ago, he'd been robbed of everything he loved. Two things had powered his survival: the determination to right the injustices served upon his family, and a healthy anger.

Harnessing the second in service of the first, Jonah marched out of the tavern, his vexation blinding him to any semblance of the direction where he headed. It did not take long to realize he was absolutely stranded, alone in a country wilderness.

In the disorienting shadows of the soaking evening, a seed of regret at his impulsivity sprouted. As he contemplated swallowing his pride and turning back to the tavern, a preternatural cry sounded on the moor.

The ground shook, heralding a beast rising out of the fog.

Jonah wouldn't have dared called the creature a horse; that was far too earthly a comparison. It sped toward him as if it had escaped straight from the ninth circle of hell.

Unholy thoughts clouded his brain. Unholier curses tumbled from his lips. He was pleased to discover the passage of time and years of service in Her Majesty's Church had not scrubbed them from his memory.

The shriek of the wind rose over the roar of approaching hooves. This was the exact reason Jonah avoided Gothic novels like vermin; he preferred interacting with the supernatural in the controlled boundaries of the King James Bible.

Through the sheets of rain, he spotted a slight figure mounted on top of the enormous steed. Was the rider attempting to bring the monster under control? Or did he urge it on, hoping he might flatten a weary traveler to the ground?

A shrill cry sounded from the rider. Was it a warning? An apology? A prayer?

"MOVE OUT OF THE BLEEDING WAY, YOU DAFT FOOL!"

With a screeching whinny, the beast reared up before him, a black wall of menacing horseflesh. As lightning flashed around them, Jonah braced his arms over his head and curled himself into a protective crouch, precisely as the hell-beast tossed its rider from the saddle.

A moment of raw stillness followed.

The rain relented, revealing where the rider lay motionless on the path.

Jonah staggered across the short distance toward the body. With a deep breath and a short prayer, he kneeled down to examine the fallen man.

The crash of two thick skulls meeting each other upended his balance. He slipped on the drenched ground, falling on top of the rider, who protested wildly by snarling in a manner more feral than a quayside cat. The body entwined with his was as scrappy and slim as one. He had to be a young lad.

"Get off of me!"

"I'm trying!" Jonah protested as they tussled in the mud. Muck worked its way beneath the collar he'd starched himself, to make a good impression for the toffs who'd forgotten him. The potential embarrassment he'd face if he ever arrived at his destination burned energy into his limbs.

An instinct he thought he'd long retired kicked in and he rolled, quickly pinning the rider's shoulders by pressing his own weight into the lad's chest.

And therein, he discovered a very distinct set of curves that most decidedly did not belong to a young man.

The body beneath him hissed.

Jonah scrambled away and staggered to his feet. With his last remaining ounce of sense, he extended his hand to the rider.

The *woman* he'd just groped in the darkness.

"My humblest apologies. Are you hurt?"

Ignoring his attempt at civility, she rose without touching him and hastily pulled her drenched scarf closer to her face. In the darkness, he couldn't distinguish any of her features, only a dark spark somewhere in the vicinity of her eyes. An alluring scent of citrus permeated the space between them.

"You are lucky to be alive, you absolute lob."

Her voice was gruff and a little breathless, but the insult didn't sting him. He'd been called much worse.

"My sincere apologies. As you may have deciphered, I'm spectacularly lost," Jonah confessed, hoping the rider might appreciate such honesty.

Her corresponding silence implied she did not.

With a swish of a cape, she swirled past him and gathered the horse's reins. At the soothing brush of its master's hand, the stallion quieted.

Jonah debated offering to help her mount, but by the time he untied his tongue, she was already swinging up into the saddle. Once seated, she paused as if she was evaluating him. Intensely. Impossible to tell in the dim light, but he sensed, rather than saw, she was quietly fuming.

He had a somewhat unhinged notion to ask her to take him with her wherever she was headed, so that neither of them would have to face the night alone.

"I regret any…inconvenience I may have caused you," he said roughly. "If you'd be kind enough to help me get my bearings, I will trouble you no longer."

A lifetime passed before she replied, "Where do you wish to go?"

"Ravenglass Hall. Do you know it?"

"Yes."

"There was supposed to be a carriage to meet the coach," he explained. "But it seems there was a misunderstanding with the directions I received from the estate steward."

"What business have you with him?"

Cheeky of her to be so demanding of his private matters when she clearly had her own secrets to hide. He could not judge her for it. There were too many reasons why a woman might be dressed in such clothes and traveling in such haste by herself on a miserable night.

She was not the mystery he needed to solve. His own mission would fail if he remained stranded in the dark, in the middle of nowhere, lost and sopping and, now that he thought of it, starving.

"I'm Reverend Jonah Sinclair. The Bishop of London has sent me to tutor the Earl of Rochford's ward."

He couldn't determine if the snort came from the horse or its rider, or if it was merely the gusts rising again as the rain pounded.

A hazy limb extended toward the village. "Return to the Saltcoat and follow the post road east for another mile."

Glancing at the direction she pointed toward, he loosened a sigh of relief before turning back to thank her.

But she'd already vanished into the darkened lane.

Faith stole through the narrow foyer that skirted the kitchen and crept up the servants' stairs, only giving half a thought to the muddy footprints she left in her wake.

It was mildly ridiculous to keep up the pretense of sneaking around corners. There were hardly any servants left in residence at Ravenglass Hall, and the risk of someone catching sight of her was marginal.

Still, old habits were difficult to break, especially when they were rooted in older, ever-present fears. She'd never traversed these halls without a shiver creeping down the back of her neck. That was the reason her knees shook, and her breathing remained uneasy.

It had nothing to do with being thrown from her horse on a darkened road. Or the minutes she'd spent pinned beneath Reverend Jonah Sinclair.

A stranger. Bound for Ravenglass.

And she'd known nothing about it.

Faith couldn't afford to be overtaken by panic. Panic made her careless and clumsy, and she had far too much to do to allow it to commandeer her sense.

She padded down the dark corridor and slipped inside the room at the end of the hall.

"What the blazes happened ta you?"

Faith did herself the honor of not jumping out of her skin. Stiffening her spine, she replied with pointed diction, "My lady."

At the responding harrumph, Faith turned with such force, it solicited a small gust of wind.

"What the blazes happened to you, *my lady*," she continued, "is the proper way to phrase your question, Mrs. Lawless. Otherwise, one might accuse you of impertinence."

The older woman folded her arms and quirked a questioning eyebrow in the general direction of Faith's wet trousers and mud-soaked cape. "I see your mouth wasn't injured in the calamity."

"I see you continue to struggle with the boundaries of your position." Faith's tone was colder than her shuddering limbs. "No housekeeper would dare speak to her mistress that way."

"And here I was, thinkin' we'd dispensed with formality, after all deese years. With everything we've been through together."

Faith kept her expression blank, refusing to acknowledge Lawless's claim, despite the fact that it was true. Years ago, they'd made an unholy pact to keep each other's confidence. Neither of them could betray the other without inflicting harm upon themself.

They were stuck together.

"There will be no more lapses in decorum." Faith fought to keep her tone harsh, her words abrupt. She hated when women talked down to other women, as if she were trying to assume a man's privilege. There was a special circle in hell for betraying one's own sex in such a manner.

But Lawless had asked for it.

"Indeed," Faith stripped off her filthy cloak, shoving it at the housekeeper, "we must adhere to the very strictest conventions of good society. Now that you've invited a stranger into this house."

Lawless blinked. "A stranger, my lady?"

"Do not patronize me. And do not withhold a single detail in your explanation as to why the Reverend Jonah Sinclair believes that the Earl of Rochford has engaged him to tutor his young ward! Sinclair was kind enough to mention it this evening, shortly after he bewitched my horse into throwing me onto the post road."

"Dat explains the assault ta your wardrobe." Lawless sighed. "He wasn't supposed ta arrive until Thursday."

"Today is Thursday!"

"Are you sure?"

Faith hurled her shirt onto the floor. "A ruddy priest, Lawless! What in the world were you thinking?"

"May I remind you of your orders?" Lawless thrust her nose in the air. "'We must do whatever we can to secure Master Adam's education.'"

The crone had pitched her voice a higher octave for emphasis.

"There's plenty of time to prepare Adam for school," Faith countered. "He's only just turned ten and the one in the village—"

"We can't afford ta put it off, my lady."

The fierce look in Lawless' dark eyes made Faith's chilled bones freeze.

Reaching into her apron, Lawless retrieved a rumpled letter and handed it to her mistress. The note carried the seal of Crockfeathers Gentleman's Club. One of the most notorious gaming hells in London.

Notice of indebtedness for T. Doland in the sum of one thousand pounds.

"Good God," Faith murmured.

"Don't bring God in ta this. He's got no influence over Troy Doland. Dat man only takes from the devil."

Faith couldn't decipher if Lawless was referring to Lucifer himself, or his lordship Geoffrey Trenton, the Earl of Rochford. "And he drew on Rochford's accounts for his stake, no doubt."

"The steward's privilege," the housekeeper rasped in a disturbingly accurate imitation of Doland.

The git had been syphoning the estate's coffers. He'd started off small: a few pounds skimmed from a tenant's rent; an extra sum padded to a withdrawal for machinery repairs. But rounding the seventh year of the earl's absence from Ravenglass, Doland had become brazen.

Faith had tried to limit the damage. She'd assumed the role of a steward's apprentice to intervene in the estate's management. But for every farthing she recovered, Doland stole a guinea.

A thousand-pound loss to Crockfeathers was more than a debt. It was a path to ruin.

Her ruin. And Adam's, if they didn't enroll him in school before the money ran out to pay his tuition. It was the only provision that his father, the prior earl, had made for his illegitimate son. And Faith was determined her nephew would receive every cent he was due.

She handed the threatening note back to the housekeeper. "As dire as this is, it doesn't explain why you wrote to the Bishop of London for a tutor."

"He has a vested interest in the estate's preservation."

Faith huffed an exasperated laugh. "And you're testing his patience with this stunt. Ravenglass doesn't belong to the Church." At least, not yet.

Her attention caught on her wedding portrait hanging above the fireplace. The sweet young woman with curling brown tresses and creamy skin, sitting devotedly next to her handsome husband, taunted her. Neither of them bared any resemblance now to the people caught on that canvas.

What a naïve twit she'd been, trusting Geoffrey Trenton's dashing figure and charming attentions. After her marriage, the small fortune her uncle had bequeathed to her became entwined with the Rochford estate. Now, it was as inseparable as she and her husband were meant to be.

And unless she provided the earl with an heir—which she had yet to do—upon her husband's death, the Rochford's estate would go to the Church. It was an odd directive that some pious ancestor in the previous century had maneuvered through Parliament. Perhaps he'd had a premonition that his descendants would disgrace the Trenton name.

"Askin' the bishop was a brilliant idea," Lawless argued. "He's got all dose little petals at his beck and call. Educated parsons beggin' ta be of service. And it only costs us room and board."

"Not here. We cannot risk—"

"We'll have ta," the housekeeper insisted. "Don't have the luxury of wastin' time." She pointed to the date on the bottom of the credit note.

Less than six weeks to find a way to pay Doland's gambling debts.

It would take drastic means to raise the sum, and they couldn't risk Doland dipping into the trust allocated for Adam's education. Lawless was right: they needed to settle Adam at school as soon as possible.

Faith shook her head. "This is an enormous bet."

"So we'll stack the deck." Lawless filled the bath with cans of hot water. "I've never met a curate who wasn't as moldable as putty."

"This one is decidedly unmalleable."

"You gleaned dat from your brief encounter with him on the dark road, did you?"

Faith turned away to hide the flare on her cheeks as she recalled how Sinclair had subdued her with the power of his body.

It hadn't been entirely unpleasant. As she replayed the moment in her mind, reliving the impact of his weight atop hers, she felt rather the opposite of unpleasant.

Baffling was what it was. Usually, a man's proximity roused her fear. But everything had transpired too fast for her to become frightened. He'd moved more adeptly than any clergyman she'd ever met, as his chest had crushed against her breasts.

No, not a petal. The man was a thorn.

"Sinclair is observant," Faith grumbled as she stripped off the last of her sopping clothes and submersed herself in the tub. The gorgeous sting of hot water against her skin made her hiss with satisfaction. "He will ask questions about the earl's absence."

"No different from what we're used ta."

"Except that you've invited him to stay here, and his intelligence is far above average. When he finds us out, financial ruin will be the least of our worries."

If anyone discovered what they'd done, they were headed for the gallows.

Lawless toppled another can of hot water into the tub and smiled menacingly when Faith yelped at the scalding temperature. "Well, den. Come up with an alternative."

"I will."

"You won't."

"Do not test me, Lawless." Faith raised her chin. "The man will depart before the evening is out."

Chapter Two

On his long, sodden walk, Jonah had plenty of time, and cognitive fodder, to form an expectation of Ravenglass Hall.

The reality was ghastlier than he'd imagined.

He almost missed the turn to the winding lane leading up to the estate. The path was overgrown, obscured with brambles and gorse. He couldn't fathom how a horse, let alone a carriage, could cut through it.

Squinting through the lashing rain, he prayed the bobbing lights in the distance belonged to a stone and mortar house, not some creation of his desperate mind.

Lord, he wished he'd had more time to prepare. The summons from the earl's steward had demanded his immediate departure to Cumbria, leaving no time to research the elusive Lord Rochford. Hopefully, Christopher would uncover something soon; his friend had promised to write him by the end of the week.

He pushed away a nagging skepticism about the reliability of the local postal service and plodded his way toward the front sweep leading to the house.

The mansion rose out of the shadows, medieval and brooding. A sexagenarian footman in tired-looking livery answered his knock and ushered him into a dim foyer. The servant didn't blink twice at Jonah's disheveled state.

He returned with an invitation for Jonah to follow him up the wide staircase and down a drafty corridor full of sharp twists. Eventually, the footman stopped and unceremoniously tossed a hand at an open set of doors.

Inside the darkened drawing room, a woman sat by the fire. Her modest dress and cap, and the spectacles perched on her high-bridged nose, hinted at middle age. Her light-brown skin and dark eyes suggested she might be of Arab or West Indies descent.

"My word."

The stare that she gave Jonah was pure authority, the kind one would expect from the Countess of Rochford.

"Forgive my intrusion, ma'am." He was appalled to discover he was slightly breathless. "I am Reverend Jonah Sinclair. Mr. Doland, the steward, is expecting me."

A beat passed before she replied, "Indeed."

"I must also apologize for my present state of disrepair." Jonah gestured to his filthy clothes. "No carriage was available to meet the post. The walk from the village was rather damp and muddy."

"I see."

That came out as crisp and hostile. Had he accused her of inhospitality?

He cleared his throat. "If you would kindly direct me to Mr. Doland—"

"I cannot. He is away on estate business."

"There must be a misunderstanding." He made a valiant attempt at patience. "Perhaps you may help me clarify this perplexing situation, my lady."

"I beg your pardon." The woman's voice transformed, adopting a distinctive lilt. "You weren't mistakin' me for her ladyship, now, were you?"

"Forgive me." Just how many times could a man apologize in one conversation? "It has been a long, confusing day. You have me at a disadvantage."

"Mrs. Lawless, housekeeper." She gave him a wicked grin as she rose from her seat with a faint grunt. "You'd best follow me, Mr. Sinclair."

Lawless did not put him out of his misery by escorting him to a chamber with a hot bath and somewhere to hang his sodden clothes.

Instead, she steered him into another suite of rooms, and in a booming voice bellowed, "Master Adam!"

A young nurse ducked out of the bedroom. She blushed as she bobbed a curtsy to Sinclair, her eyes widening at the dirt stuck to his collar.

"Mrs. Lawless. I told Master Adam that Mr. Sinclair has come to be his new tutor. He went all quiet-like, as he does, and…" She nodded toward the wardrobe at the end of the room.

"That's all right, Peggy." Lawless gave Jonah a wry look and shouted, "Not hidin' from strangers, are you, Master Adam?"

A faint rustling sounded from the wardrobe.

"Now, boysie, come out and greet Mr. Sinclair." The housekeeper sniffed. "Even if he's covered in muck."

The wardrobe door creaked. "What kind of muck?"

"Lord if I know. You should see the state of him." Lawless let loose the kind of low whistle Jonah had only heard at the docks. "He's absolutely filthy."

"She speaks the truth, Master Adam," Jonah chimed in, hoping to draw Adam out. "I am completely unpresentable."

Curiosity overcame the boy's fear, and, needing to inspect Jonah's dishevelment for himself, Adam darted out of the wardrobe and halted a few feet before them. He studied his new tutor with the same silent scrutiny as the rider on the road. Jonah wondered if it was a Cumbrian custom.

When Adam sighed, as if in disappointment that there was much less muck than promised, Jonah imagined that the boy would have folded his arms across his chest to underscore the sentiment. Had he not been missing the lower half of his left arm.

He could feel Lawless's eyes on him, expecting him to react with visible horror or disgust. Perhaps if he'd led a different life, the sight of a missing limb on a child would have horrified him. But he'd grown up with children like Adam. He'd known a few who had lost the use of more than one limb.

"Sand and gravel," Adam pronounced, gesturing to a clump on Jonah's shoulder. "With a bit of red clay, I should think. Although it's hard to tell until it's dried out."

"Very keen assessment," Jonah agreed. "Would you like to take a sample, and we can mark your observations tomorrow?"

With as much gentleness as he could collect in his bedraggled state, Jonah slowly crouched down to the boy's level. "Take your time. You have my permission, Adam."

Glancing at the housekeeper and his nurse, the boy inched forward and grasped a clump from Jonah's shoulder. He pinched it between his thumb and forefinger and giggled. "It's sticky."

As Peggy fussed with a handkerchief to catch the mud, Jonah said, "I'm delighted to see you take in interest in the area's soil composition. Very important for a farming estate."

Adam squinted at him. "How did you get it in your ears?"

He couldn't confess it was due to a tussle. With a woman. Though he was tempted to bring up the question of a young man with a terrifying horse to see if there was a connection to the estate.

"Has the mud migrated that far? Perhaps I should excuse myself to attend to it."

"I daresay you should," Adam advised. "Before you meet Lady Rochford."

Lawless scowled. "Now Master Adam—"

"Is correct," Jonah interrupted, silently offering a prayer of thanks for the unfiltered mouths of children. "Her ladyship is expecting me."

Truthfully, he doubted the countess knew anything about Doland's plans for the boy. But he didn't trust the wily housekeeper to present him in the best possible light to her mistress.

And he needed the Countess of Rochford to form a high opinion of him. Otherwise, he'd have no chance at convincing her to betray her husband.

"Mrs. Lawless, if you could show me to my quarters, I must do as Master Adam has instructed," Jonah insisted.

"I'll let Lady Rochford know you're coming!" Adam raced out of the room before Lawless could stop him.

The housekeeper evaluated Jonah warily before she led him to a bedroom, where he found his trunk had proceeded him. He didn't have the mental strength to question how it had landed there.

"You'll be close to Master Adam here," Lawless said. "I don't need ta tell you he's a curious boy. Likes ta find his way in ta things. Peggy minds him, but he's your charge. Do not leave him on his own, especially by the river. It's crestin' with the spring runoff."

"I understand."

"Keep the boy away from the north wing, too. The third floor is under repair. And don't you go pokin' around there either, lest you bring the roof down on us," she added, before slamming the door.

The furnishings in his quarters had been worn out in the previous century, but the pitcher of steaming-hot water which sat on the rickety chest of drawers was a welcomed luxury. Peeling off his ruined suit and shirt, he seized the soap to begin the arduous task of de-mucking.

As he dipped the small bar in the hot water, the room was awash with a familiar aroma of oranges and lemons.

The very scent worn by the mysterious lady rider.

Chapter Three

The moment Sinclair entered the library, Faith realized she'd made a grave miscalculation.

Not from Lawless's grin when she'd announced him. (Though it was maniacal.)

Nor from the elegant nod he offered. (Thankfully, he hadn't extended his hand and expected her to shake it; he possessed some sense of propriety.)

Rather, from the space and attention the man commanded merely by walking into the room.

He was surprisingly well-attired. While simple, the cut of his black suit reflected the hand of an expert tailor, and his white collar was starched to perfection. But it was coals to Newcastle compared to his sheer physicality. Sinclair possessed a build of perfect proportions: broad shoulders, trim torso, fine legs.

And he carried himself with an authority that implied he was well aware of it.

She'd misjudged him on the dark road. Had she perceived him like this, she never would have offered to meet him in her private study. It was too close.

Too intimate.

Sinclair lifted his head and sharp blue eyes met hers. "Lady Rochford, upon my honor to make your acquaintance."

The assessing way he studied her, and the desk she took refuge behind, undermined the politeness of his greeting. If she wasn't careful, this attentive man would see right through her, and the deceptions she'd constructed.

"Would you like a refreshment, Mr. Sinclair?" She gestured to the miniature glasses next to the crystal decanter filled with amber liquid.

He acknowledged the offer with another polite tilt of his head and crossed the room, giving wide birth to the crackling fireplace. After offering her a glass, he raised his in salutation and sipped slowly, drawing her attention to his well-shaped mouth.

She had an appalling sense of what those full lips were capable of, beyond reciting the Lord's Prayer.

"Lady Rochford?"

Faith blinked. "You were saying?"

"Madeira. It's unusual to serve it as an apéritif."

"Heavens, I hope we haven't caused a scandal."

"Only if generosity is considered outside of the rules of good society." A charming grin spread across his face. "This is a very old Madeira, and you do any guest a great privilege in sharing it."

Pretty words. Delivered with an even prettier smile. She may have overestimated his intelligence if he believed such insipid overtures would lower her guard.

"Are you a connoisseur of spirits?" she asked. "I thought most members of the clergy frowned on imbibing."

"You'll find that I subscribe to more liberal views."

An understatement if ever she heard one. The man was overly familiar in his manner. She suspected his liberal views were the reason he wasn't ensconced in a parish of his own.

"Madeira is a favorite of mine," Sinclair added. "My father was a merchant, and it was his primary trade route."

"It must have disappointed him that your calling prevented you from following in his footsteps."

"Fortunately, he didn't live long enough for that particular disappointment. He died when I was young."

His tone was teasing, but the tightness in his eyes felt weighty to her.

"My sincere condolences," she murmured.

"Am I correct in understanding that you once called the island home?"

It never was home, she almost confessed, rattled that he was so well-informed. Had the bishop prepared him, or did he have other sources? Surely, the scandal sheets weren't still writing about her missing husband.

No, she'd wager he'd done his own research. Throughout their conversation, Sinclair had scrutinized the room as if he was compiling a mental inventory. But his focus was divided; his gaze kept sliding back to hers. Likely, because she'd inhaled a little too much Madeira, a little too fast, for it not to be scarring her cheeks with heat.

She couldn't recall the last time an attractive man had paid her such attention.

"It was a long time ago," she eventually responded to his question. "And very far from Cumbria. But so is London."

"The journeys are comparable," he replied with mock solemnity. "And I must get used to leaving London. My orders will take me to Manchester soon. Unless, of course, you find my services indispensable here."

He flashed another brilliant grin, which did nothing to assuage her flush. His presumption that such a flirtation might have an effect on her made her more self-conscious.

The man had to leave. Immediately.

"It is those services that we must discuss, Mr. Sinclair. I am afraid that your invitation to Ravenglass was, regrettably, under false pretenses."

"False pretenses," he echoed in a soft tone that was more than a little scary.

And Faith knew a great deal about soft scary.

She refused to let it discompose her. "Master Adam doesn't require a tutor. He is presently enrolled in school."

"Ah, yes, the one in the village." Sinclair nodded. "I'm sure it's a fine institution. But Master Adam is a special lad. He has a curious, bright mind. Combined with his physical disadvantages, he requires specialized instruction. The kind that, to date, has been sorely lacking in his education."

A few minutes with Adam and the arrogant peacock believed he knew what was best for her nephew's future.

She was going to enjoy tossing him out on his ear.

"And who gave you permission to make such an evaluation, Mr. Sinclair?" No amount of salt in the world could have melted the ice in her voice. "Who instructed you, sir, to interview Adam without his guardian present? Do you conceive that I have so little regard for his welfare that I'd permit him to converse with a strange man without my knowledge or consent?"

Sinclair's head drew back; she'd surprised him.

She relished the victory.

"It is quite a presumption to enter a house without invitation. But accosting a young child—"

"I beg your pardon," he bit out, seething at her accusation. "I would never do anything to endanger a child. I consider it part of my vocation to protect children like Adam."

"You know nothing about him."

"I know what it is to be forgotten." His sharp blue stare bore into her. "And what one must do to survive in spite of it."

How *dare* he.

Faith had withstood everything from cold snubs to scathing insults since she'd become the Countess of Rochford. But the insinuation that she'd neglected Adam's care—made by an interfering idiot—was not to be borne.

"'Do not judge, and you will not be judged.' That's somewhere in Matthew's gospel, isn't it, Reverend? How quick you are to assess us. One brief meeting, and you claim to understand Adam completely." She laughed blackly. "You must know how hard he fought during his first six weeks of life just to learn how to breathe."

That revelation stunned him into silence.

"And three years later, after his mother died," she went on. "You must recall that he wouldn't stop shouting, 'Mama! Mama! Where have you gone?'"

Sinclair had the decency to hold his tongue, but his cheeks colored with every poisonous word she threw at him.

Leaning forward over the desk, she rasped, "And of course you remember last year. When the boys in the village blackened his eye. He demanded we explain to him what a bastard was."

A log popped in the fireplace, and Sinclair recoiled. The crack in his otherwise unflappable countenance unnerved her. She paused to consider if the sparks in the grate or her ferocious declarations had made an impact.

It didn't matter. Nothing would deter her from playing the advantage.

"If there is one thing I can assure you, sir, it is that Adam never has, nor ever will be, forgotten. Not by me, nor any member of this household."

As she loomed over the desk, unleashing her tirade, Sinclair angled himself toward her. He stood close enough for her to detect the spray of freckles across his nose and forehead, which she might have found endearing, if his brow wasn't pulled so tight in judgment.

"Lady Rochford, if I have offended—"

"Considering the circumstances, it would be best if you departed tomorrow."

He straightened, commanding every inch of his full height. "I'm afraid that is not possible, ma'am. Not until I clear up the matter with Mr. Doland, since it was he who wrote to the bishop. At the instruction of Lord Rochford himself."

Bloody, meddlesome Lawless. No arguing with a forged missive written on behalf of the earl.

"Mr. Doland is away on the earl's business," Faith countered. "I don't know when he will return. It could be weeks."

"Perhaps, my lady, if you had a word with your husband, he could clarify his wishes about Master Adam."

There it was. The blow she'd been bracing herself for since she'd knocked heads with this man on the road.

Sinclair's real mission was to solve the mystery of her missing husband.

His bishop had a vested interest in learning the truth. Without an heir, the Church stood to inherit the Rochford estate. And Sinclair was exactly the sort of man who could persuade a vulnerable wife that it would be in everyone's best interest to proceed with the declaration of the earl's death.

But as he stood across from her, eyes blazing and chest pumping, Faith sensed that something beyond professional duty had drawn him to Ravenglass. His determination and impassioned speech implied a personal agenda for finding the earl.

Given the extent of her husband's crimes and the people he'd harmed, there was no telling what even a clergyman might do for retribution.

Faith could not allow such a threat under her roof. She had to find a way to convince Sinclair to leave, without intrigue or incident.

"Thank you for the suggestion, Sinclair, on how I should interact with my husband. You are most helpful," she clipped. "Tell me, are you this impertinent with your own parishioners? Or is this a new form of spiritual counseling that I'm unacquainted with?"

She didn't permit him a breath to respond, before adding, "I will write to Lord Rochford directly. Whether he deigns to respond is at his discretion.

Sitting down on the chair, she dismissed him with a wave of her hand. "That will be all."

CHAPTER FOUR

ANGER WAS NO FRAME of mind to deliver a Sunday service.

But as he stood by the altar of the village chapel, Jonah could not summon the solace required to lead a parish in prayer. Instead, he was consumed by a fury that had been on constant simmer since he'd arrived at Ravenglass Hall.

From the small pulpit in the freezing stone church, Jonah suppressed his inner turmoil and stared out at the congregation, which numbered seven: three female elders, their glowering sons, and a surprisingly adept organist. If he was being honest, he was shocked that anyone had turned up. When he'd inquired about Sunday services, he'd received blank stares and shrugs from the servants. Lawless had cackled.

The countess hadn't voiced an opinion. She'd avoided him completely after their confrontation in her study.

His cheeks burned at the memory of his own lack of restraint. He'd overplayed his hand during their too-brief interview and ended up alienating the one person who could lead him to Rochford.

This search for answers about his father was consuming him, impeding the very vows he'd made to prayer and service. He couldn't forget that divine intervention had led him here. Jonah had supervised the bishop's correspondence on the day the earl's missive had arrived. With shaking hands, he'd reached into his pocket and pulled out an old newspaper clipping about Lord Rochford's entanglement with an illegal import enterprise. It had shared the same address as a warehouse that had belonged to Jonah's father.

That business was long-since shuttered, but the newspaper clipping—which he'd received from a friend only weeks before—was the first promising lead on his father's death in years. One Jonah was compelled to follow. He'd convinced the bishop to send him to Ravenglass as a final assignment before his move to Manchester by promising a quick resolution to the matter. It left him with less than a month to investigate.

The possibility of failing, when he was so close to uncovering the truth, was intolerable.

Staring out at the small flock gathered in the church, Jonah battled an uncharacteristic sense of unease. He felt more out of place than when he'd arrived at Harrow School, an obvious charity case without a spare set of boots. The men in the congregation—bigger and burlier than they grew them in London—regarded him with a mix of suspicion and disdain that he'd done nothing to earn.

It took the better part of his self-control to rein in his temper. Rather than continue to fight it, he decided to channel his outrage with fire and brimstone.

A reminder of God's wrath usually spurred repentant hearts.

Turning to a passage in Isaiah, he drew a deep breath. "See, the Lord is going to lay waste to the earth and devastate it; he will ruin its face and scatter its inhabitants. The earth is defiled by its people; they have disobeyed the laws, violated the statutes and broken the everlasting covenant."

A pricking sensation at the back of his neck made him raise his eyes from the reading.

The countess stood in the church aisle, holding Adam's hand. A watery ring of light surrounded them, making her glow against the gray stones of the ancient chapel.

Her walking suit of burgundy wool wrapped her in an exquisite sort of armor. Simple silver embroidery highlighted the attractive fit of the bodice. A small postilion hat decked with only a slim ribbon brought attention to her glossy, dark hair and the elegant curve of her neck.

There was no trace of the lithe rider he'd held briefly in his arms. Or the haughty aristocrat he'd offended with his callous accusations.

Only a beautiful woman, who stunned him with a vulnerable look that penetrated his very soul.

Faith was caught in Sinclair's gaze like a rabbit in a snare. The first jolt of pleasure at the intensity of his full attention was soon eclipsed by an inordinate sense that she was intruding.

For all intents and purposes, she was. The old chapel was a place of sanctity. *His* place of sanctity, and he had every right to resent her invading it after the way she'd treated him.

In the aftermath of their interview, she'd hated herself more than a little for allowing her fear to dominate her decisions. And then Lawless had swooped in and pointed out the error in alienating the one person who could help secure Adam's future. Faith was so ashamed of her behavior, and so completely befuddled about how to rectify it, she'd hidden from him for days.

She'd buried herself in the estate's accounts, searching for a way to raise the funds she needed for the river repairs. Against her better judgment, she re-read an old letter she'd received from her uncle's man of business, referencing one of his investments that was excluded from her marriage contract. Faith's solicitor had cautioned her it could take years to find anything, and the assets could be worthless. But she'd written again, desperate for any hint of progress.

Then Peggy had reported that Adam had outgrown his new boots, and a blinding fear had seized Faith. If she didn't stop Doland from embezzling from the estate, soon there'd be no money to clothe the boy.

She had to get Adam settled in school as soon as possible, and she couldn't do it alone.

For her family to survive, she'd have to rely on help from Jonah Sinclair.

As she stood before him in the middle of the church, she felt like she was surrendering to an enemy. A trickle of perspiration gathered at the base of her spine as everyone was watching him watching her.

When was the last time she'd attended services? It had to have been years ago, before she'd taken up her disguise as the steward's apprentice. She was making up for lost time now, as she stood there, thunderstruck, like some helpless damsel.

She tried vainly to summon the gravitas to earn their respect.

All she could manage was to meet Sinclair's eyes and silently beg for mercy.

A tense silence followed.

Then, ever so slightly, he shifted his weight on the balls of his feet.

His expression remained carefully blank as he walked around the lectern, to the front of the pulpit.

"The Lord will punish the powers in the heavens above and the kings on the earth below." Sinclair resumed his oration, speaking the words from memory while he strode toward her, maintaining her gaze, which was equally assuring and disarming.

"The moon will be dismayed, the sun ashamed; for the Lord Almighty will reign on Mount Zion and in Jerusalem and before its elders—with great glory."

He paused before the small Rochford party. With a gentleness that belied the apocalyptic passage he recited, he clasped Faith's elbow and guided them to the family pew.

Thankfully, the organist struck up a hymn comprising of baroque trills, drawing the attention of the tiny group of worshippers away from where Faith had collapsed beside Adam and Peggy.

Bending her head over the Psalter, she fought to regain control of her breath. She'd had a plan; one that did not include allowing Sinclair's kindness and his touch to unravel her. She was a woman with an independent will and a firm control over her emotions and her senses.

There was no reason to fear the man. He was a parson, for God's sake. Not Don Juan.

As the service ended, Faith rose from the pew. She admired her own restraint as she waited for Sinclair. He attended to the altar items and his vestments in a swift and graceful dance around the pulpit that was nothing short of captivating.

She decided the open door might be a better place to cool the flush on her cheeks while he finished with his duties.

When she turned, she found Martin rushing toward her, winded, as if he'd run the entire way from Ravenglass.

"I'm sorry, milady," Martin rasped. "The master's phaeton's just passed. It's headed toward the house. I thought you'd want to know."

Faith froze. She had enough sense not to turn back to Sinclair, knowing that fear was plastered all over her face. For his own protection and hers, she'd let him think she was still his adversary while she marshaled her defenses.

"Quite right, Martin, thank you." She controlled the shake in her voice. "We must return to the house. Swiftly."

Doland had returned.

Chapter Five

Jonah was wrestling his way out of the frail white surplice, wincing as he popped a few delicate stitches in his haste to get it over his head, when the countess bolted.

Frantically, he threw aside his vestments and scrambled around the pulpit. He couldn't let her leave without speaking to her.

He sprinted down the aisle and staggered outside. On the road ahead, the Rochford coach sped away as if a pack of hellhounds hunted it.

Hard not to be offended that she hadn't bothered to wait half a minute. Especially after all that effort she'd gone through to attend the service.

After she'd slayed him with that *look*. That silent, desperate supplication hinted at the possibility she wanted him to stay. It had extinguished the fury that had been burning in his belly for days and replaced it with something equally intense: a craving for action.

No word had arrived from the earl, which made him question if the countess knew where to send Rochford any type of missive. A woman in close contact with her husband did not need to ride around disguised as a man, in the shadows of the evening.

That sort of woman—no matter how fiercely elegant—needed help.

So why wouldn't she accept his? Why flee before he had the chance to apologize?

"Afraid you missed them, sir."

The voice came from a circle of men standing in the shelter of the church eaves. Those who'd attended the service offered a nod or a tilt of their chin in recognition.

"Indeed," he replied to whoever had remarked on his employer's repudiation. "Perhaps I shall interpret the sudden departure as constructive criticism of my sermon."

That drew a smile from a man with salt-and-pepper hair. He removed his pipe and said, "It's been a while since we've had service here. No vicar, you know."

"None since the old dowager died," another added. "Been at least ten years, has it?"

"Fifteen."

Heads bobbed all around.

"The ladies usually go into Haynesford, to their church," one man said.

The market town was a ten-mile journey round-trip. Battling the spring rain and mud, the travel there and back could take most of the day. "That must interfere with household chores and other commitments," Jonah remarked.

The men gave a collective huff.

Now he was getting somewhere. The countess's slight had roused a semblance of sympathy from the villagers. They might talk to a man who they perceived was on their side.

They might even betray a few confidences about the earl.

Guilt pecked at him, as he acknowledged his thoughts had leapt to his obsession with the past, rather than what he might do to be of service to this small semblance of a parish. True, they were a prickly sort, but Jonah enjoyed standing with them beneath the shelter of the roof, listening to them talk.

The serenity of the moment broke when a man came tearing down the main road of the village. He ran at a fast clip, a feat given his advanced age and frail frame.

"Here now, Anders." Someone seized the man's arm. "What's the matter?"

"Carriage," the older man wheezed, whirling back on the group. "Was it his? Rochford's?"

There was an exchange of worried glances among the group before the man with the pipe replied, "Aye, 'twas his."

Anders's countenance transformed into something wolfish, and a monstrous growl erupted from his throat. "Then the earl is back."

Jonah's head whipped to the road, as if to assess that the accusation could be true, when he himself knew it was false.

Unless, during the service, Geoffrey Trenton had finally returned home after seven long years? It would explain the countess's abrupt exit. While his pulse sped at the prospect, Jonah doubted that Rochford's arrival had made her flee. Anders had to be mistaken.

When no one counteracted Anders's wild assumption, the old man growled before setting off in a frenzy down the wet road.

The men shouted and grumbled after him to stop, but no one could deter him.

"He's very distressed," Jonah said. "May I be of service? Perhaps I could relay a message to Lady Rochford."

His voice trailed off as the men's expressions darkened. The burliest of the bunch grunted and set off after Anders.

The others turned and headed back to the village without another glance at Jonah, the church, or the medieval manor rising in the distance.

Faith thanked the divine universe for the loyalty of her servants.

She'd done very little to earn such fidelity. Other than treating them with the humanity and dignity her aunt and uncle had instilled in her. And handsomely paying them to guard her secrets.

There was also the distinct possibility that they pitied her. She wouldn't allow herself to indulge in self-pity, so she supposed it was nice that someone felt that way.

When they returned from church, Peggy whisked Adam upstairs, and Faith marched into the dining room, where she found Lawless pouring a bottle of claret into a decanter.

"Martin saw the phaeton pass," Faith said without preamble.

The housekeeper's eyes darted to the hallway, and she gave Faith a tense nod.

Doland was back then. Earlier than they'd expected. The blackguard must have run out of money.

"Now 'oo do I gotta kill to get a drink around 'ere?"

A wheezing guffaw heralded Doland's arrival.

"Ladies." He ground out the word like an insult as he crossed into the room. Even after a decade at Ravenglass, the experience of sharing four walls with the man's menacing height and heft unnerved her.

His brow strained at the dim light from the window, and he gingerly passed a hand over the base of his skull.

Faith preferred when Doland showed up pleasantly inebriated, rather than brutally hungover. His present condition, combined with the added strain of travel, made him edgy and argumentative.

When his eyes clapped on the table and the decanter of wine, he seized it and poured himself a full glass. In one long gulp, he drained half the contents and sneered.

"Need to 'ave a word wiv that tosser of a wine merchant. This plonk is worfless."

Thanks to Lawless's machinations to water it down. They couldn't afford for him to drink the cellar dry.

The steward's poor opinion of the wine's quality didn't prevent him from refilling the glass before turning his attention to Faith. "What's all this I 'ear about some niminy-piminy parson come to tutor the li'il bastard?"

Usually, Doland's questions were of a rhetorical nature, and as a matter of practice, Faith pretended that the man and his inquiry did not exist.

He rumbled a phlegmy laugh. "I do enjoy your sulks, Lady Rochford. Reminds me of when you was a girl, puttin' on airs like Mrs. Brown, the Empress Mother 'erself."

His voice had grown thicker and slurred from the wine. "Back before you became an heiress. And a countess."

She didn't acknowledge his bullying. Nor did she need a reminder that besides ruining the estate, he also knew enough of her secrets to destroy her.

With a jeer, Doland refilled his glass and lumbered out of the room.

Faith and Lawless waited without moving for the space of several minutes, before either of them dared to move.

"I suppose we'll be doin' dinner," Lawless said.

"Do we have anything suitable?"

"There's a side of ham, some early vegetables, and a lemon tart."

When Faith raised a surprised brow, the housekeeper sniffed. "If you were goin' ta the trouble of attendin' Sunday service, thought we might as well have Sunday dinner."

"Complete with the parson?"

"Did you forget we need his help?"

For a very brief moment that morning, Faith had fooled herself into thinking she could depend on Sinclair. When she'd frozen in the church aisle, his steady and gentle response had surprised her.

Doland's arrival was a reminder that if she placed her trust in a man again, she could expect nothing less than betrayal.

"Oh, I nearly forgot," Lawless said. "The parcel from the modiste arrived. She found trim with dat Madeira lace."

It was a coded reference, in the event that Doland was listening in on their conversation. Faith's solicitor must have written with information on the Madeira interests.

"It's in your bedroom. Thought you should unpack it yourself." The house-keeper smirked. "Since it's full of unmentionables."

Chapter Six

Jonah's black mood darkened on his sopping walk back to Ravenglass.

Lady Rochford had not sent her carriage back to spare him from slogging through the terrible weather. The plausible reasons for this frustrated and alarmed him.

Could her husband truly have returned? The ancient Mr. Anders was convinced of it. And was prepared to wring the earl's neck, which was extreme. The earl's neglect of his estate likely had caused aggravation among his tenants. But their genuine fear and loathing of Rochford was something else altogether.

Upon his return to the house, Jonah retreated to his room and was in the middle of extracting himself from his drenched dress shirt when the footman knocked at the door.

"Dinner will be served in a quarter of an hour, sir."

"Will it now," Jonah replied, working to contain his surprise. The countess had hosted no formal dinners since his arrival. Her return to civility was likely connected to whatever had caused her flight from the church.

It made him deeply suspicious.

The servant maintained his stoic expression as he lifted Jonah's wet shirt and jacket. "I'll see that these are laundered. Your other clothes have been refreshed."

In the wardrobe, Jonah found his suit and shirt freshly washed, dried, and pressed. The countess's presumption irritated him, but it was a relief he would not have to sit through a full dinner service in damp garments.

"Thank you, Martin."

"My pleasure. Shall I stoke the coals for you?"

"No. It's fine." The servants must have thought he was batty for banking the fire each night, but he couldn't sleep with it roaring away. He'd rather freeze.

"Very good, sir. You received a letter in the post. I left it on the desk."

Christopher had bloody well taken his time with the promised research on the Rochfords. The benefit was that the missive was not thin by any means: his friend's well-placed connections had proved fruitful. As desperate as Jonah was to tear the thing open, he wouldn't tempt the countess's temper by being late. He tucked the letter into his prayer book and hastily changed clothes.

By the time he'd finished making himself presentable and wandered downstairs, he'd regained most of his typical steadiness. At dinner, he'd be the epitome of good manners. Hell, he'd be downright charming for whichever version of the countess showed up to greet him.

Or whoever else might join them.

As he made his way to the drawing room, a man lurched into the hall. He loomed over Jonah with bulk and muscles designed to intimidate. His shoulders were nearly bursting out of his scarlet velvet jacket. The luxurious garment was at odds with his unkempt beard.

"And 'oo the bloody 'ell are you?"

The fellow's voice was more of a conundrum than his wardrobe. Jonah had spent his formative years in Cheapside. Much of his education had consisted of scrubbing dropped h's and flattened vowels from his vernacular. He knew a fellow Cockney when he met one.

And this man was Cockney, down to his pores.

"I beg your pardon, sir. I'm Reverend Jonah Sinclair."

"The tu'or." The man squinted at him with menace.

Jonah envied his ability to deliver such a glower with restraint.

Without a word, the well-dressed ruffian marched past him into the dining room.

"I see you've met Mr. Doland."

Jonah turned, and it took him a stark moment to remember to offer a bow to the countess. He took his time with the gesture to keep from staring at the way her gown hugged her figure. The sapphire silk dress lacked the daring necklines that Christopher's sisters were so fond of, which was a pity. He suspected that Lady Rochford had a lovely *décolletage*.

"You've received your wish for an audience with the steward, Mr. Sinclair."

Though she maintained a detached tone and blank expression, she couldn't hide the wariness in her eyes. It pinched his breath, and he regretted for the hundredth time that they hadn't spoken after the service. At the moment, he wanted it more than a conversation with Troy Doland.

"My lady." He offered her his arm to escort her into the dining room.

She brushed past him with her chin held high. He debated whether the slight was meant to put him in his place, or if it was merely demonstrating strength before her brute of a steward.

In the dining room, Doland positioned himself at the head of the table.

Before Jonah could protest the arrangement, Lawless bustled in with a platter of cold salads. The housekeeper's speaking look was more of a silent shout for him to hold his tongue.

Without a word, he sank into his own seat. The countess maintained a guarded expression, but her posture remained stiff and locked. Her fury seemed tightly laced alongside her corset. he would have delighted in provoking her just to see it unleashed.

They proceeded through the first course in fraught silence. Lady Rochford offered neither a look nor a word to her steward. Her leg bobbed frantically beneath the table, causing Jonah's hackles to rise.

He recalled the way she flinched the first time he mentioned Doland's name, and his stomach clenched. Her refusal to broker a meeting between them wasn't a punishment for his impertinence; it was an effort to protect him from the steward. Anyone who spent a moment with the man could sense his inclination toward violence.

Lady Rochford assumed that as a man of God, Jonah wouldn't defend himself by harming someone else.

How wrong she was about him.

How much he looked forward to proving it.

The tension in the dining room broke with a rattling huff from Doland. "So, Sinclair. You're 'ere at my summoning? Funny fing, is, Rev, don't recall writin' to your bishop."

"That does not surprise me, sir. A man of your station, running an estate and enterprise of this size. You must have a mountain of correspondence."

It was an extreme effort to dampen the sarcasm from his voice, and Jonah wasn't sure he'd succeeded. But when the countess's bright eyes swerved toward him, he consumed the little spark of warmth in her gaze like a tasty morsel.

"One couldn't possibly keep track of every missive," Jonah went on, "could they, Lady Rochford?"

"Certainly not."

Doland drained his wine and gestured to a footman to refill it. "That's where we disagree. A steward's only worf 'is salt if 'e stays atten'ive. My job is to oversee *all* the earl's business. Even the itty-bitty 'ouse accounts." Doland flexed his thick fist for emphasis. "I was just remindin' Lady Rochford of that this evenin'."

In response, the countess violently ripped her bread apart into pieces.

Jonah offered a thoughtful nod. "Quite a substantive charge of duty, sir."

"Don't I know it."

"How lucky the earl is to have someone who takes their responsibilities so seriously. He must trust you completely."

"Aye. We've a long 'istory, Lord Rochford and me."

"Depends on you to protect 'is bees 'n honey."

"Too right."

Doland had replied mechanically; the wine had dulled his wits. Jonah's use of "bees and honey"—which in Cockney rhyming slang meant "money"—caught him out.

It was possible for a man to reinvent himself; Jonah had. But the likelihood a Cockney would secure an influential position managing an ancient agrarian estate like Ravenglass was slimmer than a slip of paper.

No, it was far more likely that Doland shared Rochford's connections to the underbelly of East London. After ten years of searching, the charlatan might finally lead him to the men who'd betrayed his father.

It took every defensive maneuver Jonah had acquired in his twenty-nine years to stay in his chair.

The steward bellowed for more wine.

Lady Rochford's frosty glare issued a silent counter order, and the footman hesitated.

In a deadly low voice, Doland uttered, "I asked for more wine, din't I?"

"There isn't any left."

Doland's meaty hand smacked the table.

The countess covered her wince by staring daggers at her dinner plate. Jonah found her thinly veiled animosity endearing. Neither one of them wanted to be at Doland's mercy, but neither one of them was foolish enough to risk a confrontation.

Though Lady Rochford wanted it as badly as he did. Her lips pinched together, turning her mouth white at the corners.

With the edge of his thumb, Jonah tested the dull blade of his knife, weighing his options.

A tremendous banging and a loud thud echoed from the foyer.

After which, shouting ensued.

Lawless barreled into the dining room. "There's been a slight disturbance in the front hall."

Jonah and the countess rose to their feet in the space of a breath, but Lawless obstructed their path. "You should stay here, my lady, and finish your dinner."

"Allow me to be of service," Jonah insisted.

Doland hauled himself from the table. "I'll 'andle this."

The countess attempted to follow him, but Lawless tugged her back. "Let him deal with it."

"He will make things *worse*."

The break in her voice spurred Jonah to action. He pushed past Lawless and chased after Doland.

In the foyer, Martin bracketed the staircase with the groom, defending the hallway from the ancient Mr. Anders.

"Stop hiding, Rochford!" Anders bellowed. "I know you're here, you coward. Have the bollocks to confront me if you dare!"

"Pipe down, ya daft codger," Doland commanded. "Or I'll silence you m'self."

Anders scoffed. "You do his dirty work, covering up—"

Doland wrapped his thick hand around Anders's throat. The older man choked for breath.

"That's enough," Jonah cautioned. "Let him go."

"You got your du'ies, Rev, and I've got mine. It's my responsibility to protect this 'ouse."

"Kindly remove your hands from Mr. Anders's throat, Mr. Doland, if you intend to protect yourself from me."

The steward flashed his cracked teeth. "Try me."

Removing his suitcoat, as if he had all the time in the world and was not frantic about Anders dropping dead on the carpet, Jonah rolled up his shirtsleeves. "Unhand Mr. Anders. Or I will be obliged to apply *my* protection."

Doland wheezed. "Ya gonna knock the stuffin' outta me, parson? What would the bishop say?"

"A few choice words to correct my left jab, I should think."

"*Enough*."

The countess's voice rang through the foyer, punctuated by the unmistakable click of a pistol disarming.

Lady Rochford stood on the stairs with her elegant arm extended as she pointed a multi-barreled Lancaster at the three men in the hallway.

"Mr. Doland, release Mr. Anders."

The steward cursed.

The countess adjusted her aim.

Reluctantly, Doland eased off his grip.

Jonah caught Anders as the old man staggered back and coughed. "I must see your husband, my lady."

"That's not possible, Mr. Anders."

"I'm owed, my lady. He owes me the decency of an audience."

"You are. But it's not possible tonight."

She'd said it softly, with respect and a steely authority that roused a peculiar ache beneath Jonah's ribs.

Slowly, she lowered the pistol. "What I can promise, Mr. Anders, is that I will deliver any message you wish to the earl himself."

As Anders stood quietly quaking in the foyer, Jonah had never felt so divided. He empathized deeply with Anders's demand to see Rochford. But he could not ignore the primal need to defend the woman who stood alone against that fiend of a steward, and perhaps the entire village.

Gently, Jonah placed a hand to steady the older man's shaking shoulders. "Mr. Anders?"

"I will relay whatever message you wish to tell me," Lady Rochford repeated, catching Jonah's eye. "And then Mr. Sinclair will escort you home in my carriage."

At the mention of the coach, the older man's expression darkened. Drawing a breath, he shouted, "You can tell your devil of a husband that he killed my daughter."

Chapter Seven

A STEADY DRIPPING SOUND woke Faith from an uneasy sleep.

She stifled a groan. The last thing she needed was a leaking roof.

Dragging herself out of bed, she inspected her quarters as well as she could in the lamplight. Rain lashed in torrents against the windows. It had been ceaseless all spring. The river had crested early, endangering six of the tenant farms that bordered the east side of the estate. She needed an engineer's opinion on whether a dam might help, but engineers and dams were expenses she couldn't afford.

When her surroundings proved dry, she pulled on her wrapper, withdrew from her room and proceeded through the corridor. She paused by the faded tapestry that shrouded the door leading to the north wing and debated the merits of going through. It was unlikely the leak stemmed from the third floor since they'd repaired that section of the roof last year.

She crept away quickly. She couldn't linger by the hidden door while Sinclair remained in the house.

After the debacle of a dinner, she'd have to invent some excuse to make him go. It had been a miracle she'd avoided his questions about Geoffrey this long.

Treading down the staircase and past the library, she ducked into her study. From her pocket, she withdrew a small key and opened the hidden compartment beneath the desk where she housed her copies of the estate's accounts. Earlier that day, she'd filed away her correspondence, including the missive from Emrys Kane, her solicitor.

She reserved Mr. Kane's letter for last, hoping that by doing so she'd usher in some good luck as to its contents, knowing the rest of the letters carried no good news.

Doland's visit to London had been eventful. He'd broken several display bottles at the wine merchant and ridden a horse lame at the Mayfair stables.

One hundred pounds in damages needed to be paid.

God only knew where she would find it. She'd sold off everything, including the jewels she'd received from Geoffrey as wedding gifts. The gems themselves were worthless paste fabrications, but the genuine gold settings had paid for six months of dry goods and a decent pair of working boots.

She pushed aside the miserable bills and turned to the note reminding her of Dr. Blake's upcoming visit. There was a letter enclosed with it from Lady Cora Longworth, presumably a friend of the doctor's, inviting Faith to attend an upcoming meeting of the Ladies' Discussion and Improvement Society. They must have been desperate for patrons. Her husband's scandalous reputation usually barred her from such invitations.

Faith glanced at Mr. Kane's letter. Part of her dreaded receiving more disappointment. But a larger part of her hoped he'd found something that would lead her out of her predicament.

She searched for a letter opener to break the wax seal. Discovering it had fallen to the floor, she crouched beneath the desk to retrieve it.

"What 'ave we 'ere?"

A light bobbed across the Persian carpet as thick footsteps approached.

"Is the mouse readin' its books?"

The traitorous sounds of her own breath made Faith clamp her hands over her nose and mouth.

A phlegmy cough reverberated above her. "Readin' your fairy stories, mouse? Always liked those, din't ya?"

As Faith's shoulders shook, she was furious at herself for reacting like a child. If only she'd brought the pistol. She hadn't thought she'd need it. With the amount of alcohol Doland had consumed, he should have been unconscious.

"Too shy to come out? Guess I'll 'ave to find ya." His thick hand slammed on the desk. "And I better not catch you wiv anyfing that little mice shouldn't be playin' at."

Jonah sat at the small, battered writing desk, staring at Christopher's unopened letter.

Although it promised insight into his preposterous situation, he couldn't bring himself to read it. Not until he'd sorted through his own troubled thoughts. His desire to confront Doland—preferably with his fists—was a palpable thing.

Pummeling the blackguard wasn't an option. Jonah needed to coax Doland into revealing Rochford's possible connections to the criminals who'd killed his father. For that, he needed the filth alive.

Although, for the countess's sake, he'd consider the alternatives.

The moment she'd appeared on the stairs and brandished her pistol, he'd felt a sense of pride, and a crushing blaze of lust he'd had trouble shaking off. She'd displayed the strength and self-possession he aspired to. Anders's scathing accusation that the earl had killed his daughter had hardly ruffled her.

But it had unsettled Jonah.

His thoughts still raced. He'd be up all night if he didn't find something else to capture his attention. An ancient historical. And possibly a nightcap.

He ventured to the library in search of both, but the moment he arrived downstairs, the unmistakable rattle of Doland's chortling echoed from the direction of the countess's study.

Jonah strained for a signal that she was well. The only sound that carried from the far end of the hall was the steward's muffled voice.

There was no way on earth he was leaving her alone with the brute.

He flew down the hallway to the study, where he found Doland swaying over the desk with his hand curled into a fist. The countess stood opposite him, wielding a silver letter opener.

Jonah cleared his throat. "Good evening."

They flicked their eyes to him as if they were swatting away an insect.

Doland's body oscillated as he fought to gain his balance, which was no surprise given the sheer volume of drink the man had consumed at dinner.

"Is aught amiss?" Jonah persisted with the pretense of civility, hoping the mental struggle would force Doland to retreat.

"Blimey, Rev," Doland wheezed. "You look primed for a finality!"

The countess frowned at the unfamiliar reference, but Jonah knew exactly what Doland had meant.

London gangs had code words and expressions they used to cover up their less than legal activities. A *"finality"* was a reference to Finality Jack, the discourteous nickname for the former prime minister, Lord John Russell. Its translation rhymed with the word omitted: Jack.

In certain circles, a *"finality"* meant an *attack*.

There were a dozen people in the world who knew the meaning of that word in the context in which Doland had delivered it. They'd all been part of the Skinner's Lane Lads, a crime circuit responsible for the ruination and death of Jonah's father.

Which meant *Doland* was a member.

And quite possibly, his murderer.

The absurd elation Jonah felt with this discovery made him laugh. A deep, long belly laugh that captivated the steward's attention.

Doland whirled around and advanced. In his inebriated state, the steward lost sight of the edge of the carpet Jonah had flipped up with his boot. He stumbled over the rug and crashed to the floor.

Where he ceased moving.

Jonah crouched down to examine the damage.

"Is he breathing?"

Lifting his head, Jonah found himself face-to-face with the countess. She knelt on the other side of Doland, clutching the letter opener. She regarded him without the wariness he expected from her, and her proximity allowed him to catalogue the amber flecks in her brown eyes.

He turned back to the steward. "Yes, he's breathing."

"Are you sure?"

"Quite sure. His condition is due to inebriation, rather than a blow to the head." He'd survived enough brawls himself to know the difference.

"Thank you."

The softness in her voice could not be mistaken for warmth or weakness, but it was genuine and Jonah was moved by the terse words of gratitude. They were as intimate as a confession.

Slowly, he rose to his feet and lifted her with him. For a moment, they stood in the circle of each other's arms.

"Are you well, my lady?" he whispered.

"That is a relative word."

"Did he—"

"He didn't touch me." She exhaled. "He never has before."

"That gives me no consolation."

"Then we are in agreement."

She withdrew and walked back to the desk, still gripping the letter opener. Her hands shook as she shuffled papers into a pile.

Reaching across the desk, Jonah gently placed his hands on hers. "Allow me."

After a moment's hesitation, she surrendered the small knife. He placed it on the desk so that it was within her reach and gathered the papers together.

"Lady Rochford, I must ask something of you."

Her expectant stare unsettled him more than the tumble with her steward.

"When you first invited me here, I spoke too plainly about Master Adam," he said. "I was misguided in my judgment of how you and the household care for him. Please forgive me."

"I accept and appreciate your apology, Mr. Sinclair, but it's unnecessary."

"It is if I'm to stay. I intend to write to Bishop Alcott—"

"Indeed. After this evening, you'll have so many things to report."

The disdain in her voice stopped him short.

"I expect the bishop will want to know everything," she continued. "No detail spared. No reputation spared either."

Her accusation made his stomach churn with shame.

With one letter hinting at the struggle she faced with Doland, Jonah could destroy everything she'd been working to preserve.

Of course she wanted him far gone. He could ruin her.

It was the furthest thing from his mind.

"No, my lady. You mistake—"

"Good Lord!" Lawless exclaimed, as she and the footman careened into the room. "I suppose it's too much ta hope he's not breathin'."

Neither Jonah nor the countess chided her for voicing her wish aloud.

The countess waved a dismissive hand. "Please escort Mr. Doland to his cottage. You should retire too, Mr. Sinclair." Her eyes flicked to his. "No doubt the events of the evening have exhausted you."

Jonah needed to hit something, and only resisted slamming his bedroom door for fear he'd wake Adam.

Now that he knew Doland's seedy connections, he was torn between remaining in the house to stand guard and chasing the footman and the groom to wherever they'd taken the steward. If he could extricate enough information from the lout, it could lead him to evidence that would clear his father's name.

And then, Doland and his associates would pay.

But before either of those things could happen, he needed to calm down.

As he paced the narrow space between the bed and the small writing desk, he spotted Christopher's letter poking out of his prayer book and seized it with a small growl.

My intrepid friend,

Well, you have landed in the thick of it.

Excellent. A reminder of the direness of his situation was exactly what he needed from his most faithful ally.

"Not helpful, Christopher," he mumbled.

You're probably grumbling to yourself, "Not helpful, Christopher!" And as you well know, I am unhelpful on most matters, including the organization of my own life. Since you are not here to remind me of my shortcomings, that particular task has fallen to my mother. I humbly beg you to get on with solving this great mystery, so I do not have to face one more tirade about my future existence.

Jonah smiled. With two successful older brothers, and a sister married to a viscount, Christopher's lack of self-direction was an anomaly among the Wilde family.

I can, when I put my mind to it, prove very helpful indeed, which I shall demonstrate in my response to your inquiry about the Earl of Rochford.

All reliable sources report that generations of the Trenton family have eschewed London society. My mother can't recall the last time one of them attended the Season, and she remembers everyone and everything.

Luckily for you, a break in the case came when I invited Griffin to join me for a very old cognac on offer at Sunderland's. You recall my eldest brother has more clarity about the world when imbibing and at the mention of Rochford, something jogged his memory. He introduced me to a gentleman who claimed an acquaintance with the family.

After a brandy or three, he made some disturbing accusations about the Trentons. Allegedly, Rochford and his brother Charles, the former earl, were infamous among those elements of London society who indulged in gambling and prostitution. And they were more than just hobbyists.

Many unsuspecting aristocrats embroiled themselves in illicit schemes to fill their estate coffers. But gambling hells and prostitution rings were the territories of professional racketeers and London gangs.

It explained how the brothers had entangled themselves with a crook like Doland.

But how in the world did the countess become entangled with them?

At this juncture, you are likely pondering how your current Lady Rochford came into the picture.

The Metropolitan Police were watching the Trentons, and the brothers learned that Scotland Yard was planning a raid on one of their establishments. They fled the country before getting caught, but the demise of their criminal businesses left them in serious needs of funds. That problem was rectified by Geoffrey's engagement to Miss Elisabeth Faith Morton, the sole heiress to a wealthy merchant in Madeira.

"Elisabeth Faith," Jonah murmured. He couldn't wait to ask which one of her parents had insisted on the virtue moniker. Unlikely she'd surrender that information, no matter how hard he pressed.

The engagement was arranged while Miss Morton's uncle was on his deathbed, and on the day of his funeral, she and the Trentons departed the island with apparent haste. Charles and Geoffrey made enemies in Madeira and were eager to return to England.

And here is where the tale turns dark.

It is more than a correlation to say that deaths followed the brothers. Shortly after their return to the family estate, Charles's wife, the former countess, succumbed to a wasting disease, enabling him to take up with his mistress, the mother of your young pupil.

Two years later, Charles was thrown from a horse and died, making Geoffrey the next Earl of Rochford.

And a year after that, on his way to Madeira, Geoffrey disappeared.

This mystery has intrigued both of my brothers, and they are making discreet inquiries. I hope to write soon with more information, if only for your safety.

The cloud surrounding the Rochfords and their misfortunes cannot be due to carelessness alone. All jesting aside, I advise you to proceed with caution. And if I, of all people, am writing the word "caution," please know that I do it with no small amount of discomfort.

Be careful, Jonah.

I remain, dear sir,

Your loyal friend,

Christopher Wilde

Jonah scrubbed a hand down his face and resumed his pacing. He'd wear the woolen carpet bare before the end of the night.

If half of what Christopher had written was true, Geoffrey Trenton was a fiend and a criminal. And if the earl hadn't followed his brother into hell, they all faced the danger of his return.

But the more pressing threat was that his accomplice, Doland, had ready access to the countess, her family, and her home. The thought of something happening to Elisabeth Faith Trenton at the hands of these cretins made Jonah's chest tighten.

It was folly to fixate on the simmering attraction he felt toward her. In that fleeting moment that he'd held her in the study, he knew she'd experienced the frisson too.

Neither of them would act on it. He'd never committed his heart to anyone, and he certainly wouldn't now, with someone else's wife.

But unlike her husband, Jonah wouldn't abandon her. He couldn't leave a child and a woman in such circumstances.

Somehow, he had to convince the countess to allow him to stay.

CHAPTER EIGHT

FAITH KNEW THERE WERE places in the world where rain was scarce.

Her uncle and aunt had a fellow acquaintance among the Society of Friends who'd once described a rain dance ritual performed by American Indians in the Western American territories. And of course, she'd read her Bible. The Old Testament was chockful of references to people wandering deserts in search of an oasis.

No one had ever shared with her a method to *stop* the rain. If she still possessed her inheritance, she would have paid half of it to find one.

Today's inspection of the eastern end of the property revealed that without a permanent fix for the riverbank, a flood would be inevitable.

She had no idea how she was going to pay for a dam. Hours of riding around in the rain had provided no inspiration. As she stood in the greenhouse's shelter, staring at a lone candle left burning in the kitchen window, she couldn't bring herself to return to the house without a solution.

Thank God Doland had turned tail and slipped away while she'd been out surveying the grounds. Perhaps Sinclair's confrontation in the study had scared him off. If she was lucky, she'd have a few weeks of relative peace to sort out a solution to the estate's solvency.

A hot drink. That was what she needed. Something warm and spiced to get her blood moving, set her thoughts to rights. Things were always better after a little rest and a hot nightcap.

Faith entered the house through the servants' door and hung her sopping mackintosh on one of the hallway hooks. The thing did a fair job protecting her from the rain, but her shirt, trousers, and waistcoat were damp. Every draft sliced through to her bones as she ducked into the kitchen.

Sinclair stood at the stove in nothing but his shirtsleeves and trousers, stirring something in a small iron pot. His silhouette dwarfed the modest furnishings around him. The curving lines of his broad shoulders, melding into his narrow torso and trim waist, seemed to take up all the free space in the room.

A different type of shiver crept down her spine.

At the sound of her footsteps, he turned around, holding a wooden spoon in front of him as if it were a saber.

They both stared at the utensil for an inordinate length of time.

Eventually, her eyes drifted to where Sinclair's shirt collar splayed open, displaying a healthy part of his neck and chest. An alluring hint of dark hair exposed at the vee of his shirt was a blatant invitation to stare.

"Mr. Sinclair."

There. No one could accuse her of not attempting to diffuse the awkward silence.

How unfortunate she was at a loss to follow through with anything else.

"Lady Rochford. Good evening."

A similar plague tied his tongue. She wondered if he was embarrassed at being caught in his shirtsleeves but dismissed the thought. Sinclair had confessed that he wasn't prudish.

She needed to withdraw, but she couldn't gather enough wits to leave. The only thought that kept turning over in her mind was that Sinclair hadn't glanced twice at her trousers and waistcoat.

Had he known her secret, since their first exchange the night he arrived? She'd been so diligent about donning her disguise and maintaining a careful distance from others when she was out on estate business with tenants.

The prospect that Sinclair had told others—including the bishop—solicited a violent shake of her limbs.

His brow wrinkled. Discarding the spoon, he ducked into the linen press and returned with an old tablecloth.

"Allow me," he said softly, not bothering to wait for her reply before he unfurled the worn cotton and circled it around her shoulders.

Warmth engulfed her—more from the heat of his hands than the soft, worn fabric. His unobtrusive gesture should not have overwhelmed her the way it did.

"Wh-what are you making?"

He shuffled back to the stove with a sheepish grin. "I was heating some milk."

"For Adam?"

"No, for me."

"Trouble sleeping, Mr. Sinclair?"

His lips quirked. "Something like that."

Her fingers pulled at the tablecloth, revisiting the spot where his hands had been moments before and finding it cold and damp instead.

She was chilled and flustered. A servant could walk in and find them at any moment.

But she couldn't leave without finding out what was disturbing him.

Nodding to the kettle, she asked, "Is the water hot?"

"Yes, it was steaming when I walked in."

Good old Lawless. She'd known Faith would want something when she returned.

"Then I believe I have a remedy that will serve better than warm milk. I'd appreciate if you could stoke the burner for me."

Sinclair gave an exaggerated bow and turned to the stove. His expression turned pensive as he took a poker that was twice the length of the stove and stirred the coals. He looked like a lion tamer cautiously approaching a great cat with his chair. She supposed he was one of those Londoners who maintained a healthy caution around an open flame, for fear of burning down the entire city.

Faith stole into the pantry, found the bottle Lawless kept hidden behind the oats, and retrieved a small tin of mulling spices along with a jar of honey. Depositing her quarry on the long wooden table, she pilfered two mugs from the servants' shelf. She poured a dram from the bottle into each mug, then sprinkled in the mulling spices and honey before Sinclair filled the mugs with hot water.

As she wrapped her fingers around the cup, the heady scent of cloves and orange peel mingled with the fragrant wine, and she released a deep breath. Now that she had what she came for, she would take her warm potion and retreat. She'd postpone dealing with the reality of Sinclair knowing her secret, and what he might do with it.

He turned to replace the kettle on the stove, and the faint candlelight gilded the contours of his shoulders. Her imagination did not have far to travel to picture what was beneath his lawn shirt: fine muscles, both strong and soft to the touch. Golden skin so warm, the heat of it against hers would chase away her shivers for good.

Faith's knees buckled. She sank into the nearest chair with a clatter.

"Did you hear that?" Sinclair's head snapped to the window.

"No," she replied hoarsely. "What was it?"

"Something scuttled outside. I heard it earlier, but when you arrived, I thought it was your footsteps across the garden."

"Probably a fox, creeping through the fence. There's a warren at the edge of the property I must see to."

Sinclair peered into the darkness outside for a long moment before turning back toward her.

No escaping him now. Not without looking like a complete coward.

Which she was. If she had an ounce of the courage she thought she possessed, she'd have given him the dismissal note from Geoffrey she'd forged after he'd left her study last night.

Willing her hands not to shake, Faith extended one mug toward him. Sinclair took it without brushing her fingers with his own, which was not something a married woman of her position should have noticed.

Taking the seat next to her, he extended his glass in a toast. "To a lasting peace?"

"Queen and country might be safer."

He grinned. "To Queen and country."

She indulged in a small sip. The spices and alcohol warmed her instantly.

Sinclair also sipped his drink slowly, while his eyes remained locked on the bottle. Eventually his attention swung back toward her, and his gaze turned evaluating, taking in her steward's garb.

A slow flush progressed from her forehead, down her neck. "How long have you known?"

When he cocked his head in question, she gestured from her neckcloth to her boots. She wouldn't speak her secret aloud, especially when he was trying to play coy.

"Since the first night I arrived at Ravenglass," he conceded. "Although, I doubt I would have recognized you, if you had not fallen from your horse and resisted when I attempted to help you."

"Resisted? I believe you fell on top of me."

"Indeed."

He had an appalling lack of shame. Surely all curates couldn't be this arrogant.

Despite her irritation, she didn't press the matter further; she'd say something more inappropriate, and they were flaunting propriety enough as it were.

Really, why were they bothering with common etiquette at all? They were a breath away from each other in the dark kitchen. His shirt gaped open, and she was dressed in breeches, with her hair tumbling down her back.

They'd left propriety behind the second she'd walked through the door.

If she was being honest, they'd abandoned decorum completely when he'd come to her rescue by rendering Doland unconscious. Despite his clerical vows, Sinclair had few qualms about inflicting physical harm on another in her defense.

The manipulation, the careful use and restraint of his strength, had been wildly alluring.

"How much of...all of this have you shared with your bishop?" she asked.

"I wrote him that I arrived safely, and that Master Adam's unique talents required some time to evaluate the best lesson plan to fulfill the earl's request."

That was quite the evasion. "You're obscuring the reality of the situation."

"Everything I wrote was true. Adam is extremely bright, so it's difficult to assess what pockets of his education are missing, but where they are, he is very behind. It will take work to get him up to scratch."

She scoffed. "So you'd lie to your bishop, compromise your conscience?"

"To ensure I have enough time to complete my duty to prepare Adam for school, yes. I know the value of discretion, how easily a stray comment in a letter can snowball into gossip." He held her gaze. "Is it so difficult to believe that I'd want to shield you both from it?"

"You must have something to gain here."

His eyes left hers and rested on the Madeira. The damned bottle fascinated him. She recalled him referring to fine vintages when he mentioned his father's business.

A tingling sensation at the back of her neck warned her against examining that shared connection to her former home too closely. But to protect Adam, and her secrets, she needed to know Sinclair's agenda.

Slowly, she pushed the bottle across the table toward him. He examined the thing with the same intensity as an archeologist unearthing a fossil.

Turning the bottle, he pointed to a faint but intricate stamp at the bottom of the label.

Imported by Sinclair & Associates, Ltd. Pier 37. London.

"What a peculiar coincidence," Faith murmured.

"Not particularly," he replied. "My father imported half of the bottles of this vintage."

"It must have been quite an enterprise. That stamp is extraordinary."

"Yes, it was plate pressed. An engraver made it in exchange for renting out part of my father's warehouse."

Sinclair traced it with his finger. "When I was seven, the first wave of the oidium blight hit. A little nefarious American parasite destroyed grape cultivation in half of Europe. Most of Father's clients were ruined. And so was he."

"I'm sorry. I remember when it peaked in Madeira. It was terrible."

He nodded. "My father made some extremely poor decisions trying to recover. Trusted the wrong people and ended up at the Queen's Bench."

Debtors' prison, in London.

Faith fidgeted in her seat, unsure of how to acknowledge such an honest confession. It must have been freeing for him to live so openly.

"My mother and I lived across the street from the prison for a time," Sinclair said. "We were determined to find evidence to clear his debts and his name."

She didn't enjoy picturing him as a child navigating those filthy narrow lanes, teaming with criminals and cutthroats, the needy and neglected.

"Despite our high hopes," he continued, "my father died within a year of his indenture."

He revealed this with a steady voice, which made her envious, and a familiar pain in his eyes, which made her soften. "That must have been devastating."

"Not just for us. Our extended family were tradesman who'd all benefitted from my father's success, and his failure equally devastated them. If some relative could, they'd take us in for a short while. When they hit a rough patch, we'd bounce around to another house. Until Mother took a sudden fever. It was a blessing that it happened so fast; she didn't suffer."

He'd said that first night that he knew what it was to be forgotten, and she hadn't believed him. Regret churned her stomach. "No child should have to endure that kind of loss."

It was easier saying it to him, rather than believing it about herself.

Sinclair sighed. "Adam and I have a great deal in common. I grew up in a house that was as fine as this one. Nicer, actually; not so many drafts."

"It's the drafts that lend Ravenglass its character."

His mouth twitched. "I understand what it's like for Adam. To have to depend on someone else's mercy to survive, knowing it could all evaporate in an instant. And that the world can be inhospitable to people on their own."

There was a preachiness to his tone she resented, as if he was scolding her. "If you're withholding the truth from your bishop because you empathize with Adam's position, I confess, I struggle to believe that anyone is that altruistic."

"You wouldn't be the first skeptic I've met."

"And you wouldn't be the first parson I've met looking to advance his own cause." Frustrated with his moral superiority, she scrambled to her feet, sending her chair back with a bang loud enough to echo beyond the kitchen, into the yard. "Tell me truthfully. Why are you delaying your orders to Manchester for this? What do you have to gain from this assignment?"

With deliberate slowness, Sinclair rose from the table. In one stride, he crossed the distance between them and turned the sharp focus he had paid to the bottle on her. "I suspect your husband and his associates have made you many enemies, my lady. But I am not one of them."

His passion was convincing, but his nearness was discomforting as his attention lingered on the places where her damp shirt and trousers clung to her curves.

Faith had experienced attraction once before and it had done her no service. Her unreliable desires would not betray her in such a way ever again. While part of her wanted to believe Sinclair posed no harm, that was impossible. He held a position of influence. In her entire life, she'd yet to meet a man who hadn't used that against her.

"You say you are not an enemy," she pressed. "Do you consider us friends?"

"Yes."

"Then as a friend, I will write the bishop and recommend that he release you from this commitment. Surely, the Church needs you to attend to more important work."

Sinclair had the audacity to lean closer. "And what if I refuse to leave?"

The low rumble of his voice made her mouth dry. "What in the world would compel you to stay?"

His response drowned in a violent shattering of glass that drew their attention outside.

Where molten orange flames devoured the kitchen yard.

CHAPTER NINE

The winter gardens were ablaze.

Fire bloomed from inside the glasshouse. It was several yards away from the house, but one stray spark could turn the mansion into an inferno.

And all Jonah could do was watch the disaster unfold before him.

He'd torn out of the kitchen, but halfway down the steps to the lower garden, the stench of smoke and paraffin assaulted his nose and stymied his limbs.

A familiar panic gripped him. Despite the rain biting at his cheeks, soaking his shirt, he felt the flames as if he stood within them.

He tried to call out, to move, but every motion was suspended. How he was getting breath in and out of his lungs was a complete mystery.

"Mr. Sinclair!"

The voice called from miles away, seeking his father. Rescuing people was a job for grown men. Not him.

He was only a boy.

"Sinclair!"

Whoever was calling to him needed help. *He* needed to help them.

But the wind and the roar of the fire crowded his ears, trapping him on the slick stone steps.

"Jonah!"

Lady Rochford's hoarse and melodious voice, with its familiar undertones of annoyance, yanked him out of the past.

"I need you to collect yourself, Jonah. Open your eyes."

Unaware he'd clamped them closed, he blinked at the flames rising in the dark night.

"Look at me. Not the fire, Jonah. Look *here*."

Obeying the command, he found the contours of her face, registered those brown eyes that were lit from within by their own spark. A warmth rose within him that chased away the paralyzing fear.

"Breathe with me, Jonah."

She counted to four as he inhaled, and again as he exhaled. It took several attempts before he could clear the dregs of his memories and ground himself to the present crisis.

He rattled his head. "My lady. Forgive me—"

"No time for apologies. I need your help, or I need you to get to safety. Which are you capable of?" Soot stained the back of her shirt, and despite the roaring inferno that was eating away the outer buildings, she remained unnervingly calm. "Mr. Sinclair?"

With a shaking breath, he replied, "I am at your service, madam."

"Mount a horse and ride to the village. If we can't contain the blaze to the outer structures, we'll need more hoses and men to save the house."

"Martin's on his way there, my lady." Mrs. Lawless emerged from the house, wheezing a breath. "I'll take Peggy and Adam to the Saltcoat."

"Go now—don't tarry. I'll send for you when it's safe." The countess dismissed the housekeeper with a wave. Lawless glanced at Jonah before fleeing into the night.

"You too, Sinclair. Hurry."

Then she promptly tore off into the smoking shadows.

Jonah's pulse continued its frantic pace, spurred on by the shame of his fear. The countess was willing to throw herself into the fire because she had no one else.

He was her only source of help. And that was more terrifying than the rising fire.

It left him no other choice but to chase after her on shaking limbs.

"My lady," he shouted. "It's not safe."

To prove his point, a crash pierced his ears as the glasshouse roof imploded into the flames.

"If we don't contain the fire now, it will spread," she replied.

"How can I help?"

"I do not wish to put you in harm's way."

"But you would risk yourself, and all those who depend on you?"

She turned as if to contradict him again, but the scowl he threw her stopped her short. "There is a fire hose—a long rubber contraption located on the west side of the garden. It attaches to the water engine in the upper gardens. We can wheel it to reach the glasshouse."

As she darted back into the night and the smoke, Jonah had a firm word with his galloping heart to quiet down.

It was ineffective.

Locating the hose proved a challenge, and lifting the thing was even more difficult, since its weight was equivalent to a small freight train.

Hoisting the hose over his shoulders, he staggered back down to the lower gardens, and after more fumbling around, attached it to the water engine.

Dragging the machine toward the house, he was grateful his years of training now enabled him to direct his strength toward something better than bare-knuckle fighting.

As he approached the glasshouse, he couldn't locate the countess. He didn't hide the panic from his voice when he shouted her name.

"Stand back, Sinclair!" Lady Rochford emerged from the darkness with a copper barrel strapped to her back. "Stay there," she shouted. "Don't move from that spot!"

A spray of white froth erupted from the tube attached to the barrel and the ensuing cacophony drowned out his protests. Following the trail of foam, the countess walked straight into the fire.

Jonah was tempted to chase her. Mostly, to see if it would make her half as furious as he felt for the little regard she had for her own life.

And also because her audacity impressed the hell out of him.

As she advanced, the flames receded. She forced the fire back to the far edge of the yard before the canister spurted, emptied of foam.

"Now, Sinclair!" She discarded the contraption and gestured to him. "Bring over the engine and hose."

They scrambled to wheel the cart closer.

"We need a third man to manage this," he insisted.

"There's no time. I've done it before with two. You man the pump—I will aim the water." She gathered the hose and nodded toward the handle. "Ready?"

Not even remotely. "Ready."

He seized the handle and, with all his strength, worked the lever back and forth.

"Easy," the countess warned. "Pace yourself."

A deluge burst from the hose, but the countess held it under her control.

"Keep pumping!"

He paid little mind to the ache in his arms; he'd worked through pain before.

Eventually, the volume of water diminished the fire. When the engine emptied, they ferried leather buckets from the garden pump until all that remained were embers.

By tacit agreement, they paused and stared at the smoldering ashes.

There should have been a sense of accomplishment in the victory, some riotous joy in saving the estate and protecting its people. But Jonah felt strangely bereft by the crisis ending.

Beside him, the countess stared at the smoke with an equally empty expression on her soot-marked face.

He'd never seen anyone who needed a friend more than this woman.

"Lady Rochford," he croaked, his voice raw from the smoke and shouting and the near-death. "Let's go inside."

She didn't acknowledge him, or his suggestion.

"The danger has passed," he added. "And we have you to thank for it. It is time to get out of the cold."

The countess responded with an exhale. Her body shook with the force of it. He was having a terrible time resisting the urge to fold her into his arms and clasp her tightly enough to cease her trembling.

"Forgive me, ma'am." Jonah's voice took on a scolding edge. "But you are attired in your, ah, working wardrobe. Which, besides being ruined by soot, will raise far too many questions when help arrives from the village."

Staggering to the edge of the engine cart, she sank down. "No one is coming from the village."

She slowly raised her eyes to meet his. The sorrow he found there made his legs so weak that he sank down beside her.

"No one has ever come."

The wind rose and she swayed along with it; her shoulder brushed against his. And it was as natural as drawing breath for Jonah to enfold her into his arms.

She rested her head on his shoulder, as if it was too heavy for her to hold up on her own. In her exhaustion, he doubted that she even realized she'd allowed herself the indiscretion.

An entire community of people had turned their backs on her. So had her husband. She was used to being abandoned. Tonight, she all but dared him to forsake her too.

But he wouldn't. He couldn't.

"Where is your husband, Lady Rochford?"

The only reply she gave was another deep sigh.

"Whoever did this wanted to send a message. Of intimidation and fear. I cannot believe that you were the intended victim, my lady."

"Why, because I am a woman? You think I have no enemies?"

"I think tonight was an act of retribution for crimes committed long before you arrived at Ravenglass. I believe your husband was the true target, and you probably know why."

"You think I'm innocent of whatever these crimes might be."

"Yes." He patted the engine. "This is not a small investment. And you know exactly how to operate it." In a softer tone, he added, "Because it's happened before. And when no one came, you knew it would happen again. And you'd be powerless to stop it."

She said nothing, but Jonah felt her shudder as if it came from within him.

"The earl has neglected his duties as master to this estate," he continued, his voice gathering strength. "And he's neglected his duties as a husband. To protect you. To safeguard and keep you."

"Keep me." She huffed a laugh. "That he has done."

She caught his gaze, and Jonah saw an ember of her familiar spark.

And something else that compounded a growing ache in his chest.

"My lady, I must know...after all that happened tonight...why would a man leave his greatest treasures unguarded when his enemies clearly mean to do you harm?"

She withdrew and angrily shook her head.

He stopped it by cupping his palm to her cheek. "Do you know where your husband is?"

With a slow and steady voice, she replied, "Yes."

CHAPTER TEN

FAITH STARED AT THE sun rising outside her bedroom window, contemplating what to do with her restless feet.

Outside, the rosy light of dawn crept over the horizon, chasing away the mists that gathered at the wild edges of the lawn, where the grass met the scraggly forest. Now that the rain had ceased, she couldn't afford to pass up the chance to inspect the river.

As she dressed quickly in her breeches and shirt, she avoided looking at the wretched engagement portrait. One day, she'd work up the nerve to sell it. God knew she needed the funds.

Instead, she stared at Sinclair's cape draped over the chair.

When she returned to her room after their ordeal, she hadn't been able to surrender his cloak. Beneath the damp and the smoke, other scents lingered: soap and leather and some other unspoken ingredient that belonged solely to Jonah Sinclair.

The way he'd drawn her into his arms was as natural as rain falling. She'd surrendered her defenses, and Sinclair had played the advantage by demanding an explanation for her husband's abandonment.

She wished for a scenario where she could confess everything to him and still protect them both.

Shaking off her troubled thoughts, she left a hurried note for Lawless in the kitchen and set off toward the barn to saddle her horse. While the chill in the air was enough to catch her breath, the rising sun warmed her cheeks, and she turned toward it, closing her eyes for an indulgent moment, before entering the barn.

A soft *tap, tap, thud* echoed from the far stall.

Faith froze.

When they'd extinguished the fire last night, she and Sinclair had combed the grounds and house and found no signs of the intruders who lit the flames, but she hadn't shaken off the fear that the arsonists might have concealed themselves somewhere else.

The rhythm continued. *Tap, tap, thud.* Then, *shuffle, shuffle, tap, tap, thud.*

Her drumming heartbeat clashed against the tempo. Seizing a horseshoe hammer she crept toward the end of the barn.

Tap, tap, shuffle, shuffle, tap, thud.

She detected panting, punctuated by heaving gasps that reverberated in the cavernous stable.

Marshaling her own breath, she peered around the corner of the stall.

Sinclair stood with his back to her. He wore a faded linen shirt untucked over a trim pair of trousers that clung to his powerful legs. Above him, a twenty-pound bag of oats hung from a wooden beam.

With a *tap, tap,* his powerful arms jabbed at the bag.

As it swung back toward him, his feet expertly dodged its impact.

Shuffle, shuffle.

It was an elegant dance, a demonstration of strength. What power he'd contained in the confines of his simple black suit.

Abruptly, Sinclair went on the attack.

Tap, tap, tap, tap, THUD.

He punctuated the final thrust of his rippling shoulders with a low growl, primal and proud, like the snarl of a predatory cat.

The hammer tumbled from Faith's grip.

Sinclair spun around, chest pumping, eyes ablaze. His shirt was undone; rivulets of sweat ran from his neck down to abdomen.

"Forgive me—"

"I am sorry, I didn't think—"

The competing apologies were stunted by the fact that their gazes had collided and seemed unwilling to surrender to each other.

Without conceding, she found her voice first. "I heard noises and was afraid the intruders from last night had hidden themselves better than we thought."

Shaking his head, he removed his padded gloves, which he mercifully held close, covering his exposed chest. "I searched everywhere again this morning. No trace."

"You were prepared in case you found them." She nodded t at the gloves. "I didn't take you for a pugilist."

"No?" He teased with feigned surprise. "Not aligned with your image of a dutiful parson?"

Not at all.

Her eyes traced the makeshift punching bag. "I'm no expert, but you appear to know what you are doing with all this."

He hummed in agreement. "There was a time in my life where I thought this," he raised a fist, "was the only way I'd be able to earn a living."

"But something set you on a different path."

"A curate." The corner of his mouth kicked up. "From St. Mary's Le Bow. Found me one day after I'd lost to a boy twice my weight. He paid for a doctor to stitch me up and agreed not to tell the relatives looking after me if I promised to work off my debt at the church and studied as his pupil. In the end, I preferred the violence and gore of ancient Rome to roughhousing in Southwark."

"How old were you?"

He scrunched up his face in thought. "Couldn't have been more than ten."

Adam's age. And far too young for a boy to be thinking of how to survive on his own.

They stood in the stall, staring at each other for a long moment. For what was there to say after the events of the previous night, and all of their confessions?

There were no words to sum up her gratitude toward him for making her feel a little less alone. Even if it was for a fleeting moment.

She'd be foolish to put her trust in him. It was more than likely that her husband and his associates had contributed to the ruination of his father. Sinclair wanted answers, and if she allowed him to stay longer, he'd find them.

Along with the secrets that could destroy her.

Her eyes caught on his gloves. His strong fingers flexed around the leather as he held them pressed close to his chest. Last night, he had stayed with her, fought his own demons to protect her, and the estate.

She wondered what else he would be willing to fight, what he would sacrifice in exchange for answers he'd been chasing for decades.

There was little chance he'd ignore her admission about her husband. Perhaps wrestling with the oat sack had been easier than wrestling with what he was going to do about it.

"Thank you," she blurted. "For your help last night." Her voice caught. "I couldn't have done it alone. I am in your debt."

"Rubbish. There is no debt. And you did all the work. It was extraordinary." He shook his head. "I'm only sorry that I wasted so much time by freezing up. Fire and I are not friends."

"I know you have questions. If I was in a position to answer them, I would."

He held her gaze for a long moment, before acknowledging her assertion with a small nod.

When he turned to button up his shirt, she sighed in relief. She could select her words more carefully without the distraction of all that skin.

"Lord Rochford has adversaries. The Trenton family have mistreated, neglected, and abused their tenants for generations. The current earl and his late brother perpetuated that cycle."

She laughed sharply. "From Cumbria to London, the people who wish us ill must number in the thousands."

Sinclair spun around; no doubt surprised by the frankness of her words. "That can't be true."

"You know the rough edges of the world." She nodded at his gloves. "And what people do to gain what they want."

Sinclair frowned. "And Doland? How does he fit in?"

"He is party to their crimes. But he also has his sticky fingers in his own pots. And entwined Rochford in his dealings."

"Which gives him leverage over the earl."

How polite they were being by referring to Geoffrey by his title, avoiding calling him her husband, as if neither one of them wanted to accept the fact.

She wandered a little way down the barn, her hand skimming the rough wood stall. "I have done my best to intervene on behalf of the tenants' needs. But I cannot stop Doland from withdrawing on the estate accounts without the presence of the earl. He's run up significant debts. The kind that are usually resolved with drastic action."

"Or intimidation tactics to extract payment."

"Exactly."

Sinclair curled his fist tightly around his boxing gloves.

"It is a matter of months before we have nothing left," she whispered. "Which is why I must get Adam to school and pay his fees in advance."

"Eight years of tuition is a very large sum."

She nodded. "When Adam was born, he was sickly. Charles and Geoffrey did not believe he'd survive past infancy. At the insistence of Adam's mother, Charles agreed to amend his will to provide for a trust for Adam's education. The money is secure for now."

But it was only a matter of time before Doland weaseled his way into the account.

"And what becomes of you?"

Sinclair's soft, thoughtful tone was nearly her undoing.

She refused to let herself go to pieces by his demonstration of kindness. Instead, she reached for anger, giving him her most vicious glare, before turning on her heel.

He deftly snaked around to stand in front of her, blocking her retreat from the barn.

"Please, my lady, humor me. When your wayward steward defrauds you of your fortunes, what will you do?"

She shook her head.

"Do you think your husband deserves to lose everything because of his notorious past and previous crimes?"

Raising her chin, she lobbed back, "There isn't enough money in the world to balance the scales for the harm and misfortunes he's caused."

"And yet you would protect him from standing trial for them by concealing his location."

"It's not that simple. No matter how much I wish it were."

His gaze was unrelenting as he advanced precariously close to her. "You didn't answer my question. What happens to you if the estate folds?"

"I will survive."

The sharp look he gave her and the tension in his shoulders indicated that he wanted to shake some sense into her.

Perhaps she should let him.

"And what if the earl's enemies track him down, and decide to enact their own justice by taking his life?"

"It won't come to that." She hated how small and feeble her voice sounded. "Adam must go to school. I am doing everything in my power to help him."

She drew a deep breath and was irritated by how much her chest was shaking with the effort of it. "I cannot do it alone."

To his credit, Sinclair didn't smirk or grin. His smooth expression was marred only by a small wrinkle between his brows.

"You said yourself that the village school won't do, and I am too preoccupied with keeping the estate afloat to be of much use to him," she added.

"It's more than that."

Lord, he was insufferable. She'd made every concession she was capable of, and yet he demanded more from her.

Holding her gaze, he said in a low voice, "Why are you asking me to stay, my lady?"

"I want Adam to have every chance at success. He excels at so many things, but society is a mystery to him. To thrive, he must learn how to make friends, how to be social with other boys while protecting himself, and I can't teach him that."

"What makes you think I'm the right person to do it?"

"Because you know what it's like to have the deck stacked against you."

"I do," he agreed. "And I can show him how to overcome it."

She raised her chin. "If you stay, I need your promise of discretion."

"You have them both—my help and my discretion. Along with my word." His voice carried the same weight as if he was making not just a promise, but a sacred vow. "I will not let harm befall anyone as long as I am here."

Sinclair extended his hand to seal their arrangement, as if she were a fellow gentleman.

She had a thousand reservations about taking it. A curt nod was what she was accustomed to.

And the very last thing she wanted.

Faith reached out and clasped his hand. His grip was strong and sure.

She was the first to let go.

CHAPTER ELEVEN

As Jonah traversed the road to the village, he squinted in the bright sunlight.

Eyeing the clear sky with suspicion, he searched for some trace of the dark clouds that had haunted the county for the last month. The disappearance of the dependably miserable weather was mildly alarming and teased him with an optimism he couldn't afford.

When the countess had asked him to remain at Ravenglass for Adam's benefit, he'd cautioned himself against forming high expectations of his sudden turn in favor. Or to read any meaning into the connection they'd forged through a literal fire.

God, she'd been magnificent last night. It wounded him that he couldn't pay her the compliment directly. He'd come close to confessing it and more in the barn. And when her gaze had raked over the gape in his shirt, he'd momentarily forgotten that she was married.

To a man in league with the criminals who had taken everything from him.

She didn't trust Jonah with the truth of Rochford's whereabouts, and he couldn't blame her for it. She was too clever not to suspect he had ulterior motives for wanting to stay at Ravenglass. And too wise to confide in an interloper she barely knew, when everyone she'd depended on in the past had betrayed her.

Yet, she was willing to take a chance on him to help safeguard Adam's future. It was a mission he would not allow himself to fail.

"Why did we have to leave so early for the village?" Adam asked.

"I've some letters for the morning post."

He also wanted an early start to round on every establishment in town. He wasn't leaving until he obtained a thorough explanation for why the entire town had abandoned the countess's call for aid from the fire.

"I thought the post didn't leave until ten o'clock."

Jonah sighed. "I have a number of letters; it will take some time to stamp them."

"Who are you writing to?"

"Adam, it is not considered polite to ask someone such a personal question."

"Why not?"

"I suppose because one's correspondence is personal. It is at another person's discretion how much they choose to share with you about their life."

When they entered the village, a cloud passed over Adam's face. Jonah was dreading this visit himself, but he soldiered on. If he had to bring the bloody Spanish Inquisition upon these so-called neighbors, so be it.

As they turned onto the main road, Adam halted. His eyes locked on a group of boys who were building a stone fence at the edge of the miller's shop.

"Why don't you go see what those boys are up to?" Jonah suggested. "It looks like they could use some help with that wall."

"I wish I could. Look at those lovely slates." Adam stared with longing at the rocks, like another child would look after a puppy or a kitten. "But they won't want my help."

"How do you know if you don't offer?"

"They don't want me bossing them around." He frowned. "They'll leave, and then I'll be stuck there, and the wall won't be finished. Because I can't even lift one of those stones on my own. They don't know how lucky they are."

Jonah crouched down so he could look Adam in the eye. "Why don't you tell them that? I reckon they don't have a clue what kind of treasure they're tossing around."

Adam gave him a skeptical look. "I think I'll just come in and post the letters with you."

Jonah did not want the boy tagging along with him into the shop, because he intended to confront every last one of the cowards who'd refused to answer Ravenglass's emergency bell, and he didn't want the boy to see him get angry.

It would not be pretty.

"I have church business to attend to. It will take some time."

At the mention of church, Adam rolled his eyes. "I'll see what they are doing. But I am warning you, it won't go well."

"Prove me wrong then."

"Fine," Adam agreed and set off down the road to where the boys were working.

Initially, they ignored him, which Jonah supposed was a good thing. Then Adam pointed at the slates and one of them stared at the fence and scratched his head. The others looked similarly perplexed.

Adam placed his hand on his hip, defiant.

The boys exchanged glances, gestured to Adam, then started to take apart the slates.

Jonah gambled that the brokered peace would hold up long enough for him to wreak his own havoc at the mercantile.

He entered the shop, bracing himself for the wariness and avoidance he'd met on his previous trips to the village.

"Good morning, Mr. Sinclair."

Jonah swung his head to the counter, where the shop mistress—Mrs. Clarence—nodded. The two customers she was waiting on tipped their hats in his direction.

"Can I be of help to you with those letters, Reverend?"

Bobbing his head between the letters and the surprisingly welcoming expression on the shopkeeper's face, Jonah murmured, "Good morning. Yes, thank you."

The shop bell rang, and a man entered in a bedraggled state. Jonah recognized him as the parishioner with the pipe, who he'd spoken with after Sunday service. Dirt coated the man's shirt and his trousers were stained to the knees in dried mud.

"Morning, Mrs. C.," he greeted the shopkeeper.

"How are the boys going up by the river, Mr. Holland?"

"Grand. The retaining wall is holding. First shift has gone for some rest."

"Jamie has the rest of the supplies in the back. I'll get him to load the wagon."

"Thank you kindly."

Holland turned to Jonah. "Begging your pardon, Mr. Sinclair, for the scruffy attire."

"Not at all, Mr. Holland. You're at work very early today."

"Not sure that it's early or late." Holland gave a gruff laugh. "Not when we've been up all night."

Jonah stiffened. "Whatever for?"

The other man frowned. "No one at the big house heard about the riverbank? Upper portion subsided, flooded the far eastern fields."

"Dear God, was anyone hurt?"

"No, thank the good Lord. We cleared out all the families last night before the worst of it. Every able-bodied man in the village was out, so we were able to stanch the flow. Otherwise—" Holland shook his head.

They'd avoided a total flood because of it, but no one had heard Lady Rochford's call for help.

Immensely unsatisfying, that. It left no victim for Jonah's fury. No one to eviscerate for their neglect.

"Why did no one send us word at Ravenglass Hall?"

"But we did," Holland pressed. "Two travelers were up at the Saltcoat. Offered to go up to Ravenglass themselves."

Two strangers, willing to travel to the estate. And most likely the perpetrators Jonah was searching for.

"Mr. Holland, do you know anything about those travelers? Their names, where they hailed from?"

Holland shook his head. "Afraid I didn't speak with them myself."

"Of course."

"The barman said they sounded like London folk like—" he paused, and Jonah knew what the man was afraid to say.

They sounded like Troy Doland.

Jonah sighed. "I'm afraid those men delivered an entirely different type of message."

"Sir?"

The countess wouldn't want to advertise the details of the attack. But the villagers had a right to know that there were threats to Ravenglass. And perhaps if they knew the countess was as much a victim of the earl's and the steward's machinations, she might win a few allies.

With a sigh, Jonah related the events of the evening. Holland's frown deepened, and the man muttered a curse beneath his breath, followed by a quick apology.

"It's happened before. There was a small fire in one of the gardens, must have been about a year after his lordship set out on his travels. A tree was struck by lightning. They rang the bell, but Doland had been passing through the village, said to pay it no attention. Afterward, when the steward's own young man told us about the fire, many of us were ashamed. Mrs. C. skinned us alive, made us promise to set up a rota, for when a call came again."

The older man shook his head. "I swear to you, sir, had we not been at the river, help would have arrived."

"It was a well-planned attack," Jonah managed in an even tone, an accomplishment given the rage he was swallowing down. He was forming very specific designs for his next encounter with Troy Doland.

"Everyone in the county knows the river's been vulnerable with all this rain," Holland said. "But Doland won't engage an engineer to inspect it. Have half a mind to write to the earl myself to ask him to do something. Though we all know he won't. Only one from that household who's ever shown a genuine interest in the people and the estate is that apprentice."

Jonah wished the countess could have heard the warmth in the man's voice.

Holland glanced at his mud-caked gloves. "Not sure if you knew, Mr. Sinclair, that I'm a mason by trade. My nephews handle most of the work these days, but I'd be happy to take a look at the damage, make some recommendations for the Ravenglass repairs. That is, if the countess would allow it."

"I imagine Lady Rochford would be most grateful, sir." Jonah extended his hand and Holland accepted it.

They stepped out of the sunshine together, and Jonah's eyes travelled to the far end of the street, where Adam was working with the other boys. None of them appeared to be killing one another, and Adam was wearing something close to a smile.

"He's a sharp lad." Holland nodded.

"He is indeed." Jonah called for Adam to join them.

The boy ignored him.

Jonah raised his hand to his mouth, but Holland stayed him with a pat on his arm. "Give him a minute."

The work on the wall slowed. Adam uttered some final words to the remaining boys and scurried down the street to join his tutor.

"We built almost an entire wall!"

"Did you?" Jonah herded him onto the road.

"We would have built the entire thing, but they started it all wrong and we had to fix it. Mr. Sinclair, did you know there's going to be a fête tomorrow night?"

"Aye," Holland said. "Callum is holding a nuptials celebration for his niece and her new husband." In a lower voice, he added, "The wedding was at Gretna Green."

"I see," Jonah murmured.

"They're going to have music and games and dancing under a marquee." Adam sighed. "I wish we could go."

Jonah exchanged a look with Holland. "Mr. Holland, do you know who's invited to the fête?"

Holland scratched his chin. "Why, I expect that the bride and groom would be honored to have Lady Rochford and her, uh, family attend."

Adam's mouth gaped. "Would they?"

Holland nodded, as if convincing himself.

"And it would be impolite to refuse the invitation, wouldn't it, Mr. Sinclair?"

The boy's face was alight with expectation. Jonah recognized what lay beneath it.

A need to be a part of something.

As they retreated from the village, Jonah mused the countess had more allies than she realized.

And if they were going to combat Doland and his adversaries, she'd need every one of them.

Dazzling sunlight glinted off the remaining half of the winter garden's glass roof, nearly blinding Faith as she crossed the yard to survey the extent of the damage.

"Stop makin' dat face," Lawless chided. "You'll get wrinkles 'round your eyes if you keep dat up."

After so many weeks of rain, the sunshine was foreign, disorienting. Faith could have donned a hat, but the only one she owned which shielded her face belonged to her apprentice disguise. While she suspected that most of the servants were silent co-conspirators in her ruse, she maintained the pretense of her position within the boundaries of Ravenglass. Which meant no trousers at the house. At least crinolines had gone out of fashion, thank God, and her at-home dress made of deep-blue muslin allowed her to forgo a corset.

Lawless sidled up beside her to assess the wreckage, and she blew out a heavy sigh. "If you'd been any closer, it would have blown you both ta bits."

"I can't decide if it was pure luck on our behalf, or incompetency on theirs."

"This was professional." The housekeeper sniffed. "They could have gone for the back of the house easily and they weren't shy of fuel."

It was a message, then. A warning about what the perpetrators would destroy if their demands weren't met.

And she'd bet a fiver that what they wanted correlated with the notice of Doland's debt to Crockfeathers.

"How long can we put off the repairs?"

"Three months, maybe four," Lawless said. "Dere's a fair bit of work here. But it won't be easy finding someone to make the repairs in the middle of harvest."

"It will take me time to find the money." Faith shook her head. "I'll need to sell something."

It would need to be small and expensive to escape Doland's notice. For a drunken lout, he maintained a disturbingly close eye on the house's inventory, plotting which of the valuables he himself would plunder.

"The dowager's enamel snuff boxes might do nicely," Lawless suggested.

"We sold those to pay for the plumbing in the north wing. It will have to be the silver service, then. The third best."

The housekeeper shook her head. "I just gave them ta Dr. Blake to pay off our outstandin' accounts."

"I thought the good doctor refused the payment on the grounds of our long-standing friendship."

"Yes, but the good chemist insisted he be paid," a lilting voice said with amusement.

A willowy blonde woman in an elegant gray walking suit crossed the garden. Faith offered Elyse Blake her hand and a genuine smile. "Dr. Blake. We weren't expecting you until next week."

The doctor accepted her hand with a friendly squeeze. "I have to go to London at the end of the week for the Ladies' Discussion and Improvement Society meeting. I hope you'll forgive me for coming earlier than planned."

"Only if you forgive my having to pay you in cutlery." Faith ground her teeth around a smile.

"My dear, I wish you would allow me to do more—"

"My dear doctor, we already owe you more than I can ever repay in a lifetime."

In other circumstances, Lady Blake and she might have been the closest of friends. They were the mistresses of neighboring estates in a county with few other members of the aristocracy. As such, it was customary for Elyse to call on Ravenglass occasionally. But more frequent visits to the scandalized Rochford residence would be a risk to Elyse's reputation.

Faith would not allow it.

Elyse's eyes clapped on the ruined glasshouse and her frown deepened. "The servants said there was another fire. I'm relieved to hear this time, you were not caught on your own."

Faith's skin flushed. "Yes, we have a recent addition to the household."

The doctor arched an eyebrow. "While I'm happy to hear that Adam now has a devoted tutor, I can't help but wonder how you can trust anyone sent by the bishop."

She'd been asking herself the same question all morning. The devastation of the riverbank was a blow, one that threatened to tip them into ruination. It was sheer luck—and the hard work of her tenants—that the damage hadn't been worse.

All of her attention should have focused on the crisis. Yet, as she'd toured the river, and visited the displaced tenants, Sinclair had preoccupied her thoughts.

"I don't know if I can trust him," Faith confessed. "But I'm not sure that I have much of a choice."

"Lady Rochford!"

They turned around to find the man himself crossing the garden. Quite a clip he was running at too, his long legs sending up gravel behind him, his hat clasped in one hand as his jacket billowed behind in the breeze.

He was practically breathless by the time he reached them.

"Are you well?" Sinclair rasped.

Faith blinked up at his flushed face. "Indeed, I'm fine. Are you?"

"Quite." He swallowed visibly. "Martin said the carriage in the drive belonged to the doctor."

"Now that you've caught your breath, Mr. Sinclair, may I present Dr. Elyse Blake."

If Sinclair was surprised at discovering the doctor was a lady, he hid it well between a polite smile and smooth bow. "An honor to meet you."

"Dr. Blake attends to Adam and the household regularly," Faith added. "Whenever she's in residence at Broadmoor. The county is fortunate to have someone with her skills as our neighbor."

Elyse gifted her a radiant smile as she pulled on her gloves. "Since you both report to be in very good health and humor, I must see to my other patients."

"I'll show ya through," Lawless offered, but her eyes caught Faith's in a silent warning.

They needed Sinclair's attention away from Elyse and her rounds at the house.

Luckily, he seemed content to stand outside in the garden.

"How brightly the sun shines this morning," he remarked. "Quite disorienting, isn't it?"

"We're retreating to discussing the weather now?"

He gave her a smile that was entirely too devilish for a clergyman, which caught her off guard. She'd wanted him to be abashed, awkward about the shaky intimacy that they'd experienced, working together to save Ravenglass. That was how she felt about it.

"I gather you heard about the river during your trip into the village."

Sinclair nodded, his expression sobering. "Apparently, two travelers at the Saltcoat offered to bring us the news directly last night."

"Did anyone recognize them?"

"No." He made a predatory noise in the back of his throat, the same sound she'd heard when he was punching his bag in the barn. "The only thing we know is that they were Londoners who spoke like Doland."

Cockneys like him. The prospect made her shudder.

Sinclair marked it. He glanced back at the house and stepped closer. "How long have you known Dr. Blake?"

"Years and years. Since she became mistress of Broadmoor."

"Is she related to Lord Antony Blake? The Member of the House of Lords who was a physician?"

"She is his widow." Faith nodded.

"No one took over his title?"

"They had no children, and he had no other heirs."

"So there is no one for us to counsel with on the matter of the traveling arsonists. Other than the local magistrate and constabulary."

"We won't be alerting the constabulary." The coolness in her tone countered the anxiety heating her blood. "Or anyone else."

His mouth coiled in protest.

Leaning closer, refusing to hide the fear in her voice, she said softly, "Would you risk drawing those villains back here with all that attention?"

"My lady!" Mrs. Lawless rushed into the yard, her breath heaving. "You're wanted straightaway to help with Master Adam's lesson."

Faith exchanged a puzzled look with Sinclair, who appeared as confused as she was by Lawless's request.

"The boy asked Peggy for dancin' lessons." Lawless gulped a breath. "In the ballroom."

The one place in Ravenglass Adam had never ventured to. Besides the north wing.

Ignoring the confusion plastered on Sinclair's face, Faith seized her skirts and ran into the house.

As she chased Lawless down the corridor, Faith silently repeated the same direction over and over, like a mantra.

Do not look at the wall. Do not look at the wall. Do not look at the wall.

At the door to the ballroom, she and the housekeeper halted, sharing the same uneasy stare. Lawless murmured a colorful curse, but Faith raised a hand to silence her. Sinclair's footsteps advanced quickly down the hallway.

She tugged her skirts back into place, smoothed a hand down her bodice, then nodded at Lawless to precede her into the ballroom.

"Her ladyship has arrived."

Adam let out a whoop. "Thank Jaysus."

His name echoed as the four adults—including a winded Sinclair—shouted at him in unison.

"We had a conversation just this morning about blasphemy," Sinclair chided.

"How is thanking Jesus showing contempt for God?" Adam persisted.

"Because you are making something holy—a prayer of thanks—irreverent."

"I don't think—"

"Adam," Faith interrupted, failing to school her impatience. "Can you please illuminate the reason you summoned me here with such great haste?"

"Forgive us, Lady Rochford." Peggy flushed. "Adam is learning to dance."

Faith turned to the man she blamed for the upheaval. "A word, Mr. Sinclair." She gestured toward the door, hoping to ease him completely out of the ballroom, but the infuriating man stopped short of the door.

"There is no need to get angry with the boy."

"I thought I made it clear that you must discuss any new lesson plans—such as a deviation from the schoolroom setting—with me ahead of time," she retorted.

"Don't give out to him, Lady Rochford!" Adam shouted, and it was all Faith could do to avoid hushing him for raising his voice. "It wasn't Mr. Sinclair's fault. I didn't ask him to use the ballroom."

"Adam—" Sinclair warned.

"There's going to be a fête," Adam continued. "With contests and lawn bowling and bonfires and," the boy drew out the last word for emphasis, "dancing."

He was beaming as he turned to Faith. "And *we're* invited. *All* of us. So, you see, I have to learn how to do the reels, or else they won't invite us back."

A fine, sensible argument, delivered in Adam's fine, sensible tone.

Faith's eyes stung at the unspoken sentiment beneath it: he couldn't bear to be excluded.

"It's true," Sinclair confirmed. "The boys he was playing with today in the village told him about it."

"He played with a group of boys today?" she whispered. "And he didn't, they didn't—"

"Kill each other?" Sinclair whispered back, grinning. "No, it was rather harmonious. He was nervous at first but, by the end, I had to drag him away."

"That's wonderful." It lifted the dread weighing on her a little to think Adam was making friends.

They'd included him in the fête and, knowing how hard it was for him to have earned the invitation, Adam was fearful of disappointing them.

That possibility roused such an ache in her chest that when Sinclair asked if they should proceed, she nodded.

"Excellent." Sinclair sprang on her approval, and motioned to the pianoforte, where Lawless sat, eyeing them warily.

"Peggy taught me the steps. But we need four of us to do all the passes," Adam said. "And we need music."

In the empty ballroom, even the faintest tune from the piano would echo throughout the house. A knot fisted Faith's stomach. "Perhaps we'll practice the steps first."

"But I've been doing that for ages!"

"Mrs. Lawless, you'll play for us, won't you?" Peggy asked.

Faith cleared her throat. "I don't think it's appropriate—"

"Please, my lady," Adam begged. "Just once through. Then Peggy and I can practice on our own."

She glanced at Lawless, but the old bat sat silent, forcing the decision on her mistress.

Sinclair too, was unusually quiet. It was as if he was as unsettled as she was about the endeavor, which was ridiculous. What did he have to be nervous about?

Don't look at the wall.

"Once through," Adam insisted. "And then we'll practice the rest on our own."

"In your rooms," Faith countered, not bothering to elaborate why. She was the Countess of Rochford, for God's sake. She shouldn't have to explain herself to a ten-year-old.

"Once through, then we return upstairs." Sinclair made the final offer before Adam could force another protest.

Adam gave another whoop as an excited flush colored his cheeks.

She'd have to have a heart of stone to refuse such a simple request and watch that joy fade from his face. Or tell him to hush his voice.

"Lady Rochford, you must partner with Mr. Sinclair, since Peggy and I are better matched for height."

Sinclair offered her his arm.

She stared at it for an inappropriate amount of time, hesitation her last attempt at maintaining control.

Gently, he took her hand and threaded her arm through his. As his bare hand grazed hers, she felt a current pass between them.

"You know the polonaise, don't you, Lady Rochford?" Adam asked.

"Yes, I know the steps."

Sinclair leaned forward and murmured, "Then you can help me along."

The rumble of his voice so close in her ear sent licks of heat down her neck.

"Now, Mrs. Lawless!"

The housekeeper began to play and, to Faith's relief, she kept the damper pedal down to reduce the sound.

"Count us in, Master Adam," Peggy encouraged.

"Louder, Mrs. Lawless!" the boy shouted. "I need to count us in!"

With a sigh, Lawless released the damper. The music rose above Faith's protests, and then Sinclair's warm hands were upon hers, and he swept her into his arms.

"To the left!" Adam called, flinging himself and Peggy into a circle.

Sinclair guided them to follow, pulling her in the opposite direction they were supposed to move, then spun them around so they landed on the right beat.

"That's it, Mr. Sinclair." Peggy nodded. "Keep counting, Master Adam."

"Now we spin!"

Adam reached for Faith's other hand, and Sinclair linked them together, grasping Peggy's, and they skipped in a circle to the music.

"Now right!" Adam called, and they shifted direction in time with the song, all of them finally stepping together and in rhythm.

"The ladies!"

Faith met Peggy at the circle center while Sinclair and Adam looked on, Sinclair clapping and Adam grinning as they waited for their chance to step into the center and meet the ladies. When it was time for them to switch partners, Adam confidently reached for Faith, crossing is right arm over his body to meet hers.

Their hands clasped. The delighted giggle that escaped from Adam's throat was the most beautiful sound Faith had ever heard. She tipped her own head back and laughed as they twirled, and Adam delivered her back to Sinclair.

As Faith fitted her hand into his, his grasp tightened around her, and her breath caught.

He tried to ease off his grip, but she clung to him, unable to tear her gaze away from the way his fine cheekbones heated with color and the beautiful curve of his mouth.

Later, she would admit to herself that she was besotted.

Had she not been, she would have heard the footsteps and the familiar creaking sound.

Before the north wall of the ballroom split open and a white-clad figure stepped out and cried, "Faith and begorrah!"

The music halted. Lawless staggered to her feet, exchanging a panicked look with Faith, as she'd flung herself away from Sinclair.

Do not look at the wall.

"D-did you need somethin', Dolly?" the housekeeper asked.

Dolly scanned the room, registered Faith's presence, and bobbed a curtsy. "Pardon me, my lady. I heard—"

"Yes, thank you, Dolly," Lawless said quickly. "You're not needed here."

She stared pointedly at the door everyone else had used to enter the ballroom.

Do not look at the wall.

Do not look at Sinclair.

Faith could feel his eyes pegging her with a stare, but she kept her own gaze pointed at the servants.

Lawless cleared her throat. "I remember, now, I need you downstairs, girl. Come with me."

The housekeeper rose from the piano and sent the maid a scathing look as she curled her fingers in a beckoning motion.

Dolly's eyes widened to saucers, but she trailed after Lawless, giving Faith another curtsy on her way out.

Adam was halfway across the room before Faith had the sense to summon him back.

"Adam, come here."

He paused. "Did you know that wall was a staircase?"

"Adam." She pointed to the place on the floor before her. "Now."

Reluctantly, the boy followed her command.

"What direction do we face?"

Adam glanced out the door. "The north."

"And what do you know about the north wing?"

His shoulders sagged with a sigh. "That there was damage to the attic ceiling."

"And?"

"And until we replace the beam, it's dangerous for anyone to go up there."

She nodded, forcing herself to swallow the bitterness of the lies she was about to tell. "That is where the staircase leads."

"Then why was Dolly up there?"

"Adam. Is it your place to question Lady Rochford?" Sinclair's tone was forceful and, from the way he'd emptied his expression, Faith would bet that he was as annoyed at having a part of the house forbidden to him as Adam was.

The boy's mouth drooped; the joy of the dance lesson squelched by being disciplined. It pained her to take that pleasure away from him.

But if he went wandering up there, she hated what he'd find far more.

"I believe it's time to continue the lesson upstairs," she said, gesturing to Peggy, who gathered Adam to her and urged him out of the room.

Sinclair remained, his eyes scrutinizing the wall and her in equal measure.

"My lady—"

"Mr. Sinclair, I must ask that you restrict Adam's lessons to his rooms. As you can see, it has upset the household."

He stiffened at her terse tone. "Forgive me. We meant no harm—"

"Thank you. That will be all, Mr. Sinclair."

For a fraught moment, he remained unmoving, staring at her, before he bent slowly, offered her a stiff bow, and backed out of the room.

Faith knew by his lack of protest that he was plotting how to uncover where the ballroom staircase led.

She would have to find something else for him to chase.

Chapter Twelve

Buttery late-afternoon sunshine filtered through the trees bordering the village green as Jonah and Adam joined the crowd of villagers at the fête.

Adam's head darted in all directions, taking in the tables of sweets and savories, the barrels for apple-bobbing, and the large white marquee erected on the back half of the square.

"Did you see that man with the rubber balls?" The boy's mouth dangled open in pure wonder. "He's throwing them in a circle."

"Juggling." Jonah smiled. "My, he is clever."

"Can you do that, Mr. Sinclair?"

"No, never learned myself."

"Well, it's not too late to start."

Jonah laughed. "And where would you like to start today?"

"Apples. I've been practicing in the tub."

Peggy nodded sheepishly. "It's true, sir."

"And then maybe the bowling pins," Adam continued. "Although we didn't have much a chance to practice those, but if it's anything like pall-mall, I should do fine."

He turned to Jonah. "Do you think I should try the shooting too? I haven't practiced. Lady Rochford won't let me touch a gun."

Rightly so. "Let's start with apples and see how we go."

The boy flashed a smile and skipped across the green to the barrels, with Peggy trailing behind.

"Welcome, Mr. Sinclair." Mrs. Clarence waved him over to a table stocked with pastries. "Can I interest you in tarts and punch?"

"I'd be delighted to try the pastries, ma'am, but I'll hold off on the punch for now."

"Pacing yourself, that's wise of you." The shopkeeper handed him a small apple hand pie. "Dancing will start at sundown."

A wagon pulled up to the edge of the green, bearing three large casks of the Saltcoat's ale. The proprietor, Callum Burns, and the ancient barman struggled to lift them from the cart.

Jonah nearly flattened three people as he fled across the square to reach them. The publican was his best lead on the Cockney travelers who'd set fire to the Ravenglass gardens, and he'd hoped the celebration would provide him with a chance to question Callum.

When he approached the wagon, the men readily welcomed his help.

"Can you manage carrying it to the tent, Mr. Sinclair?" Burns asked.

"No troubles," Jonah said, although his muscles burned when he hoisted the barrel onto his shoulder. "It's a short distance."

He followed them both inside, and Burns directed them to a large oak table. He acknowledged Jonah's assistance with a brusque nod. "You're strong for a parson."

"Spent as many years lifting those as I have with the Church."

"Did you now." The older man eyed him with something close to respect. "Didn't think city folk worked that hard."

"My city folk did."

The tavern owner's mouth twitched in an approximation of a smile, which Jonah interpreted as a divine signal to press his case. "If I may, Mr. Burns. I was hoping you remembered something about the two travelers who were at the Saltcoat, the night that the river flooded."

"Don't recall much." Burns mopped up the condensation that leached from the casks with a rag. "Two men. Good sized, they were. Londoners, but not gentry." He curled his lip. "Talked just like Doland."

"They said they had business up at Ravenglass?"

"Aye. Said the steward was expecting them." Burns frowned. "Didn't think it odd then, but it seems strange now. Doland left town the day before. Hasn't returned since."

"Is it common for the steward to receive such visitors at Ravenglass?" Jonah hoped his question implied the subtext: *Without an invitation from the countess?*

"Doland does a fair bit of business at the pub, with a variety of sorts," Burns replied. "Keeps that lot away from the big house. As he should."

With that judgment rendered, Burns strode away, leaving Jonah with more questions than answers. He searched the tent for the Saltcoat's barman and barmaid, hoping to grill them to uncover something Burns had left out, but was distracted as the musicians took up their fiddles, pipes, and drums and began to play.

Adam rushed into the tent, accompanied by a ginger-haired girl. "Time for dancing, Mr. Sinclair!"

"One dance. Then we must be going." Lady Rochford had stipulated that they were to return at dark. Given recent events, he understood her concern.

"Two dances," Adam insisted. "One fast and one slow."

"Adam—"

"Please, sir." The girl interrupted him. "Only a few boys know the steps. We're always wanting partners."

Adam nodded, giving him a searching, buoyant look that crumbled Jonah's resolve.

"Two dances," he conceded. "And then we must go."

Adam bolted with his new friend into the crowd of dancers.

As more people joined in the merriment, the air in the tent grew stuffy. The adult women also suffered from a lack of dance partners, and Jonah found himself the subject of more than a few stares.

He could dance, although he was unpracticed. But dancing was an activity for courting and wooing a wife. Something he couldn't commit himself to until he found justice for his family.

His mind flashed back to the abbreviated practice in the ballroom, and how the countess had smiled as she'd clasped his hand. He could still sense the heat of her skin, felt himself growing flushed and hard at the memory.

When Dolly had walked through the passageway, and Lady Rochford had abruptly tossed him out, the cut hadn't stung him. Not the way it would have, if another woman had promised him friendship and then dismissed him like a servant.

He'd spent enough time with the countess to garner that the maid's arrival had frightened her. He wished that she'd trusted him enough to tell him why.

Dear God, it was warm in the tent. He needed some air.

Across the dance floor, he met Peggy's eyes and motioned that he would take a turn outside. She waved happily and returned to watching Adam, clapping along as the boy leapt and twirled.

Ducking out of the tent, he drew in a deep breath of cool air. The day had faded to black. Men clustered around the scattered bonfires, sipping ale and puffing on pipes.

They'd stayed later than planned. If they dawdled longer, he'd anger the countess. The idea of her rendering him a tongue-lashing, her cheeks aflame and her brown eyes afire, roused a wave of pure lust the evening breeze couldn't tamp down.

A break in the music provided a moment of rare silence. Above the far-off crackling of fires and murmured voices came a faint, menacing whinny.

The same sound that had nearly announced his death a few weeks ago.

He whipped around, searching the dark pockets of the village square. At the edge of the green, below the branches of the great chestnut tree that guarded the front of the churchyard, he made out a familiar silhouette.

The rising moon and the faint torchlight guided him through the darkness. As he rounded the church, the countess remained beneath the tree boughs, staring out at the green.

"Good evening, my lady."

She stiffened at the sound of his voice, then her shoulders relaxed. He relished a small thrill that she recognized him, and a greater disappointment that she remained facing the other direction.

"Are you armed?" he murmured.

At that, she turned toward him, brows arched in surprise.

"It's dangerous to be out here, alone, in the dark." He stepped closer, forcing her back under the shade of the tree.

"It is equally dangerous to be caught out here with a man," she whispered.

"Ah, but not dressed as you are."

She was in her apprentice attire, but her neckcloth dangled loose around her throat, exposing her face.

"Where is Adam?"

"Dancing with Peggy. He begged to stay for one last set."

"You didn't want to join them?"

He gave a small laugh. "As I displayed during Adam's lesson, dancing is not my strong suit. I lack practice."

"Perhaps you lack the right partner."

The suggestion might have been construed as flirtatious, in one seeking such signals.

When he edged closer to further investigate that possibility, she did not retreat.

Until something scuttled nearby, and they both froze.

Gravel scattered, preceding the sound of advancing footsteps.

"This way," a deep voice drawled.

A high-pitched giggle responded. "Where? I can't see!"

The countess threw Jonah a look of pure terror. He didn't think twice before he clasped his hand to her mouth and tugged her against the side wall of the church, shielding her with his body.

"Faith and begorrah!"

Dolly's voice echoed from a few feet away from where they hid.

In the shadows, the countess's chest pumped with her labored breaths, and her muffled exhales were hot against Jonah's palm. He struggled to avoid agitating her further by leaning in closer, but that was proving difficult. Every atom in his body begged him to draw nearer to her warmth, to the intoxicating scent of oranges and lemons permeating the narrow space between them.

"Morris, it's too dark out," Dolly exclaimed. "What are we doing here?"

"Isn't this much better than that stuffy tent now, love? No one's around to disturb us. Hardly ever get to see you, now that you're up at the big house." Morris rumbled. "Don't like you up there, Dolly. A gorgeous girl like you ain't safe with the Rochfords."

The countess trembled.

Despite his absence from Ravenglass, the earl's sordid reputation persisted among the villagers and Lady Rochford couldn't escape it. But how was Dolly connected to it? Something had spooked the countess when the maid had interrupted the dance lesson in the ballroom.

Did Dolly make her fear the ghosts of her husband's past crimes?

Jonah lifted his head, hoping to find some way to calm her, but at that precise moment, she twisted toward him. Her breasts grazed against his chest.

Beneath his palm, she uttered a faint moan.

Jonah pressed his palm gently against her mouth in warning.

"Don't be daft, Morris. I'm plenty safe at Ravenglass," Dolly insisted. "Lady Rochford is a fair mistress. She's kinder than anyone knows, especially to the boy."

"Fine, fine," Morris conceded, his voice turning soft. "But I've missed seeing your face every day, love."

His footfalls tossed up a small stone, which skittered down the side wall of the church, landing at Jonah's feet and startling the countess.

She clamped her arms around his waist and pulled him closer.

He counted it as something of a triumph, that she'd reached for him, that she wanted the protection of his body. And tempting fate, he scrounged up the courage to peer into the shadows and meet her gaze.

I'll protect you, he mouthed, hoping she could see him in the darkness. *I'll keep you safe.*

Her eyes brimmed with silent tears, but she grazed her fingers against his palm in a fleeting caress, as if to thank him or perhaps assure him. He didn't care, he only wanted her to do it again.

Jonah's breath sputtered. As he silently cursed his flailing lack of self-control, the countess's warm hands flexed at his waist. He didn't know if she was seeking or providing assurance, but it demanded closer contact.

Slowly, he lifted his arm from the wall and gently stroked her shoulder, which she tilted, ever so slightly, toward him.

The small encouragement made his pulse pound wildly. He could no longer pretend this was about her protection.

His sole aim was to keep her in his arms.

In sweet surrender, his hand traced a path down her arm, to the dip of her waist, then the curve of her hip, before winding around to rest at the small of her back. The rough cotton of her shirt chafed at his fingers, but the give of her curves against him was softer than silk.

"Oh, Morris," Dolly murmured. "I've missed you too."

"A good job can't keep you warm at night, Dolly. Not like I can."

"Come, love, give us a kiss," Morris begged. "You don't know how long I've been wanting to taste you."

The countess's breath gusted against Jonah's hand. He couldn't stop himself from stroking the dent beneath her plump lip with his thumb.

She responded with a low whimper, and clasped her own hand against his, pressing both of their palms against her mouth, as if it would take their shared strength to contain her.

As if, like Morris, she'd been pining for a lover's kiss and couldn't withstand the wait.

Across the green, the music came to a sudden, crashing halt. A clamor of voices rose from the direction of the tent.

"You come back here, you little brute!"

"Where did he go? Did you catch that hook on him?"

"I see him in the corner. He won't get away with this!"

The commotion brought with it the return of Jonah's good sense. He staggered away from the countess as she yanked her kerchief up around her throat and face.

Peering around the corner of the church, Jonah saw Dolly and Morris fleeing into the chaotic crowd, which had emptied into the square.

"They're gone," he murmured.

They both ducked beneath the cover of the chestnut tree and stared at the green.

Adam stood between Peggy and a red-faced man. Trailing behind was another boy, who was holding onto his cheek, and howling.

"Is Adam hurt?" the countess asked, her voice pitched high in alarm.

"He doesn't appear to be," Jonah replied calmly, although his gut clenched at the prospect. And at the alarm in her voice. He had to rectify it. "This is my fault; I should have stayed with him. I'll take care of whatever he needs and will bring him home safely. You should go, while they're all too distracted to notice."

"Sinclair—"

He darted away without giving her the apology she deserved. He didn't quite trust himself to linger further, with his blood pumping and his hands aching to return to her body.

No, it was much safer for him to join the noisy mob on the green and attend to the mess his own neglect had perpetuated. Adam wasn't the only one who needed social instruction.

Foolish of him to think that he could guide them both through this when he knew so little himself. Without Christopher, he'd have been utterly lost trying to navigate society.

He needed his friend. To coach him on the young gentleman's social education he'd missed out on, when his family had lost everything.

Christopher would jump at the chance to be of service. The visit would give Jonah the chance to share information about his quest that would be unwise to put down in a letter.

More importantly, Christopher's presence would keep Jonah and his tumultuous feelings for Lady Rochford in check. Although, if he invited a guest to Ravenglass, the countess would be furious with him.

Which was exactly what Jonah needed her to be.

Chapter Thirteen

As she sat in the crowded church, with sunlight filtering through the stained-glass windows, Faith berated herself for her reckless behavior the previous night.

She racked her brain for the series of decisions that had led to her colossal mistake. After the interlude in the ballroom, she'd needed to move her limbs and breathe fresh air and pretend she wasn't trapped by the weight of her past choices.

So she'd gone to watch the festivities from a distance in her disguise. Sinclair had found her in the shadows, and when he'd swooped her behind the church wall and guarded her with the shelter of his body, she'd welcomed it.

No, more than that. She'd *reveled* in his closeness.

He'd made her forget that neither her heart nor her body was free to give away. And hours later, she could not stop imagining what might have occurred if they hadn't been interrupted.

Or what could happen in the future if they were both free to act upon her imaginings.

Mrs. Clarence, the village shopkeeper, marched down the aisle and sat in the pew across from Faith. She carried a basket of posies, which she placed ceremoniously at the end of the bench, and as she straightened, she gave Faith an officious nod, and a welcoming wink.

The woman's warm reaction was as surprising as a slap in the face.

The shopkeeper wasn't the only parishioner whose hostility appeared to have thawed. The congregation had greeted her with careful smiles and nods, which she did her best to return, while she puzzled over what had caused this sudden change.

As the ancient church tower bell rang, people noisily rose to their feet. In the weeks since Sinclair's first sermon, attendance had mushroomed. Dozens of parishioners gathered for Sunday service.

Sinclair strode down the aisle, eyes aimed devoutly at the pulpit. The ceremonious white robe strained at his shoulders; the previous rector must have possessed a much different stature.

Despite the borrowed garments, there was no question that Sinclair belonged there. He fit in among the congregation like the missing slice of glass from the broken stained window.

When the service concluded, Faith did not flee the church for the safety of her carriage. They'd walked on account of the fine weather and to avoid recreating another fracas at the sight of the Rochford brougham.

Slowly, she and Adam made their way to the crowd gathered on the church's steps. She located a woman hovering next to a boy with a blackened eye. Grasping Adam's hand, Faith walked him over to where they stood, the crowd parting like the Red Sea to accommodate them.

Peggy introduced the woman to Faith as a Mrs. Woodgate, who blinked in surprise.

"Is there something you needed, milady?"

"Indeed, Mrs. Woodgate." Faith pulled Adam forward. "*We* need to apologize for what happened between Gilbert and Adam at the fête."

"I'm sorry for hitting you, Gilbert," Adam offered. "And hurting your eye. Even though you pulled Lottie's hair first—"

"Adam—"

"Apology accepted, Master Adam," Mrs. Woodgate replied quickly, pulling on Gilbert's collar. "Isn't it?"

Gilbert nodded his acquiescence and wriggled free of his mother's grip.

He turned to Adam with a calculating look. "You bring that net?"

"Of course." Adam patted his pocket. "You bring the bait?"

Gilbert jutted his chin at the boys waiting by the fence, with long poles strung over the shoulders.

Adam turned to Faith. "We're running an experiment on minnows to see if the pole or the net catches them faster."

And with a flash of a smile, the boys tore out of the churchyard, leaving Faith and Mrs. Woodgate's jaws dangling.

Peggy took off after them, murmuring something about the need to keep an eye out, and Mrs. Woodgate followed suit.

"Lady Rochford!"

Faith turned to find the shopkeeper approaching. "Good morning, Mrs. Clarence."

"And a beautiful one it is." The shopkeeper smiled. "May I solicit your opinion on a matter of fashion, milady?"

"Fashion?" Faith stuttered.

Mrs. Clarence dipped her hand into the basket and retrieved a small round of bluebells. "Are these bouquets smart enough to sell at the Cumbria Cup next week? Some ladies think they're too simple, but I believe a posy *should* be simple. After all, no one wants to be lugging a grand fountain of flowers with them on a day out, now do they?"

The shopkeeper waited expectantly for her answer. As if she truly valued Faith's knowledge of society's latest fashions.

As if Faith hadn't spent the last ten years locked away from everyone and everything.

She smothered an overwhelming urge to laugh and replied shakily, "Quite right, Mrs. Clarence. I prefer simple elegance to ornamental frippery."

"Hopefully everyone will share that sentiment," drawled a deep voice. "So that Mrs. Clarence may sell a packet of posies."

Faith did her best to ignore Sinclair's canny smile, but when the shopkeeper excused herself, there was no excuse to avoid looking at him.

"Good morning, Lady Rochford."

The second she met his intense blue stare, memories from the night before surfaced. Heat crept up her neck and into her cheeks and her tongue remained tied in knots, unable to articulate the simplest greeting.

"Pardon me milady. Reverend Sinclair."

Mr. Holland, the village mason, came to her rescue. He stood twisting his cap in his hands awkwardly, and with good reason. Faith couldn't recall if she'd ever spoken to him in public as the Countess of Rochford.

But they'd had several discussions about the estate, while in her steward's apprentice disguise.

"I believe you know Mr. Holland?" Sinclair said.

"Indeed." She forced a smile. "Good morning, Mr. Holland. I understand you oversee work on the riverbank. How is it progressing?"

"Slowly, my lady. But I have received good news and would ask for your help to pass it along to the steward, or his lad. We've found an engineer to consult."

Faith checked herself to keep from advertising her excitement. If they could get the man to survey the river before Doland returned, she'd worry about the money for the expense later.

"When is he available?" she asked.

Holland turned to Sinclair. "Mr. Wilde telegraphed he could arrive on Thursday."

Sinclair grinned. "Sooner than I thought. Poor Christopher really is desperate for an escape."

Faith maintained a smooth expression while her blood alternatively heated and froze at the prospect that another visitor had been invited to Ravenglass without her consent.

"Can't be quick enough." Holland tipped his hat. "I look forward to hearing from the steward."

She waited for the mason to retreat out of earshot before she whirled on Sinclair. "What did you do?"

"My friend Christopher is a student of engineering. Among other things," he added quickly. "I wrote to him about the river flooding. He volunteered his services."

"On whose authority did you make this request?"

Sinclair frowned. "You're angry."

"Asking for an explanation does not mean I'm angry." *Furious* was a better descriptor of the emotional edge she was approaching. "You had no leave to engage anyone without my consultation or permission."

"Christopher is my closest friend, and as any friend would when they learned of such a predicament, he offered his help."

Insolent man. Did he forget she was on the brink of ruin? That she couldn't afford to repair her own roof?

Dropping her voice, she asked, "And are *you* to compensate him for his time and service?"

Sinclair's brows lowered. "He's willing to consult *gratis*. The only thing you need to provide is hospitality during his visit."

"Absolutely not."

She stepped closer, but Sinclair did not retreat. He stared at her, baffled, while she warned, in a low voice, "Ravenglass is not your home. *You* are not its master, nor its mistress, free to extend invitations to whoever you please."

She threw him one final scathing look before adding, "Learn your place, Sinclair. Or I will see that you have none here."

Like a coward, she fled.

In a fugue of her own anger and anxiety, she ran, her worn slipper biting into the skin of her heel.

When the craggy stone towers of the north wing finally came into view, she slowed her pace. Bright sunshine beat down on her, and she was perspiring by the time she dashed up the drive. The house would have been a refuge, for once, its frigid stones providing relief from the heat, and its emptiness offering solitude. Most of the servants were away for their half-day out.

But her feet carried her past the house, through the sparse gardens, to the orangery.

Stepping inside, she drew a deep breath and the sweet citrus aroma soothed her.

In the languid heat, she peeled off her pelisse and loosened her bodice to ease her breathing, but as she processed what had transpired at the church, pressure mounted in her chest.

Making a scene in public was unacceptable. No woman of her station made such mistakes. Once again, she'd proved herself to be an imposter.

But she hadn't regretted the shock on Sinclair's face. That he'd earned for his betrayal.

Bewitching her poor unsuspecting tenants into being cordial to her. Inviting a stranger to her house.

Holding her in his arms like he desired her, and promising with his eyes and with his touch that they were both free to act upon it.

Her breath choked her throat.

"Here you are."

Sinclair's deep voice was as sultry and sweet as the air in the orangery.

His footsteps approached, then paused as if he thought better about coming too close.

"Will you turn around so that I know you are well?"

Whatever divine counsel had held him back before capitulated, and he stepped closer. The scent of wool and soap and the faint tinge of incense washed over her. "Lady Rochford—"

At the sound of her name, she whipped around to face him. "Now, suddenly, you care if I'm well?"

She'd lost control of her voice; she'd meant it to be scathing, but it came out wobbled.

"After you took the presumption to invite a stranger—one of important social standing—to *my* house, without my permission, you think to ask how I'm feeling?

"Did you not consider your friend's welfare?" she railed on. "Anyone who stays under this roof is also under threat from Doland and Geoffrey's enemies. I never knew a man could be so selfish, to ignore the best interests of his friends, his *pupil*—"

"No, my lady."

He'd barely raised his voice a decibel, but the tone had changed to that chilling cold authority that stole her words.

But as his eyes held hers, they blazed.

"I wrote to Christopher for advice," he insisted. "He offered his aid without my asking him. And I accepted."

"He'll tell tales to all of society about the poor little heiress, abandoned by her notorious husband, withering away in a crumbling estate. It could *ruin* Adam—"

Ruin them all.

"No," Sinclair repeated, shaking his head. "Christopher is like a brother to me. He is foolish in ways that most young men are foolish, but he is no cad and no gossip, and he would never be so cruel as to harm the reputation of a child. Or a woman."

Faith spun on her heel and marched into the thickest cluster of trees, where the canopy of leaves could hide her. But his determined footsteps chased after her, and she was strangely relieved he'd followed.

Even if she wanted to push him through one of the glass windows.

"It is for *your* best interests, Lady Rochford, that I am doing this."

Something pulled at his brow as he stared at her. Likely because she was shaking like a leaf.

"Adam's social acceptance depends on your standing in society." His voice softened. "You must show them that you're nothing like your husband."

"How *dare* you."

She attempted to shove him, but he caught her halfway through the motion and pulled her into his arms.

As she struggled against him, she fought to get a good breath so she could roar her protests. But the only noise she could produce was a sob.

She was a disaster.

And still, he held her. Despite her black words, and the way her breaths heaved as she gulped for air.

"I can't have him here," she choked out.

"You've every right to be afraid," he murmured. "If I were you, I'd distrust any of the male species and the entire *beau monde*. I wouldn't want them in my home either."

She laughed at the idea that Ravenglass was her home. It had never felt that way to her. Not until the last few weeks. When doors had been opened, shutters thrown back, and sunlight illuminated dark rooms.

Years ago, when she'd first arrived, she'd dreamed of it being home. She'd longed for the day when she and Geoffrey finally married, and she'd assumed the role of his lady wife, supervising a household, and tending to the tenants and the village.

It never happened. Her husband had seen to that, even in his absence.

But today, she'd walked into the church, and instead of contempt, she'd found acceptance.

Until that moment, she hadn't realized how badly she'd longed for it.

Hot tears poured down her cheeks as she rasped, "I cannot do what you ask."

"Can't, or won't?"

At his light teasing, she squirmed, but his arms tightened to hold her steady.

"Truly, I can't," she whispered. "I have no connections. All I know of how to behave in good society is from books and broadsheets."

"It's more than I know."

"But you're a parson. And a man. You can get away with it." Drawing another shaky breath, she whispered, "I don't think I can manage the act. In fact, I'm very confident I will fail."

A gentle finger crept beneath her chin, forcing her to look at him. "I have every faith you'll succeed."

She shook her head. "My entire life has been one form of pretense after another. I'm so tired of trying to keep up the facade."

He nodded. "It sounds exhausting. I wish I could advise you, but I struggle with it myself. For more than half my life, I've relied on Christopher's help to navigate society. He's like a travel guide one might hire on a foreign journey."

The thought roused her smile. Sinclair returned it with a broad grin that made the lines around his eyes crinkle.

She was standing too close to make such an observation. Within the circle of his arms, she could scent the coffee on his breath.

Yet none of what they were doing felt wrong. Which was the precise reason she should step away.

He stared down at her, his chest slowly rising and falling. "Please, my lady. Reconsider."

"You trust this man?"

"I trust Christopher with my life."

"Why?"

"Because he never needed to be kind to me. In the course of almost twenty years of friendship, he's given me far more than I could return to him, and he has never once acknowledged it."

His mouth tilted up in the corner. "And because everyone needs friends who are better at the things one finds challenging."

"The great Reverend Sinclair admits he struggles?"

"All the time," he said, without a hint of arrogance or self-deprecation.

Almost with genuine humility.

"I arrived at school with only the clothes on my back, two trained fists, and a well-nourished anger. It was enough to get by. Not enough to get ahead."

Faith had heard stories of the way boys were bullied and abused at school, and she'd prayed that sending Adam to school wouldn't be throwing him at a pack of lions.

She knew her nephew was a survivor, like she was.

Like Sinclair.

But she wanted more for him than that. She wanted him to thrive.

"You believe you succeeded at Harrow because Mr. Wilde befriended you."

"God, no." Sinclair scoffed. "We fought like crows mobbing one another over a dead field mouse. We were both nearly sent down for it."

"And how did you avoid that?"

"Forced proximity." He laughed softly. "We had to spend an entire weekend together repairing an old well. The only way to earn our freedom was to finish it. It was brutal. We couldn't agree on how the work should be done. One of us started throwing punches again, and in the palaver, we rolled into a ravine."

Faith pulled back. "A ravine."

"Ridiculous as it sounds, yes. It scared the pants off both of us. Something happens to your mind and your will when you think the end is near. It can bring out your best and your worst traits."

"Dare I ask which one you displayed?"

He responded with a white flash of teeth. "We both reacted the same way: with utter calm. And we both realized we could maul each other to death in a dark pit, or we could work together to find a way out of the trap.

"Hours later, we managed to chip away at the rock ledge covering the ravine. I wiggled through the gap and pulled Christopher out."

"He must have been grateful to you for saving him."

"We saved each other," he amended. "It was dawn by the time we walked back to the school grounds. We both stopped on the outskirts of the campus and looked at each other, and Christopher said, 'We've been missing all night, and no one came for us.'"

Faith recalled what he'd said at their first meeting.

I know what it is to be forgotten.

"We made a pact then. If one of us ever went missing, that the other would come for them."

He found her eyes. "No one had ever made me that kind of promise. Not even my parents."

Faith felt a powerful surge of envy. Imagine having that kind of loyalty from someone. For so many years. "I understand why you trust him."

She also sensed that his regard went beyond trust. Men didn't talk about loving each other, not the way that women spoke about friends of their own sex.

Sinclair's affection for his friend was something complex and deep.

Something she herself knew next to nothing about.

Had she had anyone in her life like that? Her mother, perhaps. But those memories were obscured by the years. They were more like dreams.

Her aunt and uncle had shown her affection in their own way. Devoted members of the Society of Friends, her upbringing abroad had been strict, but kind, and she'd done everything to be as agreeable as possible, knowing how indebted she was to them for raising her when she'd been orphaned.

Geoffrey Trenton was the first thing she'd wanted that hadn't fit into the life they'd planned for her. While neither of her guardians had objected to a marriage to the brother of an earl—they were both succumbing to illness and happy to see her settled—they'd worried their niece was marrying into a world far away from theirs.

She wondered if Adam felt any sense of familial connection to her, then chided herself for thinking it. He would never have regarded Faith as anything maternal. She'd never made him a promise that she would come for him. She'd promised herself she would, come hell or high water. But she'd never made it a point to say it to him.

And God above, how she longed for someone to say it to her.

"I want Adam to have that," she murmured. "He should have friends he can depend on. He deserves that."

"We all do."

Sinclair's words echoed like a vow, underscored by the clearness in his eyes, and the determined set to his full mouth.

His breath caught.

She'd been caught staring.

Leaning back, she withdrew her hand from his chest. His arms slipped their hold of her, providing her room to step away.

"Will you reconsider your objections about Christopher's visit, for Adam's sake?"

Dog with a bone, this man. It irritated her how delighted she was by his determination.

"After everything you've told me, would you put Mr. Wilde in danger of being on the wrong side of one of Doland's moods?"

"You're underestimating what would greet Doland if he found himself on the wrong side of Christopher. And no one would put their worst enemy on the wrong side of Christopher and me together."

"Isn't that in violation of your vows?"

"How I live my vows is a matter between me and my God."

Well, didn't that contain multitudes. He had to be referring to his indiscretion with her at the fête. Did that mean he had no regrets? Her knees wavered at the prospect.

He was weakening her in too many ways. She was growing dependent upon him. And that was just as dangerous as a stranger stumbling into the north wing.

"I have an idea," Sinclair said. "You don't want to allow someone you haven't met here in your home. Completely understandable. What if you were to meet Christopher and his family on neutral ground?"

"I cannot leave the estate unguarded."

"Not even for a day at the races?" He quirked a brow. "The Cumbria Cup starts next week, and Christopher's mother always hosts a box for Ladies' Day. I suspect that's why he's in the area and keen to escape. You'd be there and back in a day. If Christopher comes up to scratch, he can stop at Ravenglass on his way back to town."

She choked a nervous laugh. "Did you forget the conversation we just had? I am not equipped to handle a society event."

"I disagree," he said softly. "It couldn't be half as difficult as putting out a fire or calming a murderous tenant."

She resented how easily he disarmed her with his optimism.

If she wasn't careful, his hope would be contagious.

Turning her back on him, she replied, "I'll take it under consideration."

CHAPTER FOURTEEN

THAT EVENING, THE COUNTESS left Jonah an excellent Madeira.

The bottle was a very old vintage. A gift by any standard.

Or was it a bribe? To tempt him into relenting from the challenge he'd put before her.

Then again, it could have been an apology for her abrupt exit. The moment they'd sat down to dinner, the footman had handed Lady Rochford a missive with a tight face, and she'd taken off like a shot with no explanation. Minutes later, he'd heard the unmistakable clatter of her beast's hooves as it tore out of the drive.

He'd taken dinner in his rooms, but when Martin came to clear the dishes, he'd brought with him the bottle of Madeira and a glass, with the countess's compliments.

Jonah allowed himself a small taste, afraid to indulge too heavily while Lady Rochford was out. But as the night wore on without her return, he regretted his lack of indulgence, for his nerves were ticking away like the clock on the mantel.

Truthfully, he'd felt unsettled since she'd left him in the orangery. He'd exulted in the way she'd tried to hit him, then turned to him for comfort. It was a relief that he wasn't alone in the emotions that appeared to be engulfing them both. After all of those caresses at the fête, he hadn't known where he stood, or if he'd insulted her with those touches, despite her eager response to them.

Wildly inappropriate for someone of his position, and hers.

The appalling thing was that he didn't feel guilty about the way he desired her. He didn't even feel ashamed of his behavior. It was in service of helping her, and that gave him a roaring sense of satisfaction.

Still, he couldn't hazard taking things further. Nothing could come of it.

Finally, he detected the sound of horses, followed by a carriage. In something of a frenzy, he refastened his necktie. When there was a soft knock at his door, he answered it with one arm in, one half out of his frock coat.

"Are you dressed?" the countess whispered. He could barely make out her face in the candlelight.

"Yes."

"I have need of your help."

Seizing the lamp on his table, he followed her into the dark hallway. He didn't ask where they were going or why she'd summoned him.

It didn't matter. He would have followed her anywhere.

She led him downstairs, through the darkened kitchens and up the back stairs leading to the servants' quarters.

The countess unlocked the outer doorway and stopped at the end of the hallway.

When she turned, the grave expression plastered on her face kept him from speaking. "Behind that door is one of our former housemaids. She's very ill. Dr. Blake is attending to her."

Lady Rochford worried her lip before adding, "She suffers from a female complaint."

"I see."

"They know to come here for help, if they need it."

The poor woman could have been victimized by a man. Possibly by Doland.

Possibly by the earl himself.

Old Anders's words echoed in his memory. *You can tell your husband he killed my daughter.*

The countess opened the door to the small bedroom. A woman with copper-colored hair lay in the single bed, her slight frame dwarfed by the bedsheets.

"What is her name?" Jonah murmured.

"Frances—Frannie, they called her here."

"She's resting. We administered medicine for her pain," Dr. Blake said. "I hope I can help her, but I will need to perform a procedure in my surgery."

"May I assist with escorting Frannie to your very fine carriage?" Jonah offered.

Dr. Blake's beautiful smile lit her weary face. "If you would be so kind."

He lifted the woman as gently as he could. She mumbled in her sleep as he took her in his arms. He followed the countess and the doctor down the servants' stairs, and into the back entrance, where the landau waited.

The doctor stepped into the carriage and helped Jonah guide Frannie onto the velvet cushions before tucking a blanket around the patient.

"Thank you, Elyse," the countess said.

"I'll update you when there's news." Lady Blake's eyes flicked to Jonah. "Mr. Sinclair, I hope our next meeting is under better circumstances."

"As do I."

The carriage sped off down the drive. Long after it had disappeared, the countess remained staring at the distance.

Jonah wanted to swoop her back into the house. She was exposed out here. Doland could arrive back at any time. The enemies who'd lit those fires could be lurking in the wood.

Or her husband could choose that very moment to return.

For weeks, he'd seen the trail of ruin the man and his brother had left: the ramshackle house, the flooded river, the jaded townsfolk.

The Trentons had destroyed countless lives. Jonah's family was not alone in their suffering because of those men and their associates.

For the sake of protecting his own hide from further damage, he should forsake his desire for retribution and cease his hunt for Rochford. No good could come of the earl's return to Ravenglass. His return could put Adam in the countess in more danger than they already were.

"You must be exhausted," he said finally, hoping to urge her inside.

"I'm strangely alert."

She turned and marched across the yard to the orangery.

He found her in the back, where the mature trees grew thickest with leaves. Small, pale-orange baubles dangled from the branches.

Heaven must smell like this, he thought. Sweet and tart and exotic.

The countess lifted a watering can. "Thank you for helping with Frannie."

"Will she be all right?"

"I don't know. And before you ask—because I imagine what you are suspecting—I don't know if Charles or Geoffrey are to blame for her condition. But it is highly probable."

As she turned, their gazes locked. It made him giddy to have her attention so fixed on him.

It made him forget to filter his words.

"Leave him."

She blinked like she hadn't heard him.

He wasn't entirely sure he'd said the words out loud. Although he'd thought it so many times, to blurt it out now was absurd.

Her eyes widened in question.

"Leave him," he repeated, this time with more force. "Divorce Rochford. You would have grounds for abandonment alone."

He wouldn't bring himself to mention the other transgressions her husband had committed. He wouldn't hurt her further by voicing them.

She shook her head. "For a man of the cloth, you are very black-and-white."

"There are no shades of gray when it comes to abuse."

"Where would I go?"

"We would help you escape, somewhere he wouldn't find you."

"And what would I do? How would I survive? I have no trade, no skills." She laughed bitterly. "I can't sew a button. Or roast a chicken. I couldn't get a job as a scullery maid. And no family would allow impressionable young daughters near a governess who was a divorcée."

"You could learn a trade. You're the most intelligent woman I've ever met. Look how much you've mastered here on your own."

"No one is going to hire a woman to act as steward of their estate."

"Dr. Blake might."

"*Lady* Blake knows when to stand out and when to camouflage herself. Which includes employing and paying men of influence to protect her medical practice from scrutiny. She has money and connections, two vital things I lack."

Ducking her head, she added, "At sixteen years old, I thought I knew it all. I should have gone to school when I had the chance."

She turned suddenly to him. "I think I would have liked school. I used to love to read about ancient civilizations, philosophy. And I was good with languages."

Her head bobbed back and forth as if she was shaking herself from sleep. "For years, I've blamed Geoffrey and Charles for duping me."

"You were a child."

"I was old enough to know better," she bit out. "Old enough to owe my dying aunt some respect when she asked me to consider someone they knew for a husband, another member of the Society of Friends. But I was pampered and selfish. I wanted to escape Madeira, to have my own life. Geoffrey treated me like I was an adult. He enticed me with a promise of being part of a glittering society back in England.

"I believed him," she murmured. "Because I *wanted* to believe him. I wanted that life. And I wanted Geoffrey, with a desire that was anything but childlike."

Jonah didn't want to carry the conversation further. He'd no wish to hear the details of how much she'd cared for the man.

"And then we came here," she continued. "The former Lady Rochford—Charles's wife—had died while they'd been in Madeira. Instead of going into mourning, Charles and Geoffrey returned to London. To gamble away my engagement contract sum."

"He didn't try to get you to Gretna Green?"

"My uncle had insisted that the marriage contract stipulate that I needed to be at least eighteen and married in a church before they received the rest of my dowry. I suppose he thought it was the best way to protect me when he and my aunt had passed. I don't know why Charles and Geoffrey stood by it." She shrugged. "They had other pursuits to keep them busy."

The gambling and prostitution enterprises Christopher had written about. God knew what else they'd entangled themselves with.

"When they returned to Ravenglass, Charles had a new mistress he was mad about, a French woman named Clarisse, who was expecting."

"Adam," Jonah said softly.

She nodded. "Clarisse convinced Charles to acknowledge the child if it was a boy. Geoffrey didn't like that one bit."

A legitimate heir would have threatened Geoffrey's claim to the title.

"When Adam was born sickly, with one arm, Charles changed his mind. He agreed to educate Adam, but no more. One night, he and Geoffrey became very drunk, and I overheard them talking about my marriage contract. What was a loophole, what wasn't. Doland was with them, and he claimed he could manufacture any kind of change to the betrothal documents, so that it always looked like the contract existed between Charles and me."

Her voice caught. "Geoffrey went along with the discussion, like he didn't care. Like I was a plot of land to be bought and sold."

Because she had been. However noble her uncle's intentions, he'd handed over his niece to a pair of pretty monsters, because they'd swindled him into thinking they would take care of her.

Jonah curled his hands into fists.

"Charles didn't need to marry me for my money. He would get access to it when Geoffrey and I married. What he needed was a respectable wife to provide him with a healthy, legitimate heir."

"I imagine that was the part that the current Lord Rochford objected to."

She exhaled. "A few weeks later, Charles was thrown from a horse. Died instantly. And Geoffrey became the earl."

He wouldn't do either of them the disservice to voicing what she didn't say: that Geoffrey Trenton had likely arranged for his brother's death, to inherit his title.

"Geoffrey eschewed the traditional mourning period for his brother, and we were married within a month. Shortly after that, he left Ravenglass. Flat out disappeared for two years. He took Clarisse with him—maybe to protect her from suspicion about Charles's death. Maybe because he was besotted with her. They left Adam here with me.

"Turns out, I needed him as much as he needed me," she whispered. "We have many similarities, and one key difference. He can escape."

That was the reason she wouldn't leave her marriage. She was protecting Adam in a way that no one had protected her.

"For years, all I've wanted was to flee this place. I've never thought of Ravenglass as my home."

"Yet you've fought to keep it running."

"Only because I had no other choice. I never imagined I could have a life here. Until you arrived."

Jonah opened his mouth, but no words followed. He was afraid to say anything that would threaten her trust. And he was in grave danger of confessing what he felt for her.

What his vows and hers forbid them to act upon.

She turned to face the orange sapling. "Now that you know the sordidness that resulted from my poor choices, can you understand why I have avoided good society?"

"I will never understand, because I never had to live the horrors you have survived. But I know something of shame, how it has held me back."

In a low voice, she asked, "How could I pretend I am fit to walk among people protected from all of this?"

"Because you are." He walked in front of her line of vision. "There are more survivors among good society than you realize. I am one of them."

When she met his eyes, her expression was unreadable. "If Adam has any chance of escaping this miserable place, and having a life beyond Ravenglass, he will need to cultivate connections, and move through society. He must learn how to make friends, like you and Christopher."

Releasing a gust of breath, she said, "We will go to the races. We will go because it will help Adam. And because your friends invited us."

"Thank you." He stepped closer, but she shied back, her stiff posture countering the way she stared at him.

"It will be a lovely day, for Adam and for you," he promised. "I believe you'll enjoy it."

"Of course I'll enjoy it." She stepped under the cover of the trees. "Watching you with the people you love most will remind me of the happiness to be found outside these walls."

Chapter Fifteen

THE RACE DAY DAWNED sunny and warm, without a cloud in the sky. Songbirds chirped merrily as Faith marched Adam out of the house to the carriage.

The boy wore Ascot formal. His gray waistcoat and tie matched his coat and tails. Sinclair and Lawless had tracked down a small top hat for him, of perfect measure. Faith didn't want to know where they'd found such fine garments, or what they must have cost.

Neither did she care to learn how Lawless had produced the confection of a frock she was currently wearing. The shantung silk dress floated off her in long layers of cream and pale rose. No one would have dared to call it pink, thank God. At twenty-seven years of age, she was too old for that.

Sinclair strode across the drive in fitted trousers and morning coat, a rose pinned to his lapel. He moved with grace and a lightness she hadn't observed since his arrival, and when he grinned openly at her, her cheeks flushed.

An hour's journey found them at the racecourse. Ladies' Day was a highlight of the weeklong Cumbria Cup, and the road leading into the grounds was mobbed. The size and crush of the crowd overwhelmed Faith, but when the driver pulled off onto a sheltered path that led to the private boxes, she let out us much of a breath as her corset would allow.

"Why are we all the way out here?" Adam questioned. "We won't be able to see!"

"These are the private boxes for ladies and gentlemen," Sinclair replied.

"But neither of us are gentlemen."

Sinclair gave Faith a rueful look.

"You are not a gentleman *yet*," she corrected, and he rewarded her with a shy smile. "And Mr. Sinclair is a clergyman, which makes him a gentleman."

"Even if he has no money?"

"Adam, remember it's not polite to discuss other people's finances, especially in public."

"But we're not in public."

"We soon will be," she chided. "And even if we weren't, you should avoid bringing it up."

"Why?"

It was her turn now to look at Sinclair for help.

"Because money is a very private matter," he offered. "The amount people possess, relative to their friends and neighbors, can be disproportionate. That imbalance can make the people who have less feel like they are less."

"That's not true though!" Adam frowned. "You're the poorest person I know, and everyone finds you charming."

Faith coughed to cover her laugh.

"What if the person needed money?" Adam asked. "How can they ask for it if we're not supposed to talk about it?"

"You may talk about it privately, with your family," Faith quipped. "Now, we're nearly there. Let's straighten you up before the carriage stops."

She fussed with his cravat and his shirt to give her twitching hands an occupation. As she rehearsed with Adam the proper way to greet Mrs. Wilde and her family, a kernel of pride took root at his confident responses.

When he bounded out of the carriage with boyish enthusiasm, she couldn't help noticing how tall he'd grown in the last few months, and the way he held his head now, a mirror image of Sinclair's self-assurance. More boy than child, soon he'd be more young man than boy. Which made a painful little knot rise in her throat.

She swallowed it down as Sinclair alighted from the carriage and extended his gloved hand.

"Shall we?"

Faith took his arm, ensuring there was a respectable amount of distance between them. Martin and Peggy followed behind them with a hamper of foodstuffs to share for refreshment. Lawless had been forced to raid her locked stash of pantry delicacies since it would have been poor form to arrive empty-handed.

"Welcome, welcome, my dears!" A woman with silver hair and sharp blue eyes waved them into the suite. She extended her hand to Sinclair so that he could bestow a kiss on her cheek. "Finally, dear Jonah, you take a break from your labors to enjoy a bit of sport with us. It has been too long."

With a smile, she added, "But I see that country life agrees with you!"

Sinclair flashed her cheeky grin. "Thank you. We are grateful for your hospitality, and the chance to enjoy Ladies' Day."

"We couldn't have a parson out on any other day. What would the scandal sheets say?" Mrs. Wilde replied dryly.

Adam fidgeted beside them, exchanging his weight between his feet and trying to peer out to the lawn below the balcony where the rest of the guests had gathered.

"Forgive me, I've forgotten my manners. Mrs. Wilde," Sinclair said, "may I have the pleasure of introducing you to the Countess of Rochford."

"Lady Rochford, it is our honor."

"Thank you, Mrs. Wilde, for the kind invitation. We are looking forward to the race." She drew Adam forward. "And may I introduce my husband's ward, Master Adam Fitzcharles."

Adam gave a quick bow. "A pleasure to make your acquaintance, ma'am. Thank you for inviting us."

"You're most welcome, my dear. And how do you enjoy Mr. Sinclair as your tutor? I trust he is teaching you a great deal."

"Oh, yes. He's quite good with Latin and history, and of course Shakespeare."

"Of course. Shakespeare being required for all clergymen."

Faith smiled as she scanned the small crowd of people and willed the rapid patter in her chest to cease. At the edge of the lawn, a fair-haired man made a theatrical gesture to a pair of children around Adam's age, which incited them to tear across the yard, up the stairs to the veranda.

"I'm winning!" sang the girl.

"Because you cheated!"

"Alan, Portia!" Mrs. Wilde exclaimed, and aimed a frown at the breathless man who trailed them. "Christopher, you are supposed to be minding them."

"Forgive me, Mama, but you have a grave misunderstanding of an uncle's charter of responsibilities. I am supposed to wind them up."

Mrs. Wilde harrumphed. "Lady Rochford, may I introduce my wayward son, Christopher."

He turned his dimpled smile and bowed over Faith's hand. "An honor to make your acquaintance, Lady Rochford."

Sinclair's friend wore a dark-gray suit with a silver-blue cravat and waistcoat. Where Sinclair was contained, Mr. Wilde was overly free with his teasing smiles and his long-lashed looks. He acted the epitome of an audacious flirt.

Mr. Wilde greeted Sinclair with a slap on the back and a wink, then turned to his friend's pupil. "Master Adam. Welcome!"

The boy was nearly bursting, taking in the new surroundings, the breathless children, and the table of cakes that stood in the distance.

It was a tartaric test of his self-control and manners.

"My dear lad," Wilde said, throwing Sinclair a scheming look. "What are you doing here with these adults, when there is sunshine to spin in and sweets to partake of?"

Gripping his little top hat, Adam swallowed and asked, "Mr. Sinclair, may I be excused, please?"

"Yes, Adam. You may be excused to join Mr. Wilde's mutiny."

Adam tore off downstairs and onto the lawn, with Alan and Portia following in his wake.

"What a charming boy," Mrs. Wilde admired.

Faith smiled genuinely. "Mr. Sinclair has been relentless in his instruction on manners."

"Really?" Mrs. Wilde and her son echoed in unison.

Sinclair stiffened defensively. "Just what are you implying?"

"Jonah, there you are, finally!"

A stunning young beauty swept onto the verandah. Her white dotted Swiss bodice and skirts boasted embroidered flounces lined with ribbons to highlight the contours of her tiny waist. At her wrist, she wore a corsage of delicate spray roses, that brought out the blush in her cheeks, and made her hair more strawberry than blonde.

She bounded over to Jonah and extended both satin-gloved hands. "It's been eons since we've seen you! I thought Christopher was lying when he said you were coming."

As Sinclair bent to brush his lips to the tiny hands that lay open before him like a virginal sacrifice, Faith paid far too much attention to the warm smile that spread across his face.

"Miss Victoria Wilde," Sinclair said. "May I present the Countess of Rochford."

Victoria's doe-like eyes widened. Faith worried that the girl would do herself an injury.

"Lady Rochford." The young woman's tone shifted several degrees cooler. "How pleased we are that you are joining us."

She tossed a sly glance at Sinclair, mouth quirking. "I see now, Jonah. You're here on Ladies' Day out of duty to your mistress."

"Indeed, not," Faith insisted at the same time Sinclair replied, leaving off the second word of her response.

A tense silence fell upon them.

With a theatrical laugh, Victoria recovered herself. "Now Jonah, you've not remarked at all on how well I look." She feathered out her gown and preened. "Do you like it?"

From another woman, the words would have been a bold invitation. At the very least, a tease. Coming from Miss Wilde, in her saccharine high-pitched voice, it was merely a jest from a debutante.

To Faith, it felt like an attack.

And a betrayal. Sinclair had said Christopher had brothers. He'd made no mention of sisters. Who were young and beautiful and presumably unattached.

"The dress is magnificent," Sinclair said obediently. "Mr. Winston must have showered you with compliments. Is he joining us?"

"Business delays my fiancé in town," Victoria replied curtly. "Oh, they are parading the horses! Oh, I do love a flutter. It looks like number seven is a handsome fellow. Like the colt Father taught you to ride on, Jonah. Do you remember?"

"I hope the jockey is better at hanging on than I was."

"Let's get a closer inspection." She pulled on Jonah's arm impatiently. "Oh hurry, Jonah. I'll need your help with these rickety stairs, lest I fall and break my neck."

Sinclair met Faith's eyes with a long look. He was about to invite her to join them, out there in the crowd. To socialize with strangers who would judge her for the smallest faux pas.

Her breath trembled at the prospect of leaving the safety of the verandah. And she had no interest in vying with Victoria for Sinclair's attentions, putting him in the terrible position of having to arbitrate conversation.

She wouldn't do that to him. Not in front of his friends.

"Mr. Wilde," Faith turned her back on Sinclair, "would you join me in the shade for a cup of lemonade before the race starts? I do believe the heat and the carriage ride have left me quite in need of refreshment."

"Of course, Lady Rochford. Please." Wilde gestured to two well upholstered chairs at the balcony.

"Allow me to find a footman." His mother excused herself to see to the task, but Faith noted she trailed closely behind her daughter as she dragged Sinclair to the lawn.

Faith sank into the chair, and when Mr. Wilde joined her, they sighed together.

"Thank you for keeping me company," she said. "I am sure you'd much rather visit with Mr. Sinclair."

"Not at all," he replied with a gleam in his eye. "Jonah is the last person to reveal any important details about his life. I will get a much better picture of how he's been faring these last few weeks from you, Lady Rochford."

His easy nature made Faith relax into her seat and the ice-cold lemonade the footman delivered stopped her head from spinning. But it was doing little to loosen her tongue or shore up the nerve to tell Wilde about their problems with the river.

"Mr. Wilde!"

Two women in fashionable walking dresses mounted the stairs to the balcony, and Mr. Wilde rose to greet them.

The shorter copper-haired woman flashed Wilde a smile Faith characterized as more than practiced; it was disarming. "We didn't expect to see you here. Does that mean that Lord Andrews has joined you in the country?"

"Andrews remained in town. And I am nowhere near a proxy for him on any of his Parliamentary issues. I want nothing to do with politics or policy, so you can stop plotting right now."

He turned. "Lady Rochford, may I present Lady Cora Longworth, and Miss Amelia Hunter."

"A pleasure," Faith murmured, attempting to retrieve her mental list of conversation topics. She failed to think of anything that didn't have to do with irrigation or crop rotation.

The taller woman—Miss Hunter—replied warmly, "It's lovely to meet you. I believe Ravenglass Hall is quite close to Broadmoor Park?"

"It is. Are you acquainted with it?"

"Well acquainted," Lady Cora replied. "Lady Blake is a dear friend of ours."

"She's a member of a social organization we belong to," Miss Hunter added. "The Ladies' Discussion and Improvement Society. Perhaps she's told you about it?"

Miss Hunter sounded hopeful, and Faith regretted disappointing her. She recalled receiving Lady Cora's letter. Elyse had mentioned their group several times, but Faith had dismissed the invitations. Lady Cora and Miss Hunter must have been ignorant of Geoffrey's notorious reputation. When they found out, they'd want nothing to do with her.

"I'm afraid I'm unfamiliar with Lady Blake's affiliations in town," she replied carefully. "My duties at Ravenglass keep me in Cumbria."

"Of course, you must have many obligations," Lady Cora said. "But if you were to come to town—"

"You'd be most welcome." Miss Hunter gave Lady Cora a pointed look before turning her smile on Faith. "Anytime you'd like."

The women curtsied, and as they headed for the lawn, Mr. Wilde raised a brow. "Two of society's prestigious bluestockings fawning at your feet. What do you suppose all that was about?"

"I'm a curiosity."

"No, you're not. You're just someone new, which makes heads turn."

"And tongues wag."

"They always wag, Lady Rochford. Nothing we can do to stop it. It's a force greater than gravity."

A round of applause drew their attention to the edge of the lawn where Adam stood upon a newly erected tower of crates. He was pulling Alan and Portia up to his platform so they could see above the crowd.

"Industrious, that one," Wilde remarked. "He must run Jonah ragged."

"His energy is boundless," she agreed. "He needs a more stimulating environment than Ravenglass. It's time to send him to school."

"Don't tell him that!" he whispered with a theatrical shudder. "Or you'll have the poor lad headed straight for the hills."

Faith fought a smile. "I was told that you're a fan of school."

"A fan of *learning*. I generally despise organized education as a concept."

"I believe that you and Mr. Sinclair survived the worst of it together."

"That's one way to frame it." Wilde gave a deep laugh. "Do you have siblings, Lady Rochford?"

She shook her head.

"When you're the third and most unruly son sent to the same school as your older brothers, there are expectations."

"Head Boy and all that?"

"My eldest brother Griffin is clear-cut—to a fault—but loyal to the grave. Top of his class, *never* chosen for Head Boy, and will never let the world forget it."

"A hard act to follow."

"Now you're catching on." He smirked, but the tension around his eyes told another story. "My brother Roderick was the one who made Head Boy. He can sell snow to Greenland."

"And does he?" she joked.

"Tragically, no. That would be a lark, though, wouldn't it? He's a lieutenant colonel in the army. He's been in the Straits Settlements for yonks."

"Would you characterize Mr. Sinclair as a brother?" Faith couldn't believe she was talking so freely. Wilde must have hypnotized her. "I know he thinks of you all as family," she added in a rush.

"Does he? Now we'll never be rid of him. Perhaps you'd like to take him off our hands, Lady Rochford."

"We wouldn't deprive the Manchester parish of Mr. Sinclair's talents."

"Yes, of course."

The conversation paused while they both studied each other, admiring the other's restraint.

"Which one of your brothers do Alan and Portia belong to?" Faith asked, changing the subject to the children Adam played with.

"Those monsters belong to my sister Helena, who is also Roderick's twin."

"My word, you are a large family."

His grin faded quickly. "There used to be more of us. My younger brother Jeremy passed away shortly after his fifth birthday."

"Oh, I am so sorry." Faith meant it too. She'd longed for a brother or sister of her own and couldn't imagine losing one.

"Adam reminds me of Jeremy. He's curious about how the world works, like Jeremy was."

"Do you think," she started, then paused to shake her head, as if it would wave away her nervousness. "Having attended a prestigious school, despite living in your brothers' shadows..."

"Do I think Adam will do well at Harrow? Undoubtedly." The playful quirk left his mouth. "Surviving school takes grit, and an ability to adapt quickly. I suspect Adam comes by both naturally. But even a short time in Jonah's company will help him improve those skills."

"That's very kind of you. I suppose we shouldn't put the cart before the horse. There is the matter of Harrow accepting his application."

"That you should not worry over." Wilde's scheming grin returned. "Not if Cousin Archie has anything to say about it. He's a Harrow man himself."

Faith blinked. "You have me at a disadvantage, Mr. Wilde. I'm not sure who you're referring to?"

"Don't tell me Jonah hasn't asked him already."

"Asked *who*?"

"The bishop." Wilde's expression straightened as he regarded Faith's face, draining of color. "The honorable Reverend Alcott is Mama's cousin."

A stone dropped into the pit of Faith's stomach. "Your cousin is the Bishop of London?"

"Jonah never told you." He threw her a calculating look. "Why ever would he keep that information to himself?"

Before Faith could muster a response, Martin appeared on the verandah, red-faced and sweating.

"Pardon me, your ladyship," he huffed. "Might I have a word?"

"My dear man. You're half-winded." Wild stood as Faith also rose quickly. "Let me get you something to drink."

"Very grateful, sir."

While Wilde walked to the water pitcher to fill a glass, Martin lowered his voice and said in a rush, "I went to check on the horses, my lady. There was a man milling about the carriage."

Faith tensed. "What sort of man?"

"He's been at the house, my lady."

If Martin recognized him, and didn't want to elaborate, it was likely old Anders. And even more likely, he was still riled up enough to create a scene at the races.

"Is anything amiss?" Mr. Wilde asked, returning with the water.

"One of our former tenants recognized our carriage," Faith replied. "He's asked to convey his regards in person."

Wilde frowned. "Surely it can wait. The race is about to start."

"He's old and frail and forgets himself sometimes. I think the poor dear is a bit agitated."

"Then allow me to accompany you—"

"You're very kind, but there is no need." Faith flapped a dismissive hand. "Martin will come with me. I'll be back before the starting gun."

"I'll tell Jonah."

"No, please." Faith raised her voice, then covered it with an assuring smile. "Mr. Sinclair and Adam are enjoying themselves with your family. Don't interrupt them. I'll be only a minute."

Before Wilde could object, she skirted down the stairs and set off toward the carriages.

Chapter Sixteen

As Faith traversed the shorn grass where the carriages parked, a bugle sounded.

She was disappointed she'd miss the starting race. If she picked at the thought with enough attention, she'd have to accept the fact that she regretted she couldn't watch it with Adam and Sinclair. And because that rattled her more than it should have, she focused on shoring up her strength for confronting old Anders.

When they reached the field where the Rochford carriage parked among dozens of others, Martin pulled her into the shadow of a large port chaise.

"There, my lady," he whispered, twisting his chin to the far end of the paddock. A reedy man in an unremarkable dark coat and hat crouched by the wheel of her carriage.

"Martin," Faith whispered. "That's not Mr. Anders."

"No, my lady."

"Then why did you say—"

Martin clapped a hand over her mouth as the man turned back toward them.

"He's been to the house, my lady," Martin murmured. "With Mr. Doland."

One of his filthy gang fellows, then. Or Doland owed him a debt, and the scoundrel was expecting to catch him at the races.

The man reached behind the carriage wheel. His shoulders shifted, as if he was twisting something, and then he rose to his feet and spun around.

Faith pressed herself flat against the chaise. Eventually, the footsteps faded and when they peeked around the carriage, his dark hat bobbed farther away.

"Unbelievable," Faith gritted out. "He's interfered with the wheel. It's a scheme to disable the carriages and strand us on the road, where they can rob us blind."

Red tinged her view, and she started moving among the throng of parked carriages, despite Martin's muffled protests. When they reached the Rochford coach, a dark cloud moved across the sky, obscuring the sun.

"There." Martin pointed to the wheel. "He's gone and loosened the axel. And the washer's missing."

"The absolute devil. We'll need to inquire if there's a cartwright close by."

"I'll head straight to the stables after I escort you back to the box, my lady."

She shook her head. "I want a closer look to see if we can easily mend it." Inexpensively, she hoped. The last thing she could afford was a new coach wheel. "He won't come back. If he does, I'll lock myself in the carriage."

When the footman didn't move, she added, "We must see to this quietly, Martin. I don't want to alert our hosts or the other guests and draw unnecessary attention."

Reluctantly, Martin set off at a jog toward the racetrack.

Faith remained in the shade of the carriage, catching her breath and calming her temper. She crouched by the broken wheel to examine how the blackguard had managed the damage. The menacing cloud that had covered the sun made her inspection difficult, and she frowned up at the darkening sky. She'd fled without her parasol and there was an excellent chance rain would appear before she made it halfway back to Mrs. Wilde's box.

Her only hope was that Lawless might have packed a spare umbrella. Faith walked around the back of the carriage and reached for the door.

A sharp instrument pinched through the fabric at the base of her spine. "Don't move."

Ignoring the rasped command and every ounce of sense, Faith whirled around, hoping to disorient and disarm her attacker.

Instead, his filthy fingers closed around the silk at her throat.

"Jonah!" Victoria gave his arm a little slap with her lace fan. "Where are you? You haven't heard a word I've been saying."

Over her shoulder Christopher mouthed, *You missed nothing.*

Jonah was missing someone. He just couldn't make a show of it.

The countess had absconded with her footman for the better part of an hour, and it was burning a hole in the pit of his stomach.

When she'd asked Christopher to keep her company, he'd thought it best to give them time to converse, despite the outrageous flare of jealousy he'd experienced. Christopher would mince no words sharing with her things Jonah had trouble revealing himself. He'd have countless things to explain to her when they returned to Ravenglass.

If she spoke to him at all, after his abandonment.

He'd pledged to stay by her side, then had immediately left her. The minute he walked away he'd regretted it. But he couldn't summon the nerve to turn back, and when she'd disappeared, he realized what had been holding him back.

For once, he'd wanted her to chase after him.

"Forgive me," he said to Victoria, flashing her his best smile. "There are so many distractions."

As he glanced up at the verandah to stare at Lady Rochford's empty seat for the hundredth time, a breathless Martin stumbled onto the deck.

Before the footman could catch his eye, Jonah was already murmuring excuses and traversing the lawn.

Martin threw him a wary look. "Might I have a word, Mr. Sinclair?"

Jonah gestured to the stairs and followed the man outside the box. "Where is Lady Rochford?"

"There was a fellow lingering around the carriage. When I told Lady Rochford, she insisted I take her to him, thinking it was Mr. Anders. But she misunderstood me." Martin swallowed. "The man knows Doland."

Jonah's blood turned cold. "Martin, where is the countess now?"

"With the carriage. Doland's associate did some damage to the wheel. Gone off to do it to other coaches, I imagine. Lady Rochford sent me to find a cartwright, but I didn't think she should be alone, sir."

"Quite right, old chap." Jonah clapped a hand on his shoulder.

"What's all this?" Christopher appeared, a frown pulling at his forehead. "Where is Lady Rochford?"

The footman looked at Jonah pleadingly. In a low voice, he said, "Mr. Sinclair, I know the countess wishes to keep this disturbance discreet—"

"To hell with discretion," Jonah growled. "Go fetch the constables. Take Mr. Wilde with you—you can explain the situation to him on your way." Drawing a breath, he added, "I will see to her ladyship."

He sprinted to the field, but exercised more caution when he came upon the maze of carriages. Locating the Rochford brougham, he caught a glimpse of rose silk, and the ache in his chest that he'd worked to squash all day rose, nearly choking him.

His legs took over, and he sprinted to reach her, ducking between carriages, in case Doland's accomplice stood watch.

When the countess crouched down to inspect the rear wheel, the fiend slithered out as if he'd been hiding beneath the carriage, like a reptile waiting to spring upon her.

The glint of a knife pointed at her back. She whipped around and Jonah had to muffle his own cries with his fist as the scum seized her throat.

Jonah surged forward, scattering gravel in his wake, but the sharp turn of the goon's head was a warning to gather his wits. If he steamed ahead, the filth would crush her windpipe. Or put that knife to use.

"Afternoon, Lady Rochford. Out 'ere by your lonesome?" the man rasped. "Where's your faithful steward? I'd like a word with the fine Mr. Doland."

Jonah cursed his lack of a weapon. Pistols weren't exactly the thing for Ladies' Day at the Cumbria Cup. He searched his pockets futilely, but the only thing he found was a small pocketknife he'd confiscated from Adam before their departure. The blade was so small and dull, it wouldn't cut through butter.

The countess uttered a strangled scoff. "Doland isn't here."

"That's a shame now, ain't it, 'im givin' us bof the cold shoulder? Maybe I need to remind 'im what happens when 'e ignores us."

The rotter's hand had tightened on her throat, forcing a gasp from her, and it was all Jonah could do to hold himself back.

He needed to wait for the right position. He was exposed where he stood. The blackguard needed to turn a few more inches for Jonah to have an advantage.

"We gave your steward a chance. Sent warnin's." The man gave a phlegmy laugh. "But 'e hasn't responded. Rather rude, innit?"

Finally, the bastard turned. One more step, and Jonah would have him in range.

The man shook his head at the countess's silence and laughed. "What would good society say about that impertinence, milady?"

"You'll never find out, you cretin." Jonah thrust the point of the little knife between the assailant's bollocks.

It was enough to catch the ruffian by surprise, make him drop hold of the countess's neck, and reach inside his coat pocket for the revolver hidden inside.

Inadvertently showing Jonah exactly where to aim.

He thrust his elbow into the assailant's face and grabbed for the gun. The thug fought back with a left hook to Jonah's obliques, but the blow hardly registered. Every ounce of energy and concentration he possessed focused on seizing the weapon.

"What have we 'ere, a punching priest?"

Jonah responded with a jab that sent the man's head back on his neck, but his responding strike to Jonah's chest forced him to bend over for breath.

The man laughed as the unmistakable click of a revolver unlocking pointed straight at Jonah's ear.

He stared up at the wretch's snag-toothed smile.

"Why is it you gentlemen boxers always aim for the face?" the man asked, raising his gun and pointing it straight at Jonah.

Instead of a shot, there was a muffled sort of whack.

The gunman's eyes rolled back, and he teetered forward, collapsing face-first in the dirt.

Behind him stood the countess, brandishing the brick they kept in the carriage to warm her feet in cold weather.

"The answer to that question is quite simple," she murmured, as she lowered her arms and raised her eyes to Jonah. "Gentlemen always want to leave their mark."

Jonah staggered to her. "Are you hurt?"

She raised a hand to her throat. "I'm all right, just a little raw. Hopefully, it won't leave a bruise."

"Mr. Sinclair!"

Martin and Christopher appeared with two huffing constables in their wake. "We caught sight of him from the field, just as he was pulling out the gun! Lord, didn't that shave off a few years from a man's life. Thank God for you, Lady Rochford."

"Thank God for the warming brick, Martin."

"Your left hook needs work." Christopher clapped Jonah on the shoulder. His smirk covered the concern in his eyes.

Jonah clasped his friend's hand with a tight squeeze. "I'm out of practice."

"Did he hurt you, my lady?" one of the constables asked. "We've got him for aggravated property damage, with the intent to harm. Assault would be an easy addition."

The man *had* assaulted her. But such an accusation would require an interview and raise questions about Doland's possible involvement. And likely, the earl's.

In response to the policeman, the countess slowly shook her head.

Christopher cocked a brow, but one sharp look from Jonah prevented his friend from pressing the matter.

"Constables, thank you," Jonah said. "I believe Lady Rochford had the misfortune of happening upon the man in the act. When the weather clouded over, we decided to retrieve an umbrella from the carriage. I suppose our timing was terrible, or uncanny, depending how you look at it."

"But surely, sir—"

"Mr. Sinclair is correct," Lady Rochford interrupted. "It was unfortunate timing. At least we uncovered their scheme before they could inflict much damage."

"Indeed," Jonah agreed as the constables hauled the man to his feet. "And I would be most happy to give a full statement once I see Lady Rochford safely back to her company."

After the constables dragged the man away, the countess gripped the open door of the carriage. Color bled from her face.

The footman shot Jonah a look of alarm. "My lady—"

"It's all right, Martin, I'm quite well. It's just the excitement and the heat."

"We'll rest here a moment," Jonah added. "In the meantime, Christopher, could your driver help us track down someone to repair the carriage?"

His friend gave a courtly bow. "Leave it to Martin and me to sort out." Nodding to the countess, he added, "I'm relieved to see you are well, Lady Rochford."

"Thank you, Mr. Wilde. For your help, and your discretion."

When Martin's powdered wig had bobbed out of sight, the countess swayed. Before Jonah thought to ask, his arms were around her, lifting her into the shade and cool of the carriage.

"I'm fine," she insisted.

"Well, I'm not."

He hadn't bothered to hide the malice from his voice, and it snagged her attention.

"How selfish of me." She frowned as her eyes traced him. "I don't care how well you deflected that wastrel's blows. You should see a doctor."

A physician would have nothing to soothe what ailed him. "Your horse has given me deeper scars. The weasel didn't do much harm. Apparently, he prefers to prey on women."

"My dress took the brunt of it." Her trembling hand travelled to her throat. "He's ruined it, hasn't he?"

The silk at her collar was shredded and stained by the brute's grubby hands.

Had he told her how beautiful she looked in that dress? No, he supposed he hadn't. That would have been inappropriate in the confines of servant and mistress.

Not as inappropriate as telling her that the moment she'd emerged from the house this morning, he'd wanted to strip her of every single layer of silk, like plucking petals off a rose.

She drew a harsh breath. "How on earth am I to explain all this?"

"You could say your dress caught on the wheel when you were bending over to inspect it."

"I'll have to tear it properly, so that it looks like it caught."

She gripped the fabric and attempted a tug, but her shaking hands couldn't maintain a firm grasp.

"Here's another idea." He covered her hands. "Same story, but why don't we dispose of the evidence in a way that will raise fewer eyebrows."

He inspected the collar. "These stitches are delicate. I can remove them along the neckline. It will look cleaner. And then you can cover the rest with your shawl. It's turning colder. No one will remark on it."

Extending his palm, he offered her Adam's small knife, which, to his immense joy, solicited a soft smile from her.

"Would you do it, please? My hands are too unsteady. I might rip the thing in two. And I need you to do the back, anyway."

"Of course."

If only he could get his own hands to stop trembling.

Somehow, he mustered the coordination to remove his gloves as she turned to offer him her back.

Probably best to start there. If he caught her eyes now, he wasn't sure he could control his actions, and no woman deserved to be set upon with ardor when she'd just survived the assault of another man.

He was reprehensible to even be thinking about it. But the hunger to hold her, to never let her go, gnawed at him.

Slowly, he stroked a finger over the back stitches of her collar.

She gasped and he let loose a curse; he hoped his fingers hadn't gone cold and clammy with sweat.

"I'm sorry," he apologized.

"Go on," she murmured. "I'm fine."

"That doesn't work on me."

"Truly. I'm banishing the entire ordeal from my mind. It will be fully erased as soon as you finish."

But he would not forget so easily. Not with her citrus scent filling the carriage, and her shoulders still trembling.

Carefully, he ripped out the stitches, revealing a sliver of smooth, unblemished skin.

Unable to resist, he caressed the bare spot with his finger.

A breathy sigh escaped her.

His knife sliced through a ream of stitches, parting the fabric. Slowly, he traced the line of exposed skin, ostensibly searching for stray threads. He was rewarded with a low murmur, the kind a lovesick fool might interpret as an approving sort of moan.

"I'm remiss in thanking you," he said, pulling at more of the stitches. "For saving my hide."

"Well, you saved mine first."

He turned her to address the fabric around the shoulder. "Why didn't you come and find me when Martin first told you about the man?"

She faced him in profile and stared at the back of the carriage. "I didn't want to ruin it all. Everything was going so well. Adam was thoroughly enjoying himself. And so were you."

"No," he countered. "All I could think about was the fact that I'd promised to stay by your side and deserted you at the first opportunity."

"Tosh. That was never what you promised."

"No?"

The last thread holding the fabric unraveled, and the silk fluttered away somewhere out of his sight.

Red streaks marred the smooth skin of her throat.

Jonah vowed that the perpetrator would pay. That inevitability was the only thing allowing him to maintain a thin grip on his composure.

The countess's pulse pounded at her throat.

He brushed the mark on her neck with one finger and curled his hand into a fist.

"It doesn't hurt," she rasped.

"Liar."

"No." She covered his hand with her own. "Not about this."

"Prove me wrong then." He caressed her throat again with his fingertips.

And when she didn't flinch, when she merely released another sweet sigh, he followed the path of his fingers with his lips.

At the catch of her breath, he paused. Horror gripped him at the prospect that he'd frightened her, offended her with his advances.

As he withdrew, her hand clamped around the back of his neck, halting his retreat.

He waited an interminable length of time before she leaned forward and pressed against him, twining her fingers through his hair.

With a groan at her encouragement, his hungry mouth returned to her throat.

He fought to keep the brush of his lips soft, soothing. Her wordless murmurs of approval made everything south of his waist hard.

The grip on his neck tightened, and he lifted his chin to meet her astounded gaze.

"I was so worried," he blurted.

"I was too."

"He had his hands on you, and I wanted to kill him."

"He had a gun pointed at you, and I tried to kill him."

She surged forward to meet his kiss, her lips crashing against his with equal force. A caress and a crush. He was dizzy with it, had to school himself not to devour her.

Her lips parted to allow his tongue to sweep in, and he groaned in delight at her sweet, tart taste: crisp like lemons, tempting as sugar. When she nipped at his bottom lip, all the blood left his head and pointed straight at his throbbing cock.

Pulling back to seize a breath, he took stock of her wide pupils, swollen mouth, and flushed cheeks.

She was a glorious mess.

His glorious mess.

But only for this moment.

"Have you erased everything now?" he rasped.

She shook her head. "Not yet."

Leaning forward, he brushed a tender kiss beneath her chin. "Let me help." He trailed soft kisses down her throat, flicking his tongue against the bruises. "Let me take this pain and replace it with pleasure."

She rewarded him with another approving hum as her fingers twisted his hair and scraped against his scalp.

"Let me comfort you, Faith."

Now who was lying? With every touch, every kiss, every strained breath, he hungered to provide her with much more than solace.

His mouth moved over the front of her bodice, and his hands traced the seams around her waist, until they finally moved over her breasts.

He couldn't erase what had happened to her at the hands of a menacing stranger.

But he could ease her fears and ground her to the present moment. So she wouldn't have to worry about what lay in the past or in the future.

"Let me give you release," he half pleaded, his hands winding through the layers of silk to stroke her thigh. "I promise I will be careful, so careful. I'll show you. Let me be—"

Her fingers clamped down on his hand. "What? A distraction? A substitute for the husband who abandoned me?"

The accusation stunned him.

He had no reply, couldn't even muster a denial or repeat what he'd started to say.

Let me be of use to you as more than a friend.

She scrambled to put space between them, before he finally managed, "That wasn't what I meant."

"Wasn't it?" She straightened her dress and pushed the loose pins back into her hair. Peering down at her neckline, she traced the neatly cut collar with a finger. "You didn't mean to seduce me, by suggesting you could give me what's been missing for years?"

He wanted to call her a liar again, but he recognized her struggle, her confusion and hurt. It cut him deeply to be the cause of it. "That wasn't what happened."

She bristled. "Whatever you want to give me—"

"Comfort." *Affection, passion,* he wanted to add, but didn't dare.

"I don't want comfort." Seizing her shawl, she flung open the door of the carriage and stepped into the fading light. "I want more than that."

She leveled him a searing look. "And what I want is impossible."

CHAPTER SEVENTEEN

Faith was admiring the fashionable cut of draperies in the guest bedroom when her lungs were finally liberated from the cage of her corset.

"There." The maid smiled as Faith exhaled audibly and handed over the undergarment. "The dress fitted you beautifully, if I say so myself."

In spite of your vicious protests, she was too well-trained to add.

When Mrs. Wilde had insisted they stay the night with them at the house they were letting for the week, the only objection Faith had managed was that she'd nothing suitable to wear to dinner.

"Nonsense." Mrs. Wilde had flapped a hand. "Victoria and Christopher always bring along spare attire."

At which point, Faith had narrowed her eyes at Victoria's tiny waistline.

The maid helped her into Victoria's pink-and-white striped wrapper and she cringed inwardly at the ruffles and bows. She supposed this was fashionable among younger women.

As was the mint-green skirt and bodice the maid folded over her arm. Faith had been terrified of spilling something on it during dinner. Between that, the damned corset, and her latent anxiety over the chaos of her life, she'd barely eaten a thing.

Leaving the palaver at the races behind, dinner with the Wildes had been blissfully uneventful. To her own surprise, Faith had easily slipped back into performing the forced niceties of a formal meal. She'd smiled with her doll's mask, and made conversation with Griffin, Mr. Wilde's oldest brother before Christopher gracefully interjected and steered the discussion to the topic of wildlife at Ravenglass Hall. He orchestrated the perfect opportunity for Faith to suggest a future visit.

After his smooth handling of the events of the afternoon, Sinclair's clever friend had earned her trust.

A knock sounded at her bedroom door, and a footman entered with a silver tray bearing a small carafe of amber liquid, a single glass, and a plate of shortbreads.

"A little refreshment, in case you have trouble sleeping," the maid suggested.

A breeze stirred the trees outside and, in the distance, the low roll of thunder was a harbinger of an imminent downpour. Faith enjoyed nature's little rebellion against all the comforts surrounding her, but the maid frowned.

"Shall I close the balcony doors? It looks like rain."

"I'll see to them if it does."

The maid's frown remained as she pulled the door closed behind her.

As Faith eyed the tray, her stomach rumbled. Now that she could breathe again, her appetite had awakened.

She folded a few of the biscuits into a napkin, poured a drop of wine into the tiny glass, and ventured onto the balcony. The verandah was sheltered enough to prevent rain from seeping into the bedroom, and she welcomed the fresh breeze. Sinking down on the small chair near the door, she watched the sheets of rain pour off the roof.

"How are you enjoying the sherry?"

Sinclair stirred from the shadows. His hair was matted down with rain, as were his topcoat and trousers.

Faith didn't startle at his arrival; she'd expected it. If she'd had the freedom he possessed to move about at any hour, she would have sought him out tonight.

Glancing down at her glass, she murmured, "It's quite good. The sherry."

"I thought so," he replied politely. "Griffin is working to export it from Spain."

Had he sent the tray so she could also try Griffin's new project, or because he thought her nerves needed settling?

Faith squinted into the misty night. "Incidentally, how did you climb all the way up here?"

"Trellis."

"Of course."

"Massive thing. It extends around half of the house."

"How did you know this beast of an arbor would bring you to my room?" she asked.

"The Wildes stayed here before, one Easter holiday. Christopher and I were eighteen."

"And to whom were you paying a visit, then?"

He had the decency to stay quiet, but the cheeky curve of his mouth was undeniable.

A respectable woman would instruct him to take his fine legs back down that trellis to his own rooms. That would go a long way to erasing what had happened between them in the carriage.

She wasn't sure she could do it.

A crack of lightning split the sky, illuminating the paddock that bordered the house.

"Getting closer," he remarked, above the pelting of the rain.

She should force him back out there. He was already soaked; he could hardly get any wetter.

But what would that achieve? She'd lie awake in her bed, imagining him in the dark. Catching his death of cold.

It wouldn't prevent her thoughts from returning to the events of the day, as they had repeatedly all evening. She needed to exorcise them.

She needed to exorcise *him*. Not only from her thoughts.

From her life.

Taking another small sip of the sherry, she said, "You didn't climb all the way up here, in a thunderstorm, to discuss sherry."

"No."

"What exactly are you doing here?"

"I don't have a precise plan."

"Bollocks."

Thunder pounded, shaking the rooftops.

He glanced up. "That wasn't part of the plan."

"Perhaps it's God warning you to abort the plan."

"God doesn't speak to me that way," he murmured.

Something about the lowness in his tone pulled at the ache that was expanding in her chest. She couldn't determine if he meant that he communicated with the divine in a different way, or if he believed that God hadn't been speaking to him regularly.

And the possibility that he might feel God had abandoned him made her eyes prick.

Another bolt of lightning flashed, and she caught the tightness in his jaw. His shoulders were trembling.

"Well, one thing is for certain." She rose to her feet and approached the balcony door. "You cannot return the way you came."

She walked through the open door and tipped her chin over her shoulder. "Take off your shoes, or you'll drag muck all over this beautiful carpet. I will not have you put me in a position where I have to explain that to the maids."

"You're a countess. You don't have to explain anything to anyone."

He obeyed her directive, smoothly removing his shoes and following her into the room before closing the door. He locked it, then pulled at the door firmly to confirm it held.

"I do believe the deadbolt works," she mused.

"I do believe, after today, we cannot be too careful."

Her throat dried. Not at the reference to the attack.

But at that *we* bit.

Instead of sniping at him, she nibbled away at another biscuit.

"Mrs. Lowe's shortbreads," Sinclair whispered reverently. He stared at the plate the way a hungry dog might eye a table full of beef.

"You just ate a dinner of five fine courses!"

"And you didn't finish a single one."

He'd been watching her from the far end of the table, despite Victoria's attempts to hold his attention.

"You try sitting for three hours in a borrowed corset and see how much of an appetite it gives you."

"Are you feeling better now?"

Droplets of rain cascaded from his hair, cutting down his throat, and he continued to fight off a shudder.

"I'm well, but you won't be if you don't dry off." She reached for one of the plush towels on the nightstand. "You can hang up those wet things behind the door."

Obediently, he peeled off the damp coat and waistcoat and placed them on the hanger before taking the towel from her. "Thank you."

He applied the towel to his hair. As he turned toward the fire, she had a spectacular view of the way his shirt clung to his back. The transparent fabric revealed the lines and curves of his muscles.

Her cheeks warmed, and she took an indulgently large sip of sherry.

As Sinclair moved the towel over his ribs, he winced.

"Are you very bruised?"

"Just tender on this side." He turned with a wry smile. "I've suffered far worse."

There was one biscuit remaining on the plate—how in God's name did that happen? Sinclair assessed it with great attention.

"Go on, take it," she offered.

"Are you sure?"

When she gave an exasperated eye roll, he didn't hesitate to make quick work of it, and released a small, contented sigh.

"Clearly you worked up an appetite scaling the trellis. And securing my door."

"Someone had to."

Ah, so this was the point of his visit. Even here, in this exquisite room in this perfect house as guests of the flawless Wildes, he believed her enemies could find them.

As his gaze roved over her, he didn't bother concealing the fear in his eyes.

"There's no need to be concerned," she said softly.

"There is *every* need for concern." He thrust the towel onto the washstand. "We cannot ignore the fact that someone found you at a vulnerable moment today and assaulted you."

"Yes," she agreed. "That all happened. But we apprehended the man. Before he could do any significant harm."

"Terrifying you is insignificant?"

"That wasn't terrifying. He told me exactly what his intentions were. Terror is when you don't know what they'll do to hurt you."

His eyes squeezed shut, as if her brutal honesty caused him pain.

"I'm all right, truly," she insisted. "You didn't have to climb up here to inspect me for damage. Like you, I've suffered much worse."

"And what happens when they try again? What if next time, they succeed at doing something *significant*?"

She hated the way he drew out the last word, the shake in his voice.

"What happens, the next time, Faith? When I won't be there to protect you?"

Practically, rationally, she knew the answer. She'd withstood plenty of threats and incidents before he arrived on her doorstep. That was why God had invented pistols.

But she couldn't rouse the words to tell him. She couldn't give him the assurance he needed for one simple reason.

She didn't want to.

After ten years of defending herself against her husband and his enemies, she was so very tired of having to do it alone.

"We cannot solve that problem tonight," she managed. "Nor tomorrow. We have time. Someone will have tipped off Doland about what happened. He won't come near the estate for a few weeks, not with his debt collectors trying to track him down. We must put those shadows behind us and remember the good that has come of today."

In a softer voice, she said, "Adam did beautifully."

Sinclair's frown melted into a slow smile. "Didn't he? I shouldn't have been surprised. He exceeded every expectation."

"I was flabbergasted myself."

They both laughed.

His expression straightened. "He's ready."

"Mr. Wilde suggested that his mother's *cousin* might be inclined to write a letter of recommendation."

He sighed. "Christopher told you about the bishop."

"Why didn't you?"

"Would it have mattered?"

She started to deny it, then snapped her mouth shut. The truth was, she didn't know.

"At dinner, Griffin said that we wouldn't have to wait for the start of the school year. Adam could be settled at Harrow in May, for summer term."

"Only a few weeks, then."

His voice sounded as optimistic and wistful as she felt.

She went to the table, refilled her fairy-sized glass with sherry, and offered it to him. He took the delicate glass in his large hand—he could have managed with just two fingers—and furrowed his brow. "Dolls drink more liquid than this."

"It's a lady's glass. Rationed especially for our delicate constitutions."

Shaking his head, he knocked back the liquid in one gulp, albeit a very tidy one. "At least they left you the decanter."

"Only one glass, though. You didn't specify you'd be joining me."

Refilling the glass, he passed it back to her. "Wouldn't be much of a gesture of apology if I made that assumption."

"I thought you came up here to teach me a lesson about the threats to my safety."

"Yes, starting with me."

In the haze of her memory, she couldn't recall if he'd been the first to reach for her, or if she'd orchestrated it. Falling into each other's arms had felt very much like a joint effort.

If he'd made advances, she'd reciprocated them. Hell, she'd kissed him, hadn't she? She'd meant to.

But he was ashamed. For leading her down a path she was more than happy to traverse.

Sinclair watched her beneath hooded eyes. His posture suggested stillness, but she knew his muscles coiled tightly, bracing for a defense.

"I am the one who should apologize. For the way I reacted before I left the carriage today." She finished the sherry, refilled the glass, and handed it to him. "What I said to you wasn't fair."

Cruel, really, to offload her feelings like that, and punish him for his affection by volleying back with a grenade of her emotions.

"I took advantage." He placed the glass back on the table. "I used the excuse that I was providing you comfort when all I was doing was seeking my own."

"I don't—"

"Please." He held up both hands. "Let me finish."

She retreated half a step, but he'd anticipated it, knew her movements before she did, and grasped her hands.

"This preoccupation with righting the injustices against my father—it's consumed me."

At the reminder of why he'd come to Ravenglass, she stiffened. "I wish I could give you the answers you're seeking."

"You were willing to let me stay, despite knowing why I came, and now, I have some leads. While I'm getting closer, I can't shake the fear that I'll never uncover who orchestrated his ruin and murder." He shook his head. "Until I resolve this, my life is in limbo. It's the reason I haven't pursued courtship or marriage."

Two words she hated immensely coming from his mouth. She couldn't stand thinking of him with another woman. "That sounds like it must have been rather lonely."

"It was. And while I'm a man of the Church, I am still a man."

He exhaled. "I have kept my vows, in the strictest sense, but I haven't lived like a monk. The only connection I could ever offer a woman was a physical one. That separation, knowing that it will only happen once, that it will be fleeting—"

"That it's over before it starts," she supplied when his words gave out.

"Yes. I know the terms because I set them."

"And you don't involve your heart."

"That makes it sound so cold. It's more accurate to say I only surrender a small part of it, for a short moment in time. It will return to me when I leave."

"Because the intention is always to go."

"In the past, yes." He released one of her hands so that he could brush a stray curl that had fallen across her brow. "But today was different.

"When you said, in the orangery, that you would come to the races to see me happy with my friends, it nearly brought me to my knees. Because all I wanted was one day out with you and Adam."

She squeezed his hand again; she'd longed for it too.

"Today, I wanted to enjoy the race, standing by your side."

His fingers traced the edge of her jaw, delicately caressing the fading marks on her neck. "Most days, I walk the streets of London with a healthy amount of trepidation. It is a necessity for survival, a lesson I learned at a very young age. But I have not known fear, Faith, until today, when I saw that man choking you."

"In the aftermath of violence, it's a common reaction to need physical assurance."

"That was just the excuse to get my hands on you. To touch you." He gently stroked her throat. "I wanted to be close to you."

It was a herculean effort to resist the urge to draw him nearer and hold him so tightly, he had no cause to tremble.

"Faith." His voice broke on her name. "When I depart Ravenglass, I will leave behind my heart. Maybe not my whole heart, but a good part of it. The better part of it. And I'm not sure I will survive without it."

It was one thing to wish she wasn't alone in her quagmire of emotions, but quite a different reality to hear him voice exactly what she felt, better than she could herself. Damn his eloquence.

Their hands were braced between them, gripping each other with the same ferocity as if they were holding onto the edge of a cliff. For they both knew that there was no hope in indulging in what sparked between them.

"You will survive it," she whispered. "You have a life and opportunities ahead of you."

A wife and a family, she added silently; she couldn't say the words aloud.

Slowly, his thumb stroked over her palm. "I'm struggling to see that anything in the future would best what I'm holding at present."

She had to bite her lip to keep from kissing him, swallowing his beautiful words while worshipping his beautiful mouth. But she could not let him nurse the expectation that they had a future together.

"Jonah," she breathed. "What I said earlier today still stands. This is impossible."

Despite her attempt at emphasis, she was believing the words less and less with each minute he held her, every touch he gifted her. And each time he shook his head, refusing to believe their reality, as he did now.

If there weren't so many other lives involved, she'd tell him the entire truth. Why she could never be with him. Why they couldn't hope for the impossible.

With a bitter laugh, he said, "Do something. Please. I can't find the strength to walk out that door."

And if he didn't leave tonight, how was she ever going to let him go?

Insults didn't work. Emotional honesty wasn't doing the trick either.

But there was a way that would put enough baggage between them that could create that kind of rift.

Leaning closer, she breathed, "Perhaps I was wrong today."

His arm coiled around her waist. "I'm listening."

"Maybe your usual way of coping is exactly what we need." Winding her arm around his neck, she said, "Maybe it doesn't need to be all, or nothing."

His head wagged back and forth like a dog shaking off water. "It won't work."

"Shouldn't we at least try? Finish what we started in the carriage."

The arm at her waist tightened, pulling her closer. He brushed his lips against her ear and the warmth of his breath made heat pool between her legs as he whispered, "It won't be enough."

Leaning back to look at him, she replied, "That doesn't mean we deserve to have nothing."

His mouth descended on hers; the pull was instant and drugging. Softer than their previous crashing kiss, but just as intoxicating.

They explored each other, tasting, nipping. The sweetness of the sherry lingered on his tongue and scented his breath as it mingled with hers.

The kiss was unrushed. No trace of the urgency that had fueled their tryst in the carriage. This, she supposed, was how lovers were with each other.

He'd been right. It wasn't enough.

She needed…more. More of his skin and his strength. More building friction between them.

Pulling him closer, she pressed up against his damp shirt, crushing her breasts against his hard chest. She delighted in the impact of the intimate parts of their bodies connecting through the fabric of their clothes. And the groan it solicited from him.

Suddenly, he lifted his head. "This won't make it easier."

With her thumb, she grazed his swollen lip. "It can't make it any more difficult."

Growling, he kissed her again, harder, with the ferocity she was craving. "You say that now," he rasped, dropping kisses along her jaw. "But try closing your eyes at night, haunted by these memories. You'll long to recreate them. Over and over again."

His teeth tugged on her ear, sending a direct line of fire to stoke the flame pulsing between her legs.

She scraped her nails against his back, and his corresponding rumble nearly made her rip his shirt in half.

Fisting the fabric, he asked, "Shall I?"

At her enthusiastic nod, he whipped it off. It landed like a parachute on the floor.

She sighed deeply and took in the splendor of his bare skin. The breadth of his shoulders curled into the well-developed muscles of his upper arms. A dark swirl of hair dusted his chest, trailing down his flat stomach. Her fingers traced the line separating the two halves of his torso.

Bending forward, her lips followed the path her fingers had forged, tasting the salt on his skin. He smelled of fresh cotton and clean sweat, and she wanted to drown in it.

His hand clamped on the back of her neck, and he pulled her to face him, but held her away from the kiss she was seeking.

"What"—he panted—"is your plan, here?"

"Touché." She kissed him, and he gave an exasperated whimper before retreating.

"Help me understand."

"It's very simple." She stroked up his chest. Lord, he was finely formed, such power in his muscles. Such softness in his skin.

He stopped her exploration with his hands. "What's simple?"

"Passion," she murmured as her fingers climbed his throat and pressed gently against the spot on his neck where his blood pounded. "Or rather, acting on it. Sex ruins everything."

His hands splayed across the small of her back. "Does it?"

"Too much baggage. Too many emotions. Too much." Her fingers wove into his hair. "We'll never recover from it. All of that tension we've built up will have dissipated, leaving only empty awkwardness."

"Hmmm," he murmured, pressing his lips along her hairline, showering her with ticklish kisses that pulled at something low in her core. "Perhaps you're underestimating my abilities to satisfy you."

Her protest died as his lips clamped down on hers. There was no softness on his part. This was a command, an assertion of authority.

She gasped in relief. He swallowed it like honey.

"Allow me to demonstrate my prowess."

Another blink and he'd scooped her off her feet, swiftly deposited her on the bed, and even more swiftly, he relieved her of her wrapper.

With the back of his hand, he stroked her cheek, followed the caress with his lips as he molded his body against hers. As she wound her arms around his back, he winced.

"Your poor ribs, forgive me!"

"Small bruise...small price to pay."

He kissed her again, and she drew him closer to feel more of his delicious weight. His legs threaded between hers. Through the wool of his trousers and the fine cotton of her borrowed nightgown, she could feel how hard he was. She shifted, and his erection fit into the cove between her legs.

He shuddered. "Faith."

She rocked into him, and he cursed. "You're infringing on my demonstration."

"Lady's privilege."

His strong fingers traced her abdomen with surprising delicacy, and everything below her waist grew loose and warm. She'd forgotten how easy it was, how aroused she could become by a few well-executed caresses.

Her only experience in the bedroom was during those first passionate, chaotic months with Geoffrey. She'd never imagined she'd find such bliss in the arms of another man.

When Sinclair's wandering hands arrived at their destination, he cupped her breasts and lazily grazed the stiff peaks with his thumbs.

She moaned like a wanton.

"Is that a positive preliminary review?"

"Promising," she choked out, as he continued to stroke her through the shift.

"Then I'll continue with my work."

His mouth descended on her nipple.

It stole her breath, but who needed to breathe when there was sensation? The warmth of his mouth, the abrasion of the fabric, the pressure of his teeth were ecstasy. He altered between each of her breasts, creating two damp circles, and more wetness between her legs, where his hardness pressed into her, where she ached to be filled.

In an effort to alleviate the ceaseless throbbing, she squirmed, drawing a sharp hiss of breath.

Sinclair pushed back on his forearms, his eyes aflame with such hunger, she shivered.

"How beautiful you are." He cupped her chin. "How remiss I am at not telling you."

Her cheeks were on fire. "Your demonstration is losing marks for dawdling."

His wide, unapologetic smile cracked his face, and it hit her like a bolt of lightning.

That smile was brighter than the sunrise. And contagious. When she grinned back, his expression turned mischievous.

Fisting the cotton of her shift, he asked, "Would you prefer I remove this for the rest of our performance?"

Her hand crept to his trousers. "Will you be removing these, too?"

"No." He cleared his throat. "For the safety of our performers, those will remain in place."

It was the wise decision. While disappointment stabbed at her a little, she wouldn't let it ruin the moment.

Slowly, she lifted her arms overhead. With more patience than she'd ever imagined, he raised the fabric, gradually revealing her body inch by agonizing inch, until the nightgown was gone, and she was bare beneath him.

As he perused her in nothing but her skin, she flushed. It was all she could do not to squirm again.

"I was wrong," he whispered. "Beautiful is a poor, poor word. Doesn't begin to do you justice."

She snagged a hand behind his head, pulling him toward her. "There's far too much talking in this demonstration. Actions speak louder than words."

He voiced his agreement by kissing her. First on the mouth, then trailing a hot line from her throat with his tongue.

"We're about to reach the finale," he breathed against her torso as his hands hovered over her hips, lingering infuriatingly far from where she was aching for his touch. "Unless you prefer that we end here."

"Finale," she panted.

He laughed softly against her skin, and she shivered at the rush of his breath.

His fingers kept a slow march downward.

It was torture.

She opened her mouth to warn him against more delays, but then his fingers brushed her cleft, and she was robbed of speech entirely.

His breath came ragged against her neck, as he pressed kisses there, gently teasing while his fingers applied the same pressure between her legs.

She was going to die here. He would kill her.

She'd forgotten about anticipation. And she'd never been particularly patient. At the next teasing caress, she moved, and his finger finally penetrated her core.

He swallowed her cry with a kiss. "You're disrupting the presentation."

A second finger joined the first, and he began a subtle rhythm. Her muscles clenched around him. As she met his movements with a thrust of her hips, he murmured her name, followed by soft words of encouragement, praise.

"This is the audience participation portion," he rasped, his mouth descending to taste her breast again, and she could hear her own breath coming in gasps.

"Let go, Faith," he whispered, as his clever fingers alternated between enticing caresses and hot pressure. "Let go for me."

He pressed this thumb down on her aching bud, and her pleasure crested. She fragmented into pieces.

As drowsiness overtook her, she hoped that when she woke, she'd reap the repercussions of her bad behavior. In the harsh light of morning, she prayed she would feel awkward and empty.

At the present moment, she was awash in comfort, satisfaction.

It had to be fleeting. For everyone's sake, she needed it to evaporate, like every other good thing in her life.

CHAPTER EIGHTEEN

JONAH RATTLED THE SERVANTS by appearing shortly after dawn, hoping breakfast had been laid out. This was a foolish assumption since no Wilde in their right mind—including Mrs. Wilde herself—roused from slumber before the stroke of nine.

Coffee finally appeared, followed by grilled bread with Devon cream and marmalade. It was enough to stave off his hunger while he waited for the hot dishes—and divine revelation—to arrive.

As he slathered the jam on the hot toast, the scent of oranges permeated the room, and he looked up feverishly, searching for Faith.

This, too, was foolish of him. She'd receive her breakfast on a tray in her room, like all married ladies.

He silently cursed the hauntings of his desire. He knew this would happen when he'd agreed to her twisty, seductive words. But he wanted to believe her argument that acting on his impulse to touch and taste and possess some part of her would cure his craving.

Such pretty, pretty lies.

He'd remained in her room far longer than it had been prudent, holding her as she slept, listening to the strange popping sounds her breath made with her soft snoring. Only when the temptation rose to touch her again, to rake kisses down her throat and make her come with his mouth instead of his hands, did he force himself to creep back to his room. It took three strokes to relieve himself of his erection, but it offered him no release.

"Thank God, I thought it would be too early for coffee." Griffin Wilde strode to the table and seized the silver pot. "One day, they will invent a way for us to pour it directly into our veins."

"Where's the fun in that?" Jonah teased. "I like the bitter shock of something hot on the tongue. The scent's not half bad either."

Griffin sat down next to Jonah and addressed the bread and jam. The dark circles under his eyes were heavier and deeper than the last time they'd met.

Watching illness eat away at one's wife would do that to a person.

"How is Caroline?" Jonah asked.

"The worst part are the good days. They give us hope."

"There is nothing to be done for her?"

His jaw tightened. "The doctors now believe it is a female complaint. I find it hard to trust their opinions, given they are all men."

"Indeed. Lady Rochford has an acquaintance who might give you an alternative perspective. A lady physician."

"A lady what?"

Jonah smirked. "She trained in Switzerland and America and received her license from King and Queen's College of Physicians in Ireland last year."

"Yes, I recall reading something about that last summer. Suppose there'll be more women doctors now that Gurney's passed the Enabling Act." Griffin stared at his empty coffee cup. "Perhaps Lady Rochford could introduce us. Caroline would be delighted to meet a lady doctor."

"I'll see to it straightaway."

The arrival of hot breakfast usurped conversation as they loaded their plates with coddled eggs, diced potatoes and ham, and roasted kippers.

"I'm glad I caught you before I left," Griffin said. "I finally heard from my man about your Madeira question."

Jonah had forgotten Christopher had engaged his brother's help to search for Rochford. When he examined his conscience, he realized he'd been nursing a hope the trail remained cold, until he could resolve his feelings for Faith.

At the present moment, he wanted Faith more than he wanted to find the earl.

And if the man never was found, if death had already claimed Rochford on the way to Madeira, along with any answers the earl had about Joseph Sinclair and his business, Jonah would be content, knowing Faith was safe.

"I would have spoken to you last night, but Mother insisted on not separating," Griffin continued, his eyes fixed on the morning *Times*. "And I couldn't catch you when the rest of the party retired. Incidentally, how was that evening walk in the downpour?"

While Jonah trusted Christopher's eldest brother, he wouldn't acknowledge Griffin's insinuation. His ferocious need to protect Faith superseded everything else.

"You mentioned news of Madeira."

Griffin smiled smugly at the evasion. "After our conversation with that gentleman at Sunderland's, I recalled something about the name Arthur Lloyd. I believe he was Lady Rochford's uncle."

"Yes. I understand he was a merchant."

"A very successful one. Father had a few contracts with him before the man settled his business on a partner and retired. I had a clerk search our records, and he found something unusual."

Jonah leaned forward in his seat. "Go on."

"Mr. Lloyd and his brother-in-law were two principal partners in a joint venture company called Safra. His brother-in-law pre-deceased him, but at the time of his own death, Mr. Lloyd remained the owner of both their shares in the venture. He didn't transfer those assets to his niece when he died."

"As his next living relative, Lady Rochford should inherit his stake, shouldn't she?" Jonah asked.

Griffin nodded. "There is a third minority partner, a holding company called Fair Winds Trading. Unfortunately, there are at least fifty-two holding companies with variations of that name, so we've no idea where those lead."

"Does Safra have any holdings now?"

"Presently, it owns several hundred acres of vineyards and working farmlands in the south part of Madeira. The vineyards are worth little after the blight. But the land itself could raise a tidy sum. Somewhere in the range of twenty, possibly thirty thousand pounds."

Not a vast fortune, compared to what Faith had initially inherited from her uncle. But if she invested it wisely, she could live well on it.

"Why would Mr. Lloyd have kept it separate from the rest of her inheritance?" Jonah asked.

"It was either an oversight, or some plan to ensure Lady Rochford had investments independent of her husband and his family." Griffin's expression turned serious. "Unfortunately for Lady Rochford, it doesn't matter. Until the bluestockings can convince Gladstone and Parliament to take up property rights again, coverture stands. In the eyes of the law, the countess and the earl are one entity."

Meaning Faith's money and her land were also her husband's.

Jonah's stomach soured at the thought, and he pushed his plate away. "So this confirms that at the time of his disappearance, Rochford was bound for Madeira to settle his wife's inheritance."

"Not bloody likely," Griffin countered. "Roderick also did some digging around. There is an outstanding warrant for Geoffrey Trenton's arrest should he ever set foot in Madeira."

Working to school his temper, Jonah asked, "What are the charges?"

"Aiding and abetting forgery."

"Come again?"

"A known associate of the Trenton brothers was caught passing along forged notes from the Bank of Madeira. They were quite good, fooled many of the local tradesmen. They only discovered the plot after the Trentons had fled."

With Troy Doland, their chief accomplice, Jonah was convinced.

White sparks dotted his vision. "And the forger?"

"Also at-large. I daresay they'll never find him."

Not when he was hiding in plain sight, at the earl's own estate in Cumbria.

Jonah scrubbed a hand down his face. "Are you saying that Geoffrey Trenton hasn't set foot in Madeira for seven years?"

"Unless he was out of his right mind. There's no statute of limitations on that warrant, and Madeira is a small place." Griffin shook his head. "The man could be anywhere. But I'd bet my shirt he's not within a hundred miles of Madeira."

For the first time in a decade, Faith was relieved to return to Ravenglass Hall.

When they reached the house, it took all of her restraint not to fling the carriage door open and flee into the fading daylight. Sinclair's attention fixed on her fist at the door, and she knew if she tried, she wouldn't get far. He'd chase her to the very ends of Cumbria to find out what had kept her from uttering more than five words to him all day.

Throughout the journey, they'd both kept trying, and failing, to avoid each other's eyes.

In the end, she'd capitulated to feigning sleep. Which was far worse, because closing her eyes forced her to relive the sight of the contours of his bare chest and shoulders, his skin glowing in the firelight.

She'd been lying—to him and to herself—when she'd declared that acting on their impulses would resolve everything. What bloody fools they both were for entertaining her stupid idea.

He'd been right about it doing the very opposite of driving them apart, and she hated it. She thought he hated it too, or possibly her, for suggesting it.

Adam bounded out of the carriage, running into the house, with Peggy scrambling to follow.

"Apologies, my lady! He must have need of the facilities."

"Indeed," Faith agreed. "Go see to him."

As Lawless ushered them inside, she stared at the collar of Faith's dress. "I trust it all went well in the end?"

She gave a curt nod. "We stopped to eat dinner at the tavern in Buxbridge."

"I figured as much. We've set out wine and sandwiches in the dinin' room if you get peckish." She eyed Jonah. "Telegram for you, Mr. Sinclair."

In a lower voice, she added to Faith, "And a letter arrived from Mr. Kane."

"I think I will take a glass of wine," Faith murmured.

"I think I will join you." Sinclair looked up from reading the telegram with an unreadable expression. "If you'll permit me."

"If you wish."

In the dining room, they poured the wine and left the sandwiches untouched. The fire was low; only a few candles had been lit. The faint light obscured Sinclair's face, which Faith welcomed. It made her less distracted. Perhaps now they could both behave as adults.

She dismissed the footman and sat down at an unset place somewhere in the middle of the table to read Mr. Kane's letter.

"Bad news?" Sinclair asked.

"Is that what yours said?"

"I asked you first."

The words were playful, but his tone had that soft edge to it that meant he had something else to say.

"My solicitor is expecting news from Madeira this week," she said. "He's been making discreet inquiries about a remaining part of my uncle's estate that was not settled at the time of his death."

"Is it a substantial sum of money?"

"I don't know. But if there's even a chance it could help with Adam's education, and the other debts, it is worth pursuing."

His jaw clenched as he stared down at his wineglass. "And did your solicitor say anything about claiming the property?"

Despite the calmness in his voice, his words were a barb. She'd known it was only a matter of time before he'd chip away at the walls she'd built to protect herself, but she never imagined she'd feel physical pain, a sharpness in her chest, at his attempt to disarm her.

"That is the true crux of the problem, isn't it?" he continued. "By law, your property is also your husband's."

"Yes, we've spoken of this before." And the last time, his voice hadn't sounded so menacing.

This time, he sounded like he was making an accusation.

"What matters most is that we get the money," she insisted.

"And how do you intend to do that when the moment that the earl sets foot in Madeira, he'll be arrested?"

Faith was glad she was already seated, as her knees shook beneath the table.

He'd uncovered the truth. Part of it. The well-connected Wildes, who she'd so blindly confided in, must have used their resources to ferret out the information.

Sinclair stared at her. "The earl is not in Madeira, is he."

"I never said that he was."

"No, you didn't. You didn't say he was in Malta or Malaya either. There are warrants for his arrest there, too." He shoved the telegram onto the table. "According to records Roderick Wilde has found."

The crumpled paper landed somewhere next to his glass on the table, and Faith's heart crunched with it.

They'd finally arrived at the moment where she could no longer conceal the truth from him.

She convinced herself that she'd done it for the safety of others, but in reality, it suited her own selfish needs. Hiding her sins kept her in his regard.

And now she had to bear the consequences of lying to him, and lying to herself.

"Tell me once and for all." Sinclair's voice broke. "Where is your husband?"

Faith clenched her wobbling legs and rose from the table. Gripping the lamp, she replied, "Come with me."

Chapter Nineteen

Jonah didn't anticipate she'd comply with his request so quickly.

He certainly hadn't expected her to *walk* so quickly, either. She was halfway up the stairs to the third floor before his sluggish brain made the connection, and he had to jog to keep her bustle in view. It was an effort not to let his focus linger on the seductive motion of her fine backside.

Perhaps she was taking him to her rooms to continue what they'd started last night. Distract him from his inquiries with her delicious body. A thrill went through him as the image of her, naked beneath him, surfaced.

His bruised muscles burned as he chased her, a painful chiding to give up the ghost of those memories. He couldn't afford the indulgence of remembering. Remembering was caving. Remembering was a betrayal to his anger at the secrets she'd kept.

Finally, she paused in the dim corridor before the tired tapestry. Shoving the lamp at him, she yanked on the fabric and exposed a door.

He was nonplussed about the revelation; those drafts had to come from somewhere. But whether it was the cold air or trepidation, a shiver crept down his neck.

Lifting a set of keys from somewhere within her skirts, Faith unlocked the door, and it creaked back on its hinges, revealing a darkened stairway.

She took the lamp from him. "Wait here."

As she disappeared into the dark, alone, a thousand fears clouded his imagination. Until he recalled she wasn't alone. The house was a maze, but it connected to somewhere servants could reach.

Footsteps echoed down the stairs and the flickering of a light brought a familiar face with it.

"Here, sir." Dolly offered him the lamp. "She says you're to go up now."

The staircase was deathly steep. His knees creaked and his bruised back protested, but he mounted the steps two at a time, until he stumbled into a suite of rooms. He proceeded through a narrow galley that approximated the shelves of an apothecary. Every manner of jarred powder and bottled solution were on display. The faint sweet scent of carbolic acid and peppermint lingered.

A light drew him to the room beyond.

The walls were painted a blood-red color. An enormous four-poster bed took up the bulk of the space. Crisp white linens, an array of pillows, and several fine woolen blankets piled upon it.

Lying amongst them was a dark-haired man who stared motionlessly at the ceiling.

Jonah circled the bed and silently willed his pulse to stop skipping around, but it wouldn't settle as he stared at the Earl of Rochford.

The man's breath rose and fell easily. While his eyes remained open, he was not truly awake. He didn't seem to track their presence in the room. Nor did he appear to be in any pain.

If anything, aside from his lack of consciousness and agency, one could assume the man was relatively comfortable, if not content.

His victims should have been so lucky.

Countless questions piled on Jonah's tongue, but he couldn't bring himself to fling a single one at Faith. Voicing them would be to accept the reality of what was before him.

That the Earl of Rochford was very much alive.

Faith—his *wife*, dear God—kneeled next to the bed and stared at a worn Bible opened to the Psalms. Her lips moved silently.

Jonah's knees locked, and he sank down next to her. His hand came over hers, and when she began to read aloud, he closed his eyes.

"Create in me a pure heart, O God, and renew a steadfast spirit within me.

Do not cast me from your presences or take your Holy Spirit from me.

Restore me to the joy of your salvation and grant me a willing spirit to sustain me.

Then I will teach transgressors your ways, so that sinners will turn back to you.

Deliver me from the guilt of bloodshed, O God, you who are God my Savior, and my tongue will sing of your righteousness.

Open my lips, Lord, and my mouth will declare your praise.

You do not delight in sacrifice, or I would bring it; you do not take pleasure in burnt offerings.

My sacrifice, O God, is a broken spirit; a broken and contrite heart you, God will not despise."

"I know you are probably thinking he doesn't deserve forgiveness," she added in a low voice, as she withdrew her hand to close the Bible. "It's not his forgiveness I am praying for. It's mine."

Of all of the scenarios Jonah had imagined since he'd arrived at Ravenglass, why did he never think of this one?

The honest answer was that all of his other imaginings offered him a way that he and Faith could be together. A road out. However rocky, he would have traversed it.

Yesterday, he thought he'd never find the strength to leave her.

Now, he couldn't stay another moment.

Despite the weight of her words crushing his chest, he stood and extended a hand to help her up. Silently, they descended the stairs, and she handed the lamp to Dolly, who retreated to the shadows, locking the door behind her.

Jonah continued down the corridor without another word.

And in the same bitter silence, he departed Ravenglass at dawn.

He took the post carriage to Carlisle, boarded the last train to Newcastle, and then went on to York, where he spent the evening at a public house near the station. From there, he sent a telegram to the bishop to announce his imminent arrival in London. By the time he stumbled into Christopher's rooms in Bloomsbury later that evening, his orders awaited.

St. Clemens. Nine o'clock the following morning.

He didn't sleep—wasn't sure he would ever sleep again, for he could not close his eyes without seeing Faith. Or her husband, lying motionless in that bed, surrounded by those hideous red walls.

He'd pictured a thousand nefarious things that could have landed Rochford in his current state. His unanswered questions about Faith's involvement were the worst sort of punishment for flying off without demanding an explanation.

But once he had her explanation—*any* explanation—there'd be no turning back. That lack of control made his ire rise, stoked the embers of his lingering anger at Faith, and the secret she'd kept in order to survive.

When morning broke, Jonah rose and set out for the church, stopping at Covent Garden to wander among the flower and fruit sellers. Everything seemed dingier and smokier. The pastie he purchased from his favorite street vendor, however, tasted better than he remembered.

"Not the same up north, is it, Rev?" the woman teased with a phlegmy laugh.

"Not even close," he replied, giving her a weary smile.

At a quarter to nine, Jonah headed to Eastcheap, and another morning market. As the hawkers yelled above the peeling bells, advertising their wares and prices, he winced. He'd forgotten just how loud everything was, how close people walked and ate amongst each other.

He'd lived exactly like this most of his life. All those lonely days away at Harrow and Cambridge, he'd longed for the energy and the clamor of these streets.

Now, all he wanted was some space to breathe.

Two months in the wilds of Cumbria, and suddenly, London life was confining him. His once-familiar neighborhood now felt constricting, like a shirt he'd outgrown.

He entered St. Clemens and found the bishop, clearing away the cloth and chalice from the morning's service.

Alcott acknowledged his arrival with a nod and motioned for Jonah to sit in the front pew. When he'd completed his ministrations, he joined him in the pew and sighed. "I was relieved to receive your message. I was about to send out the guards."

"Surely you mean the hounds."

"To be perfectly truthful, Jonah, I don't know what to do with you." The bishop's smile was tight, with no trace of his normally well-developed sense of humor. "I went to some trouble to postpone your arrival in Manchester so you could expeditiously attend to Lord Rochford's request. I expected regular reporting. Not a vacuum of information. Had I not received word from Cousin Lucinda, I would have thought you'd evaporated into the mists of the lakes up there."

There was an edge to the older man's voice that warned Jonah he wasn't merely concerned about his physical well-being. And he could not afford for the bishop to be discontented with him when he needed him to provide the final sign-off on his orders to Manchester. Which was where Jonah needed to go.

Over a hundred miles away from Cumbria and the countess.

"My sincerest apologies, sir. I did not mean to cause you worry. Taking on the role of tutor, being immersed in the household...it was all-encompassing."

"I'd hoped that this service would have developed your appreciation of discipline, while giving you space and time, for prayer and reflection."

"The time passed quickly."

The bishop harrumphed. "Am I to gather, then, that you've completed the task, to the satisfaction of Lord Rochford's steward?"

Swallowing an inappropriate laugh, Jonah wondered how Faith would answer that question. "Adam—the earl's ward—is a fine pupil. He's worked tremendously hard these past weeks, and he's ready to progress to school. Lady Rochford would like to see him settled by the summer term. She hopes he might find a place at Harrow."

"An excellent choice we both would support," the bishop agreed. "I suppose he'd benefit from a letter of recommendation?"

"That would be very kind of you, sir."

"Not at all. And if the countess is keen to settle the boy, then you best get on with convincing her to proceed with the declaration."

Jonah frowned. "What sort of declaration, my lord?"

The bishop gave him an evaluating stare. "In the entire time you spent at that estate, you saw nothing, heard nothing of the earl, correct?"

Until three days ago, Jonah would have responded in the affirmative, blissfully ignorant of the reality of the man's condition. He had no idea what circumstances had landed Rochford in his miserable state. Faith had spoken about forgiveness, but he couldn't assume it was her fault. Nor could he accept the idea of her intentionally hurting anyone. And the list of the earl's enemies would paper the walls of the cathedral.

Now, he needed to tell the truth, or he needed to lie to his bishop. It was that simple.

In response to the bishop's question, Jonah shook his head.

"If the man hasn't been seen by family or friends for over seven years," Alcott continued, "it would be best to start putting things in order to have him declared deceased."

Jonah narrowed his eyes, a tightness pulling at his gut. "If you'll pardon the impertinence, sir, how are you so familiar with such matters?"

The bishop feigned a rough smile. "Are you judging me, Reverend Sinclair?"

"Merely seeking clarity and wisdom."

"Touché, dear boy." The bishop laughed softly. "It seems intrusive, but it is a necessity to know all the legalities when a directive is involved."

"I'm afraid I'm not following. I know nothing about a directive."

The bishop cocked his head. "Did I not mention it before? I'm surprised it did not come up in your discussions with Lady Rochford."

Jonah wasn't.

"The Rochford estate and title are entailed to the Rochford heir. The previous earl chose not to acknowledge Adam. And prior to his departure, my understanding is that the current Lord Rochford similarly did not name an heir."

What a carefully worded sentence. "I believe that's correct."

"There is a long-standing directive that dates back to the last century. If there is no legitimate Rochford heir, the entire estate is bequeathed to the Church."

Jonah blinked. "Everything?"

"Well, everything, that is, after any debts are settled."

A nauseating dizziness stole over him. "There is no other heir?"

"That's why we must start the death proceedings. As far as we know, Geoffrey, Lord Rochford, was the last of the line. There is even some question whether his and his brother's claim was legitimate."

The scoundrels could have manufactured anything with a forger like Doland.

"Lady Rochford employs a solicitor, a Mr. Kane," Alcott added, handing Jonah a card. "He can initiate the search, and assist with the paperwork, filings, et cetera."

"Then shouldn't Lady Rochford discuss it with him?" There was a rumble to his tone Jonah couldn't contain.

The bishop's brow raised at the sound of it. "Reverend Sinclair, it's in everyone's best interest to have this matter sorted. For once in your life, honor your vows of obedience and visit the man."

Jonah ducked his head like an abashed schoolboy.

"And let us arrange for a visit with young Master Adam, so that I may personally attest to his fitness for Harrow. A fortnight's time would be convenient. I'll expect to hear from you about the arrangements within the week."

Jonah took a circuitous route from St. Clemens to Fleet Street, choosing to walk along the quayside. The Thames could smell like the insides of hell if you caught the wrong winds on a warm day, but it was cool enough and the tide was high, and the path was pleasant.

Fleet Street was bustling with business, and Jonah marveled, as he always did, at how the buildings backed into the crooked lanes like sardines crushed into a tin.

He wandered up a side street that took him east of the Royal Courts of Justice, and north of the river, to a tidy, white-painted office with a bronze plaque announcing *E. Kane Esq.*

Fitting that it might all end here, at a lawyer's office, when this had all started with his search for justice for his family.

During his Cambridge days, as he pored over the notes from his father's trial, Jonah had entertained the idea of taking up the law instead of the Church. His tutor ungraciously reminded him that if he were to make such a change, he'd have to pay his own fees.

It had roused a terrible sense of shame in him that he'd had the audacity to question the generosity of his benefactors. He owed the Church a life debt, for rescuing him from what likely would have been an early death in the streets of Southwark.

If he walked into that solicitor's office and fulfilled the orders of his bishop, he'd uphold that debt and his vows.

And Faith would never speak to him again. But after the way he'd left, he had little hope she'd welcome him back to Ravenglass. She'd had the courage to confide her biggest vulnerability, and he coldly rejected it.

Good God, what must she think of him? She was probably frantic that he'd betrayed her and gone to the constables with her secret.

He needed an excuse to return to her. And that, more than any sense of duty or obedience to the Church, was what had brought him to her solicitor's door.

At the sound of his knock, a shout bid him to enter. He walked along a narrow corridor that opened up into a cramped reception room.

"In here!"

In the office beyond, a man hunched over a desk while his fingers traced the page of a bound set of papers. A pencil stub dangled from his lips.

At the approach of Jonah's footsteps, he looked up. "Good Lord, you're not Quincy."

"Jonah Sinclair," he corrected him, extending his hand.

"Emrys Kane." The lawyer took his offered handshake, the pencil still lodged in his mouth. "I beg your pardon. Do we have an appointment?"

"Afraid not."

"Thank God. I thought I'd lost track of the days again." He lifted his pocket watch from his fashionable pin-striped waistcoat and furrowed his brow.

Jonah was irritated to realize that it was quite a fine brow, smooth of wrinkles, with a fashionable lock of brown hair falling over it.

"I hope you don't mind my intrusion, Mr. Kane."

"They've introduced the Newspaper Registration and Libel Act." He waved a hand. "My partner is currently abroad, and I'm rather inundated with information requests."

"That sounds overwhelming. Do you consult on parliamentary matters?"

"I do. And I could do with a break from it." Kane gestured to the wooden chairs across the desk. "Please have a seat."

"Thank you. I believe we share a mutual acquaintance. I am serving in the household of the Earl of Rochford, as tutor to Adam Fitzcharles."

"Ah, yes, young Master Adam." Kane smiled. "Lady Rochford speaks of him often, and with much fondness. I trust they are both in good health and humor?"

"Indeed."

"And what can I help *you* with, Mr. Sinclair?"

Kane's slick manners irritated him. How could Faith trust such a man? How could he?

Jonah eyed the documents on the table. "Do you provide counsel to the House of Lords?"

Kane rested back in his chair, and finally retrieved the pencil stub from his mouth, before folding his hands across his waist. "May we enter into a private confidence, Mr. Sinclair?"

"If you wish."

"At the start of the century, there were barely fifty seats in the House of Lords. Thanks to King George III's generosity, now there are two hundred. Have you any notion how many of those seats are filled for key votes?"

"Don't they all have to be?"

Kane shook his head. "Most aristocracy are more interested in the life of idle gentility than power in Parliament."

"And do you charge these gentlemen handsomely?"

"Some of them," he conceded. "But others I take on *gratis*. How else is a Scottish peasant expected to influence the law?"

Few men would admit to such humble beginnings. Unless they were trying to persuade another man who might appreciate such a straightforward confession.

Jonah was not that persuadable. "And I take it that Lord Rochford's proxy is one of the many in your keeping."

Kane's smile widened. "What precisely can I do for you today, Mr. Sinclair?"

Jonah fought the urge to return his grin. If he wasn't careful with himself, he might end up liking the man. "My bishop informed me about the directive relating to the Rochford estate."

The solicitor's expression darkened. "Ironclad, that directive."

"That's what I was afraid of."

"Yes, it was a tidy piece of work." He leaned forward. "Eleven years ago, married women in Britain were granted the right to inherit property. The loophole that reformers overlooked was couverture. In the eyes of the law, Lady Rochford and her husband are one entity. Once a woman marries, she has no independent earnings, assets, or property. Unfortunately, for Lady Rochford, as beneficiary of the estate, the Church may initiate proceedings on the declaration of the earl's death. With or without her consent."

"It sounds complicated," Jonah remarked. "Any such proceedings would require a vast amount of due diligence, I would suspect."

A corner of Kane's mouth kicked up. "Indeed, Mr. Sinclair. Months. Years, even, of due diligence."

The ensuing silence punctuated their tacit handshake agreement: both men would do their best to delay Rochford's death declaration.

"I'll let you in on a bit of information we've gathered already," Kane said. "You may let your bishop know it took ages to track this down, a testament to patience in this endeavor."

"Naturally."

"We have confirmed there are no other Rochford descendants. The line ends with Geoffrey Trenton."

"Unless Lady Rochford provides him with an heir."

The solicitor gave no notable reaction to Jonah's suggestion. He might have to hire Kane himself one day. The man surrendered nothing.

"Forgive me, Mr. Kane." He stood. "I've taken up too much of your time today. I should be going."

"You're heading back to Ravenglass?"

"Yes." The pressure that had been squeezing his ribs for days eased.

There was a way out of Faith's predicament, one he could provide for her.

First, he'd have to convince her to forgive him.

Kane lifted an envelope from his desk. "May I entrust this package to you to deliver to Lady Rochford? There is some sensitive information I wouldn't want to go amiss in the hands of the post."

"I'd be delighted to assist." Jonah glanced at the darkened office across from Kane's. "When does your partner return?"

"Not soon enough. He's been delayed in Madeira for weeks." He tilted his head. "This may sound like a complete non sequitur, but you aren't by any chance related to a Joseph Sinclair, who was convicted of fraud and forgery?"

"Debts to the Crown too," Jonah quipped. "He was my father."

"Right." Kane rested back against his desk. "Extraordinary coincidence, that."

"In my line of work, I tend to think there are no coincidences."

"Your father was a merchant with business in Madeira, before—"

"Before he was set up by the men he owed to take the fall for their crimes?"

"Right," Kane repeated. "You see, his name has come up in some of our inquiries into some property Lady Rochford's uncle may have bequeathed her."

"Is it related to an entity called Safra?"

For the first time during their interview, Kane seemed at a loss for words. "What do you know of it?"

"Only what you have relayed. I have been making my own inquiries into matters in Madeira."

"I don't want to elevate your expectations unnecessarily. Most of our lines of investigation have gone up in smoke."

"Well, if it makes any difference, you have my authorization to proceed wherever the search leads you."

"I may ask you to put that in writing one day."

Jonah extended his hand. "You may count on it."

Kane took his in a firm grip. "I'll send a telegram to the countess that you'll deliver the papers to her personally."

"Good." Jonah turned toward the door, and over his shoulder added, "Let them know I'll arrive tomorrow on the evening express."

Chapter Twenty

Faith watched the collection of small glass bottles bubbling away on the stove with the pointed intensity of a Buckingham Palace guard.

Rain pelted at the windows in an odd mismatch of the steady rhythm of the boiling water. On the worktop next to the sink, a smaller pan of citrus skins steeped with gin. Fragrant steam from the warm concoction rose in visible curls.

As she inhaled, Faith held onto the scent of oranges and freshness and one more thing she'd had to surrender.

To distract herself from the prick in her eyes, she murmured the verses of "Oranges and Lemons," but that made the knot in her throat worsen, so she hummed the tune instead.

She was singing it softly, her back turned to the door, when Jonah arrived.

When she'd received the telegram to expect him on the evening post, she'd almost gone to pieces. She'd flirted with the idea of meeting him at the coach with her pistol to show him exactly how practiced she was with it. The only thing that made her think twice was his reference to a package from Mr. Kane.

He didn't say a word of greeting, and his footsteps barely made a scuffle on the stone floor, but she sensed he was there without turning around. Sparks danced down her neck; even after his abandonment, her body remained attuned to his.

Silence was his new way of operating. He quietly removed his topcoat and hat, leaving them over a chair by the table before he rolled up his shirtsleeves. He clearly meant war by showing off his exquisite forearms.

When he approached, she handed him two potholders and pointed to the washcloths that lay across the table. He lifted the pan with the bottles from the stove—at least those beautiful shoulders were good for something—and she tried not to fixate on the way his muscles moved beneath his wrinkled shirt.

Forcing her eyes back to her task, she brought her warmed pan of citrus oil over to a jug on the table fitted with cheesecloth and poured over the contents. The room exploded with the sweet pungent aroma of limonene, but now it mingled with the scents Jonah carried with him: rain and leather and him.

"Oranges and lemons," she murmured, as he removed the bottles with the tongs she'd set out.

"Say the bells of St. Clemens," he finished.

"That little rhyme was my first theatrical role." She kept her eyes on their task. "I was five years old. A man in Covent Garden had a stage outside by the fruit vendors. Punch and Judy to draw in the children. Then a play about Punch's toys brought to life. I was a doll."

His fingers grazed hers as he handed her the bottle, and she refused to look at him as she resumed carefully pouring the oil into the jars. "My mother fled her very proper, very wealthy Quaker family for the theater. She was a remarkable actress. Her Ophelia was written up in the *Times*. Although I suspect my father—the theater owner—had something to do with it."

Her hand lingered on the bottle. "They had a whirlwind romance and when they married, Father promised her she wouldn't have to give up the stage, but then I came along. And a few months later, the heart that had loved my mother so fiercely gave out on him. That's when his creditors took over the theater."

Beside her, Jonah blew out a breath.

"My mother couldn't return to the stage after that. Luckily, she'd had a talent with a needle, and Lawless found her work as a seamstress. She'd been my mother's stage dresser, you see. Before she became my companion. And later, my terrible housekeeper.

"When I grew old enough to remember lines and play a part on stage, my mother could sew costumes at the theater. And then, when she became ill and was too weak to get out of bed, it gave us something to live off of."

Jonah shifted his weight between his feet, agitated, yet taciturn. He offered no words of comfort.

She would have hated them, hated *him* for saying something trite that did nothing to alleviate her suffering. The fact that he knew her well enough to stay silent made her want to crumble into a heap.

"It's a miracle that nothing happened to me," she said. "One hears terrible tales about unguarded children. We did two shows a day. In between performances, I taught myself to read. The older children had parts they learned from books, and they were paid more. But do you know the real value of 'Oranges and Lemons'?"

She finally looked at his face. There were hollows beneath his cheeks, his hair was rakishly disheveled, and his collar splayed open as if he hadn't remembered a necktie needed to go with it.

Hunger roared inside of her, and she had to beat back the urge to reach for him.

With a shake, she reminded herself that hitting him would be more satisfying.

"All those bells, all those churches. Lawless said if I was ever in trouble, to follow the rhyme, to the bells. And when I came home one day, and my mother wouldn't wake up, that's where I went. St. Martin's was the closest. And with the help of the vicar, that is how my uncle eventually found me, and took me to live with him in Madeira."

Carefully, she removed the bottle tops from the water bath and dried them on the clean towels. In silence, they worked together to seal the bottles of oil.

When they'd finished, he gave her a long look. "What happened to the trees in the orangery?"

Very few people would have noticed their absence in the dark evening, but Sinclair was always observant. "They have taken up residence at Broadmoor, with Dr. Blake. She offered a very generous price for the lot. Save that." She pointed to a large ceramic pot by the door. "Elyse insisted I keep seedlings."

"Why sell them now?"

"After what happened at the races, I couldn't chance they would be the next target. They're far too valuable, and we need the money."

He searched the room for somewhere to direct his glare and instead found the orange sapling. "It's too dark to keep that here. Doesn't it need the light?"

"Yes," she agreed. "I will move it to my rooms."

He bent down, retrieved the heavy pot, and turned to her expectantly.

The fiend. Covering his disreputable motives under the auspices of a gentlemanly gesture. She was going to ream him for it.

The second they were behind a locked door.

Barely offering him a glance, she lifted her chin and the small table lamp and walked out of the kitchens briskly.

The orange pot was more awkward than heavy for a trip up three flights of stairs, but he managed it with his usual finesse, and she thought fleetingly it was a good thing she'd sent the carriage to meet the post coach, or he'd be dripping over everything.

At the door to her rooms, she paused. She contemplated taking the pot herself. Then she registered the angry look in his eyes and became infuriated that he thought he had the right to be angry about anything. She marched into the room in a huff that would have rivaled any true-born aristocrat.

He followed her inside and placed the pot on the chest of drawers next to the bay window. Then he turned and crossed to the door.

Faith's jaw dangled open. Of all the things she'd expected from his return, this cold reticence wasn't among them. Was he really going to leave now, knowing how badly she wanted to give him a proper dressing-down? He'd never run from a fight before. She would have sworn he'd enjoyed their past arguments.

She would have laughed, if a large knot wasn't choking her throat.

Jonah paused by the door. Slowly he raised a hand and pressed it to the thick wood, before sliding the lock closed.

The scrape of the iron twisting, and the speed at which he turned back toward her, raised an intense flutter in her stomach.

"Before we parted, the last words you spoke to me were about forgiveness. I would ask for yours, although I don't deserve it."

"No, you do not," she seethed, angered and relieved and annoyed at her own quickness to lash out. Lord, did it feel good to say it to his face.

She wouldn't yell, though, despite how satisfying it might feel. No, she had something much worse in mind for him.

"Do you know what a risk I took, baring everything to you? Have you any idea how much I wrestled with that decision?"

He did her the courtesy of saying nothing.

"And you left." Her laugh was a black and bitter sound she hated coming from her own throat. "I didn't know if you'd gone for the magistrate, or simply fled off in a huff because you were angry at me, for keeping a secret that protects everyone in this household."

His jaw trembled, but his gaze held steady.

"There were so many times I wanted to tell you everything," she whispered. "That first night, when you arrived, and you kept pressing, I was terrified I would blurt it out. And then the night of the fire, when you insisted you wanted to help, I wanted to tell you then."

"Why didn't you?"

"What experience do I have with trustworthy men?" she fired back, enjoying the way he flinched. "There are too many people whose welfare relies on the truth staying buried. I cannot afford to jeopardize their safety."

She hadn't realized she was shaking until he took her chilly hand in his warm one.

"I know that. It has been eating me alive these past days."

"That's why you came back?" she pushed. "To appease your guilt?"

"I came back because I couldn't stay away. I *can't* stay away from you."

His voice carried an edge of emotion that seeped into her, dismantling her armor. She wanted to believe what he claimed, but the moment she told him the entire truth, he'd leave her again.

Jonah's hand tightened around hers, forcing her to look at him. The tortured expression on his handsome face devastated her. "Will you tell me what happened?"

"It's safer for you if you don't know the details."

"I don't care about being safe."

She was tempted to remind him he was a gentleman curate—healthy, young, strong—and that despite his assertion, he was protected by those privileges.

But the small scar on the bridge of his nose, the rough calluses on his hands reminded her of what he'd survived as a child, and that a child's fear never faded completely.

It hadn't left her.

Releasing his hand, she walked to the small plant and traced a bud with her finger. "Orange and lemons. I asked for them to be part of my dowry and my uncle had them shipped here as an engagement gift. He thought that by the time I was of age—four years after the betrothal—they would bear fruit. Caring for them gave me an occupation while I stayed at Ravenglass on my own.

"After Charles died and our hasty wedding, Geoffrey spent the next two months here, ensuring the marriage was legal. That was the extent of our marriage before he left me again."

Her words grew softer as her throat tightened. "All that time I spent missing him while he was away before with Charles gave me a very unrealistic view of married life. At least, marriage to Geoffrey."

"Did he hurt you?" Jonah rasped.

"Not at first," she whispered. "He didn't force himself on me, if that is what you're asking. I was naïve, but not innocent, and more than willing to do my duty to provide him with an heir. Outside of the bedroom, though, he was cruel with his words, and quick to anger. He didn't hesitate to strike when he was in a temper. So I learned to be careful."

"You can never be careful enough living with someone like that."

"True," she agreed. "When it was clear his attempts had not produced an heir, he left again. I thought he'd never return, but six months later, he came back with Clarisse. She was carrying Geoffrey's child."

Something akin to a growl echoed from Jonah's chest, making her forget for a moment about the shame that swallowed her. Not just that Geoffrey had taken his brother's former lover as mistress.

But that she'd been able to do what Faith couldn't: give Geoffrey a child.

Of all the terrible things associated with that part of her past, that failure was the thing that shamed her.

Jonah stepped closer to her, his voice soft as he murmured, "What happened when they came back?"

She shook her head, but he held her eyes in his unwavering stare.

"Trust me, Faith. I have no right to ask, but I'm begging you to trust me with the truth. Please."

Knuckling away a tear from the corner of her eye, she said, "Clarisse wouldn't make the same mistake with Geoffrey that she'd made with Charles and Adam. The child she was carrying would be recognized. As his heir."

"And you were in the way."

"I don't know what would have happened had I not stumbled across the false papers and the tickets. They were planning to go to Madeira to claim the Safra land. Geoffrey under a false name. Clarisse, posing as me."

With a halting laugh, she pointed to the fireplace. "I was standing right there when Geoffrey found me with the papers. I didn't think, I just bolted out of the room. He caught me halfway down the corridor and tackled me to the floor. He got in a few blows to my face, gave my ribs a good bruising before I could fight him off."

The words tumbled out frantically. "By the time I got away from him, Lawless arrived. She was standing by the edge of the stairs, hidden in the shadows. He screamed that he'd finally figured out a way for me to be of use to him, and I snapped and struck him with a blow to his jaw, hard enough to make him stumble backward."

She shuddered. "I only meant to stop him so I could get away. But then he tripped over Lawless, and his head cracked on the banister. He tumbled down all of those stairs, landing flat on his back."

Jonah reached for her hand, and she clasped onto it like a lifeline.

"There was so much blood. He wasn't moving. At first, I couldn't find a pulse." She was proud of how detached her tone was, how calmly she described it. She supposed she was channeling the same eerie calm that had overtaken her that night.

Or perhaps it was the steady weight of Jonah's hand around hers.

"Thankfully, Lawless took over. She and Martin moved Geoffrey up to the room he lies in now. Then she bundled me into the hay cart and drove us to Broadmoor. We hid in an unused gaming cottage for days while Dr. Blake attended Geoffrey. He'd survived the fall, but Elyse couldn't gage how long, or if his affliction was temporary or permanent. Meanwhile, Lawless and I made plans for what we would need to escape, if the local constabulary found out."

"Why didn't you report it as an accident? No one would have investigated it too closely."

"Doland found out," she rasped. "He threatened to go to the London Met, unless I agreed to keep up the pretense that Geoffrey had departed on his trip."

"And you didn't think you could escape Doland, so you returned to Ravenglass."

"I might have escaped him." She lifted a shoulder. "But the day of Geoffrey's fall, Clarisse went into labor. It was too early, and although Dr. Blake was with her, there were difficulties. Clarisse and the baby died."

She sighed. "I came back to Ravenglass because I couldn't leave Adam alone in the world."

Jonah's hand migrated to her waist; the other stroked comforting circles along her back. "I hope one day he'll find out what you sacrificed for him."

"I've never thought of it that way. There was no choice. Or rather, there was only one choice. When my mother died, my uncle came for me. I don't know if I would have survived without him. And for a few precious years, I had the gift of his and my aunt's attention and love. I believe it made all the difference in my life.

"Geoffrey had already advertised that he was going away; it wasn't difficult to maintain the pretense. Men often go missing for great lengths of time, and few people question it. When it all started, I never thought it would continue this long."

"What does Dr. Blake think of the earl's prognosis?"

"He could succumb to his condition tomorrow. Or he could live like that for another ten or twenty years. She's not an expert on such things, but I can hardly engage one to see him. I live every day with the fear that Geoffrey will wake up, remembering everything. And with the equal fear he will die."

Slowly, he lifted his hand and caressed her cheek. "While I was in London, I saw the bishop. He told me about the directive. I swear to you, Faith, I didn't know."

So that was what was behind the weight in his stare, the tightness gathered around his mouth. "I realized that when you first arrived, and asked what would happen to me if the earl never returned."

His expression darkened. "I understand now why you hated me."

Her fingers crept over his. "I never hated you. Just the circumstances."

"I wish you had told me."

"Would it have changed anything?"

"Probably not. But I would feel a hell of a lot less foolish."

"Doubt it."

They both laughed softly. She couldn't bear to withdraw from his embrace and abandon the subtle strokes on her back that soothed and settled her.

In a low voice, she asked, "The bishop is starting the death declaration proceedings, isn't he? That's why you visited Mr. Kane."

"Kane and I agreed it will wait until the completion of a lengthy due diligence process."

She didn't dare indulge the small flare of joy that surfaced at his efforts to protect her. It put him in a terrible position; she would not make him choose between his duty to the Church and her welfare.

And yet, he'd already made a choice by returning to her.

With a small smile, she said, "That should give us time to settle Adam at school. We'll have to figure out what to do with Geoffrey. If we move him, we risk compromising his condition. But I suppose we'll have to, won't we? Can't keep him locked in the attic when the Church takes over the estate. If Doland doesn't burn it to the ground first."

She buried her face in her hands.

He gently pried them away. "There is another way."

"Jonah, I know you mean well, but I don't need unfounded optimism right now. I need a solution."

"You could give the earl an heir."

His hands slid up to her shoulders. "*We* could give him an heir."

Chapter Twenty-One

Faith almost asked him to repeat the words, because she couldn't completely trust that he'd said them out loud.

She couldn't bring herself to look at him and acknowledge it. This forbidden thought that he'd suddenly made real by speaking it aloud.

Wrenching her hands from his, she stepped away from him to hide the flush burning a trail up her neck into her cheeks. "After all this time, you think I'm capable of something like that? I suppose all of my masquerading made you think I'd be willing to lie to a child, and to the world, about their identity, to save my own skin."

"Never." He shook his head. "It is a way to save the estate. *Your* estate, and your inheritance, which you are entitled to. But it's also the one way I can assure that I can leave."

Jonah looked nothing like Geoffrey, and if the child resembled him, more than their reputations would be ruined. If anyone saw both of them together with a child, he'd lose his position with the Church.

A shame that the poor misguided fool believed that threat alone could keep him away. It wouldn't have stopped her from seeking her child.

"No, Jonah. It is the one thing that would assure you would stay."

At the tremble in her voice, he went very still.

"You would not abandon your own child, in any situation," she insisted. "You could not bear being apart from them."

"I would if it meant saving you."

"And how could I ever ask you, if it meant destroying you? You deserve more. You deserve a family you can claim as yours. Not some secret hidden in the shadows."

In a gentler tone, she said, "Come now, you must see the folly in this. Say it happened. Say we were together, and I conceived, and Geoffrey drew his last breath the following day."

His eyes lit and the misery that tugged on his mouth told her he'd thought of it as many times as she had.

"Were all of those extraordinary things to happen, they would never allow us to marry. The Church won't tolerate a scandalized widow becoming a vicar's wife." She pressed her hands over her own chest, adding, "You know it's true."

"It doesn't mean I want to believe it."

"I know. And I love you for asking. For believing, when we both know it won't work."

His breath caught, triggering a transformation in his posture, a sudden softening of his muscles, like ice melting on a hot day.

"Say it again," he demanded in a low voice.

She heard her own frustration register in the ask, and fury bit at her. Fine, she'd be direct, if that was how he wanted to play this. "It won't work."

He pulled her to him, a little roughly, and she shuddered with relief and excitement as his breath tickled her ear. "Not that. The other part."

The desperate expectation in his eyes made her eyes sting. "Don't make me."

With his thumb, he gently brushed away the tear that had escaped down her cheek. His gaze was unrelenting, demanding more with a look than he ever could with his voice, and she hated him for it.

Loved him for it too.

An exasperated cry worked its way out of her mouth, and along with it, release.

"I love you."

"Then we agree on one thing." His mouth came down upon hers in a fierce, all too-brief kiss. "I am in love with you, Faith. Beyond measure and comprehension."

He'd meant to stop there. Really, what more could be said beyond his confession?

It had not been his intent to tell her tonight. He'd suspected he was in love with her, after their interlude in the carriage at the racecourse. He'd denied it when he'd sought her out in her bedroom afterward.

But the way that his heart had shattered when she'd knelt beside her husband's bed had confirmed it. It was the truth he had run from when he'd fled to London.

And once he'd accepted it, he'd stupidly hoped and selfishly prayed that she might love him in return.

As he held her in his arms, admiring the flush on her cheeks and the way her delicate brow quirked at him in expectation, a giddiness rose in his chest.

This alluring, unstoppable woman loved him.

Their lips met again in a slow, languid kiss and beneath his hands, her ribs sagged with the push of her breath. He could feel her restraint slipping, the tension of her muscles easing.

Slowly, she withdrew and tucked her head into his neck. "There's nothing we can do about it, you know."

"I know."

Her fingers caressed his collarbone, slowly slipping between the folds of his open shirt, and he felt the tremors of her touch at the base of his spine. "I was wrong. Being with you that night, after the race. It didn't ease this ache."

"No." His fingers crept beneath her hair, pulling at the pins. The sable locks tumbled across her shoulders like a glossy silk curtain. "It made it worse."

His body was strung tight, roaring with want for days. Occupying the room with her wasn't enough. Now that he'd made his confession, now that she'd shared hers, there wasn't a chance on God's green earth that he was leaving without bringing her pleasure again.

And as she undid a button from his shirt, dipped her hands inside to explore his chest, he suspected she wouldn't allow him to.

Her nail caught the edge of his nipple, and he clamped down on her hands. "What do you want?"

The smile she gave him was a little shy. "Isn't it clear?"

She kissed him ardently, to underscore her point, wrapping her arms around him, pressing their bodies close enough that when their hips met, and she experienced the full state of his arousal, she gasped.

"Faith." He touched his forehead to hers. "Have me. All of me. No stopping, no restraints. Just for tonight." He swallowed to contain the strain in his voice. "One night."

"Jonah." She didn't hide the longing or fear from her voice.

He stroked her under her chin, and delighted in the way she trembled in response. "I will be gentle."

"I don't need you to be gentle."

"But you need me to be careful."

Eyes full, she nodded slowly. "There cannot be a child."

Disappointment crushed down on him, and he drew back. "Then I should leave you."

She frowned. "Why?"

"Because we can take every precaution, but the risk remains. And you said, quite eloquently, why you wouldn't claim our child as the earl's heir."

"No. I could never do that."

He took her hands from his chest, dropped a kiss on each one. "I wouldn't put either of us in such a precarious position. For all the reasons you pointed out. But mostly because I love you."

There was no time to relish the sharp intake of her breath as he abruptly retreated. His erection was rock hard, and he had a tough time maneuvering with much grace as he crossed the room.

His fingers grasped the doorknob.

"Jonah?"

"Yes, love?"

He turned in time to catch her as she catapulted into his arms.

There was nothing gentle in the way they attacked each other's lips, only urgency and heat, and it was everything the empty ache inside of him was craving. As her arms wound around his neck, he lifted her closer, pressing every inch of her body against his.

Between kisses, she gasped, "Tonight. One night."

He drew back. "You need to be sure."

"We will be careful." She pulled on his lips again. "You'll be careful."

He affirmed it with a primal growl; she'd robbed him of his ability to be articulate. Swooping her into his arms, he crossed the room and laid her down on the bed.

They pulled at each other's clothing in a manner not unlike scrapping kittens. His shirt and boots were the easiest to shed; her bodice came next, but her skirts consumed more time before they joined the pile of garments on the floor.

As she reached for her stockings, he stopped her frantic hands. "Allow me."

Blushing, she reclined, giving him a wary look. He laughed as he bent his lips to the sweet sliver of bare skin above the edge of the stocking.

She gasped at the contact. As his fingers released her garter, massaging and caressing her leg, a little moan escaped her.

He followed the path of her exposed skin with a trail of kisses all the way to her ankle, and the swirl of his tongue there made her twitch.

"Shh, be still now," he murmured, repeating the same ministrations on her other leg, stopping just short of nipping at her flesh. "We're only getting started."

Her protests turned unintelligible as his lips traced a path up her thighs, and he pulled the chemise away, inch by agonizing inch.

"I—I don't need you to be gentle, remember?" she panted as he grazed her bare skin, teasing strokes across the swell of her belly, up her ribs to the underside of her breasts.

She was so soft in all of these places, her skin like silk. The firelight danced over her body. Her pebbled nipples were lush and rosy as red pears, and he was practically salivating as he swirled his tongue over one taut peak.

She groaned, fisting her fingers into his hair, and tugged. "Too gentle."

"Too bad." He blew on her glistening tip, and she writhed as he gave her other breast similar attention. "You say you don't need gentle, but maybe I do."

As she laughed darkly, his cock stiffened to the point of pain. If he didn't shed his trousers soon, he'd do damage to himself.

When her hands crept to his waist, he wondered if he'd spoken his worry aloud, but the frenzied way her fingers prodded at the front of his pants told him she shared his desperation.

In a flash, he withdrew and peeled off his trousers and underpants, sending them to the graveyard of other discarded clothes, and rose to his knees.

The sound of her staggering breath, and the way her eyes widened as she took in the fullness of his body—as hard as he'd ever been in his entire life—made him dizzy.

Reaching for him, her soft fingers traced his ribs and moved languidly down his thighs, until they reached his rock-hard erection. Her hand clasped him delicately; her touch skimmed lightly down his shaft, caressing root to tip, painfully taunting him with possibilities.

"Too gentle," he gritted out.

"Too bad," she echoed with a sinister grin.

Mercy reached her heart, and when she tightened her grip, his cock kicked in response. She worked him over, stroking, exploring.

He'd never experienced such exquisite agony.

Until she took him into her mouth and moaned with pleasure.

For a moment, he thought he would lose not only his release, but consciousness itself.

His hips tilted toward her of their own volition and to his shock, she moaned again and sucked him in before he gained a grip on himself and roughly pushed her away, pinning her back against the pillows.

With equal roughness, he pulled off her drawers and palmed her cleft, soaked with her arousal.

"Now," she begged, a flush rising over creamy skin. "For God's sake, Jonah, I need you. *Now*."

He entered her with one thrust, meeting her soft, tight flesh. Curses fell from his lips—praises, too. He didn't recognize half of what he was saying. All of his efforts focused on not coming apart.

He'd vowed to her he would be careful.

Slowly, he withdrew. Her hands clasped his arse and her nails dug into his skin, rendering a delicious stinging.

"Too gentle," she panted.

With a smile, he replied, "Critique noted."

He thrust into her again, withdrawing and returning quickly, catching her off guard and earning another erotic murmur of approval. She caught his rhythm quickly, rising to meet him on his next thrust, and her muscles tightened around him.

Electricity lit up his spine, and he leaned in to taste her again, thrilled by the way her tongue tangled with his. Her pleasure surged. In a valiant effort to maintain his stamina, he surrendered her mouth so his lips could tease a course along her jawline. He nuzzled the soft space below her ear, murmuring words of encouragement.

He could feel her tightening, feel her climax building. It would take every ounce of his strength not to come when she did.

"Harder," she panted. "Harder, Jonah. I—"

"I know." He rocked against her, quickening his rhythm. "You're almost there."

"You won't forget?"

"I'm being careful, darling. For you. For us." He affirmed his promise with a deep kiss. "So you can let go."

Caressing her breasts, he tweaked her nipples, drawing another whimper from her. "Let it all go, Faith, for me."

Her nails dug into his arm, and the pure adulation in her eyes was worth every tortured second that he fought to maintain his control.

He reached between them, where they were joined, and stroked at the bud that guarded her pleasure, then pressed his thumb down.

She came violently, her inner muscles gripping him with such force, he had no choice but to withdraw while she was still in the throes of her pleasure.

The sight of her ecstasy brought his own climax, and he spilled his release against the sheets.

Chapter Twenty-Two

Sometime later, as Faith was dozing off, she sensed Jonah rise from the bed.

She was too deliciously sated to rouse herself. Instead, she indulged in the conceit that she was safe because he was watching over her.

Eventually, a soft clicking sound woke her. She reached for her revolver and pointed it at the door.

Jonah froze. "Good Lord, was that beneath your pillow the entire time?"

"Behind the bed frame." She blew out a breath as she locked the safety. Giving him a sheepish grin, she added, "Apologies. Force of habit."

"Permission to approach?" He carried a tray laden with cheese, fruit, and an envelope.

Overcome by an odd sense of shyness, Faith pulled the bedclothes around her and nodded.

"Now that I know you go to bed with a gun, I'm glad my grumbling stomach didn't wake you," he teased as he placed the tray on the bed.

She hadn't considered he'd been traveling for hours, likely with no food. Her cheeks burned. "You didn't stop to eat anything on your way here, did you?"

His mouth was already occupied by biscuits and cheese, but he shook his head, swallowed. "Food was not the focus of my thoughts."

Her body instantly responded to the low tone of his voice. Heat rushed through her, and the somewhat sore flesh between her legs clenched.

"Are those the famous shortbread biscuits?" she asked, to distract herself.

With a cheeky grin, he handed her a small plate piled with sliced apples, cheese, and, she remarked, a tiny portion of biscuits.

"The rest were all broken," he said defensively to her quirked brow. "I saved you the good ones."

It was impossible to stay angry with him. Not with his thick lashes curled against his cheeks, and his hair a wild mess from her marauding fingers.

"No sherry this time?" she teased.

"I had a nose around the kitchen for the Madeira but couldn't find any."

"Secret shelf in the pantry, behind the porridge oats. That's where Lawless stashes the good stuff."

The grin he gave her was so broad and dazzling, she couldn't help but return it, and the overwhelming urge to laugh produced a small giggle.

She hadn't realized she had craved this closeness, this intimacy with someone. It wasn't just sharing biscuits and caresses. It was the openness, the easiness of being with him. Without pretense. Without disguise.

And for once in her life, she wouldn't think about all of the things that could ruin it. She would enjoy this, enjoy him, knowing it was fleeting.

His grin faded, but his attention lingered. Her skin felt tight and hot under his gaze.

"Have you, that is—" she stuttered. "Has it ever been like this before for you? With your previous..." She flapped a hand, unable to finish the sentence.

"No. Never." He caught her fingers and bestowed a kiss on them. "I've only ever done *this* twice, with a worldly widow in Cambridge, before I took my vows. And I've never been in love before. Not like this."

It was a small comfort, knowing how extraordinary their connection was. And a torment, knowing that they would both have to give it all up.

That must be what was feeding into the intensity of it all. They were allowing themselves to indulge in a fantasy. This feeling of forever when they were with each other must only happen with the onset of affection, the impact of infatuation.

"I thought so." She glanced down at the tray, and her attention snagged on the envelope.

"That's from Kane."

The drop in the temperature of his tone when he mentioned the solicitor's name was a curious development. Did he hate the prospect of her having to deal with Kane about money?

He couldn't possibly be jealous of the man.

She opened the packet and perused the papers. "It's the latest report from Madeira. They're trying to track down the other partner in the holding company for the assets."

"Safra," he murmured.

"Kane mentioned it?"

"I asked him about it since it came up in my inquiries about the earl. Kane believes there's a link to my father."

Her hand reached for his, needing something to hold on to. The possibility that their families shared a connection to their pasts was too extraordinary.

"Kane thinks it's unlikely," he added. "What interests me more are the other details Griffin uncovered, about the charges against Rochford and his associates for forgery."

She flushed. "One more thing they hid from me. I was such an ignorant ninny. I never questioned why they were in such haste to leave Madeira."

"Don't blame yourself, darling. These are professional criminals we are talking about." He squeezed her hand. "It leaves no question in my mind that Doland helped orchestrate my father's ruination."

"I don't doubt it either," she agreed softly. "But we lack the evidence to prove it."

"Right now," he amended. "I will find it. And he will pay."

As she shifted through the papers, she sensed he was studying her and when she glanced up, his expression had turned a little forlorn.

"If Kane finds something, would you try to claim the assets yourself?" he asked.

"If I can. I don't know if they'd allow me to without Geoffrey. When Adam is settled and safe, I can turn my attention to it."

He pushed aside the tray. "When I saw the bishop, we talked about Adam, and I asked him to write a letter of recommendation. Alcott insisted he meet the boy in person. Christopher has written to him, suggesting that they both journey here together, which would also allow Christopher to assess the river."

"Absolutely not."

"I had the same reaction at first. Fear. Fury at Christopher for making the presumption on your behalf."

He covered her hand with his, and the weight and warmth immediately steadied her.

"Then I realized it was the best possible thing for the bishop to come here, so he can see for himself how well you and Adam have fared."

"You're fooling yourself," she said tartly. "What if he demands a tour of the house? What if a servant accidentally mentions something?"

"Faith, I consider myself more observant than the average person. I lived in this house for weeks and didn't know who was residing on the third floor. The bishop and Christopher will only be here for a handful of hours. "

"If they find out—"

"They will not find out," he said in the tone he deployed to intimidate others, the one she respected, but didn't cower from herself.

Not when he was holding her with such care.

"It puts you in a dangerous position," she whispered.

He leaned down and kissed her. If he meant it to be gentle, the intent got away from them as their lips locked, and they tasted each other deeply. His breath was tinged with the scent of apples, and the faint taste of sugar lingered on his tongue.

It was the sweetest of distractions, but she would not be deterred.

She pulled away and gently cupped his cheek. "Jonah, can you really lie to your bishop?"

"I already have."

Touching his lips to her forehead, he withdrew, taking the tray with him.

He'd left her more brusquely than he'd planned or wanted.

If he was being perfectly truthful, he never wanted to leave her again.

That was the real lie, the one he'd spoken to her, the one that had literally seduced her into his arms: one night only.

He'd promised her he wouldn't hope for more. But shutting off that thought was like cutting off an appendage. He could deny wanting it as much as he could deny loving her. The only recourse was to find some way to live with it.

His vows dictated he needed to confess the transgression he committed. And while he'd broken his vows willingly, he couldn't work past one certainty: what had happened between them was not an act of sin, but one of love.

He did not regret it.

As he entered his room, the rising sun shone through the open curtains. The servants had set up a hip bath for him last night, a thoughtful gesture he hadn't taken advantage of. The kettle of water was ice-cold and exactly what he needed. For as he stripped off his clothes, he caught the perfume of orange oil, mingled with darker, pungent scents he attributed to her skin, and he was instantly, wildly aroused.

Grinding down on his teeth, he doused himself with freezing water and shuddered.

After completing the rest of his morning ablutions, he wandered to the schoolroom and found it absent of his charge.

"He's down by the fishpond, sir," Peggy supplied. "Someone put the idea into his head that fish bite early, so he headed down there soon as the sun rose. Old Leggatt, the gardener, is keeping an eye on him."

"Thank you." Jonah gave her a sheepish look. "Is he very cross with me?"

The nursemaid shook her head. "Not in his nature."

"But I upset him. When I left."

"We told him you had urgent business to attend to in town. He didn't under-stand, sir."

"That makes two of us."

Jonah made his way out of the house and into the misty morning. The trail to the pond was as wild and unkempt as the rest of Ravenglass's grounds. He admired it with the same foreign and troubling fondness for the estate that had grown over the past weeks. From the state of things, he questioned what Old Leggatt actually did with the place. Flowering weeds and brambles marked the trail, and as he approached the pond, the grasses grew to the height of his knees.

He found Adam bent over a rotting log, staring at the water.

Jonah clomped at the gravel, so his footsteps could announce his presence. The boy slowly turned, squinted at him, then returned his attention to the pond.

Cool, calculated rejection. No question where he might have picked up that behavior.

He crossed the grass and sank down by the log beside Adam. In a whisper, he asked, "How are the fish biting?"

"Poorly." Adam frowned. "Haven't seen a single minnow in two days. Al-though I found a bunch of tadpoles in the shallows."

"School," Jonah corrected. "A group of tadpoles is called a school."

A slow grin spread across Adam's face. "Like fish, then."

"Exactly."

The boy gave a perfunctory nod and returned his attention to the pond. After a brief silence, he said softly, "I didn't think you were coming back."

Well, that dagger went straight through him. "It was very wrong of me to leave so suddenly, without telling you."

"You said you should never leave without bidding your host farewell."

"Quite right. And quite wrong of me. I hope you will forgive me for it."

Adam turned and studied him. "Why did you do it?"

"I don't quite know," he confessed, for he would not lie to the boy. He didn't enjoy lying in general, and found it especially hard with children.

"Why don't you know?"

Jonah sighed. "I was angry about something that I have little ability to control. And I let my emotions get the better of me. I needed to sort out some things on my own, and I left without bidding a proper farewell. It was thoughtless of me."

"Are you angry now?"

Oh, the pointed questions from the mouths of babes.

"No," he answered truthfully.

"Then I guess it worked for you to be off on your own. For a short while," Adam amended. "The next time, you won't make the same mistake."

"Indeed."

They watched the pond in contented silence for a while before Jonah said, "While I was away, I had a visit with my bishop. He was impressed with your progress. In fact, he is coming here to meet you, and Mr. Wilde will join him for a visit."

"They are? When?"

"At the end of the week. Bishop Alcott has offered to write you a letter of recommendation to Harrow."

"The school you attended?"

"Yes. The bishop himself was once a Harrow boy."

"And he wants to write me a letter." Adam cocked his head thoughtfully at Jonah. "Why can't you write it?"

"I am not anywhere near as respected as the bishop."

The boy wrinkled his nose as if this thought was distasteful, and Jonah felt a strange swell of pride and embarrassment.

"Will you get in trouble with the bishop if I'm not good?"

"Why wouldn't you be good?" Jonah asked.

"Sometimes I can't control it. Like you and your anger."

He was killing him today. "That's true. Sometimes our emotions are hard to manage. But what did you do the other day, with Nigel and Gilbert? When they took your net?"

"I wanted to hit them both."

"You didn't, though."

"No." He shook his head. "I took a big breath and counted to ten."

"And what happened then?"

"Then I tried to think of reasons why they might have taken my net. And I remembered Nigel ripped his. And Gilbert doesn't even have a net of his own."

"And?" Jonah prompted.

Adam flashed a bashful grin. "And I told them they had to be fast or else they wouldn't catch the fish."

"And they returned the net, didn't they? Because you decided not to let your temper rule you. You decided, Adam."

Adam hummed his agreement, but his small brow furrowed deeper. "What if I decide not to control myself with the bishop, though?"

Jonah turned the boy's shoulders so that he faced him directly. "Adam, what is it that worries you? Whatever it is, you can tell me. I promise I will do my best to help you sort it through."

"If I go to school, I'll have to leave Ravenglass. So will you. And Lady Rochford will be all alone."

"That is very thoughtful of you to consider Lady Rochford. She will miss you terribly, but she won't be alone. Mrs. Lawless and Martin will continue to help her with the house. And Dr. Blake and Mrs. Wilde are bound to visit. As friends do."

Adam pulled at the bottom hem of his coat, which was one of his habits when he was uncomfortable or couldn't grasp the right words to frame his thoughts.

"Is the bishop staying here?"

"No," Jonah said slowly. "He will travel with Mr. Wilde."

The boy nodded as his hand continued to twist the fabric. "You won't let them see him, will you?"

"Who, lad?"

Adam leaned uncharacteristically close and whispered, "The earl."

Jonah schooled himself not to flinch, and he hoped to hell his face hadn't paled; Adam was extremely perceptive to such slight movements in those he knew well.

A part of him wanted to pull the boy close and ruffle his hair. Another part wanted to kick himself in the bollocks for thinking that a boy of Adam's intelligence wouldn't cop on to what was happening in his own house. As much as Faith thought she kept a firm watch and a close hold, Ravenglass was full of drafts and cracks and hideaways.

In the end, he decided to proceed as if the boy's confession was of no consequence.

Slowly, he rose from their place at the log. "Adam, come here."

He walked a little way to the bank of the pond, and Adam followed.

"Now," Jonah said. "I want you to close your eyes. I want you to imagine a box."

Adam obeyed. "What kind of box?"

"The kind you would use to store a great treasure."

"All right. Mine is as big as one of Lady Rochford's steamer trunks, but it's silver. And covered with spikes."

"Brilliant, those spikes."

"No one will come near it."

"Marvelous. Now, I want you to imagine opening the box and putting all your worries about school inside of it."

Adam cracked an eye. "My worries?"

"Eyes closed," Jonah warned. "Tell me three things that worry you about leaving."

"Lady Rochford will be lonely."

"Right." Jonah took Adam's hand and mimed lifting and placing the worry into the box. "In it goes. What's number two?"

"Nigel and Gilbert will fish the pond dry."

"Go on then. Throw it in."

Adam tossed the imaginary rock with a small laugh.

"Number three?"

In a soft voice, he mumbled, "Everyone will forget about me."

Jonah squeezed his shoulders. "That's a big one. I better help you lift it in."

He took his hand and swung their arms. "One. Two."

"Three!" Adam cried.

"Well done." Jonah hoped his voice wasn't shaking. "Now close the lid. Do you have the key?"

Adam put his hand in his pocket and dangled his fingers.

"Go ahead, Adam, lock it good and tight."

"There's two locks, one at the side and one at the front."

"See to it then."

Adam twisted his hand.

"Now, hand me the key, please."

Slowly, the boy opened his eyes, and examined Jonah's open palm. He placed his own small hand on top of it. Jonah curled his fingers tightly, shifted the imaginary key, and clasped Adam's small hand.

"Thank you," he said gravely. "I will look after this worry box and all its contents."

Adam looked at him skeptically.

Jonah put the imaginary key in his coat pocket. "You've handed your worries over to me now for safekeeping. As long as I hold them, they are mine. I will look after them for you."

Straightening, he took the boy's hand and added, "I will look after them all."

CHAPTER TWENTY-THREE

E**VERYTHING WAS READY.**

And they were ready as they could be, given the circumstances, to receive the Right Honorable Reverend Alcott, Bishop of London.

The front trim was freshly painted. Lawless and the cook-maid had removed the dining room curtains and beaten them within an inch of their existence, removing years of dust. Jonah was surprised to find out they weren't brown, but rather a deep forest green. The garden had agreeably put forth some early daffodils and violas, and it looked as if the weather might hold long enough for them to start with tea on the verandah.

The seamlessness of it all made Jonah nervous. He had to force himself to banish the knot of dread that had taken root in the pit of his stomach.

"Can we practice one more time?" Adam asked as he stood in the foyer.

"Proceed," Jonah replied.

Adam walked to the stairs and Jonah assumed the persona of the bishop. Peggy played the part of the countess.

"It is a pleasure to meet you, Adam," Jonah offered in a booming voice, which in no way resembled the bishop's true voice—the man was actually quite soft-spoken—but Adam responded well to it.

"And you, my lord." Adam curled his arm behind his back and bowed, as Jonah had taught him. "I hope your journey here went well."

"Very well, thank you for asking. Although the carriage got stuck at one point. There is a tremendous amount of mud in Cumbria."

The boy's eyes lit up, and his mouth quirked, but he contained his thoughts about the local muck and waited expectantly.

"Now, tell me," Jonah continued. "What have you enjoyed most about your studies with Mr. Sinclair?"

"Does he have to pick one?"

Faith strode into the room and adjusted a bloom in the vase of flowers. As she bent over the table, she gave Jonah a private smile.

"Shh!" Adam said suddenly. "I hear horses!"

"The carriage is comin' up the drive," Lawless shouted from the hallway, eyeing Faith and Jonah like children caught stealing biscuits. "Best get out front."

The servants stood out in a line on the newly swept gravel drive as Christopher and the bishop descended from the carriage.

"Welcome to Ravenglass, my lord, Mr. Wilde," Faith greeted them.

"Delighted to be here, Lady Rochford." The bishop offered her a smile before turning to Jonah. "Reverend Sinclair."

Jonah called upon years of practice to school his expression, so it would not waver under the bishop's assessing gaze. He would not allow his mind to linger over his duplicity; it was in service of protecting Faith and Adam. "Good afternoon, my lord. We're pleased to welcome you to Cumbria."

"Thank you. We bring with us the blessings of sunshine and blue skies. Christopher has suggested a walk about the grounds. He's very curious about the river, Lady Rochford. I do hope you'll indulge him."

"Indeed. I will ask my man to arrange it." She tipped her head at Christopher, who offered her a glittering grin.

The bishop's attention rested on Adam, and Jonah put a gentle hand on the boy's shoulder. "Reverend Alcott, may I present to you my pupil, Adam Fitzcharles."

"Well, well, my boy, it is a pleasure." The bishop extended his hand.

Adam stared at it for a moment longer than good company would have withstood, but after shoring up his breath, he clasped Alcott's hand. "I am pleased to meet you, my lord. I hope your journey was pleasant."

"Will you both take some refreshment?" Faith offered quickly. "We have tea set up on the verandah, so we may enjoy the view of the gardens."

The countess guided them from the drive to the terrace, where a full tea service awaited them.

"Cream tea, no less!" Christopher exclaimed. "Jonah, you lucky devil. How will you ever leave this magical place?"

The bishop frowned at Christopher in a manner strikingly like Mrs. Wilde.

Adam, to his credit, withstood all the formalities of tea pouring and cake serving, along with a somewhat lengthy discussion of their visitors' journey, followed by general inquiries about the state of the spring seeding.

Jonah couldn't help but admire that despite all of her fears, Faith acted the part of a flawless hostess. She responded to Alcott's questions with a grace that charmed the bishop. When Christopher teased Jonah about fearing the wilds of country life, she volleyed back with a quiet barb about London delinquents.

Christopher laughed genuinely and threw Jonah a look that telegraphed his silent approval and his tacit questions about his friend's intentions toward Lady Rochford.

The prospect that the spark between them was so easily detectable made the sour taste of fear rise in Jonah's mouth.

"Reverend Sinclair, you're quiet today," Alcott noted.

"Forgive me, I find all this sunshine distracting," Jonah replied. "I forgot to inquire how your visit with Mrs. Wilde was."

"We left her in excellent health. She enjoyed your day at the races." The bishop turned to Adam. "You made quite an impression on my cousin, young man."

"Did I?" Adam asked innocently.

"She tells me you would like to go to Harrow School. What do you think of that?"

An interminably long pause in conversation followed. Jonah prayed Adam's response would not go too far afield of the bishop's question.

"Well, sir," Adam eventually offered, "I think it is time I went away to school."

"You do not wish to continue studying with Mr. Sinclair?" the bishop asked.

"No, my lord."

Jonah scrubbed a hand down his face. He didn't dare look at Faith or Christopher.

"Mr. Sinclair is a very good tutor. The best I've had," Adam continued. "But I wish to learn what he can't teach me. Chemistry and mathematics, and physics."

"I daresay, Jonah, he's right about that. Maths and sciences were never your strong suit." Christopher's voice was mock solemnity, but a devious grin pulled at the corners of his mouth.

Adam nodded in agreement with Christopher's assertion. "Alan—Mrs. Wilde's grandson—told me that at Harrow, the boys learn to fish and to row and ride. And he said he has a classmate who needs a special brace to walk, and he could do all of those things."

"And much more, I imagine," Alcott murmured thoughtfully.

Mercifully, Lawless announced that luncheon was ready. They rose and filtered into the house, the bishop leading the way with Faith. Jonah lingered with Adam at the end of the small parade and bent down to whisper, "Well done, old fellow."

Adam blew out a breath. "He's not really that scary. I liked him."

"I think he liked you."

Peggy herded Adam off to the nursery for his luncheon while Jonah hurried to the dining room. The footman and Lawless shuttled out platters of cold ham and cress salad, dressed smoked trout, poached asparagus, and brioche rolls with fresh butter.

The bishop cleared his throat and led them through a perfunctory grace before eyeing the food with great intent. "This is a splendid meal, Lady Rochford."

"It is simple country fare compared to London, I imagine." She stole an uneasy glance at Jonah over the rim of her water goblet.

When she looked away again so quickly, a sharp pain pricked his chest. He wanted to hold her gaze and give her signal that he was swelling with pride at how well the visit was going. Clearly, Christopher and Alcott realized what he learned over these weeks: that every small gesture Faith made, every word she spoke, was a declaration of her strength.

"I say, Jonah, you're looking a bit flushed. Are you well?" Alcott's brow furrowed.

"Only hungry, sir."

"Thank you for your kindness to Adam, Reverend Alcott," Faith quickly intervened.

The bishop smiled. "He's an extraordinary boy."

"And you believe he could do well at Harrow?"

"I do," he said proudly. "He is a credit to your efforts. I will be most happy to write Master Adam a letter of recommendation."

"Thank you, my lord." Her expression was a sunbeam, whose warmth she turned on Jonah. "We are so grateful for Reverend Sinclair's help."

"Well done, Jonah," Christopher added.

"And with your work now complete, St. Stephen's in Manchester will be very glad to welcome you." Alcott looked pointedly at Jonah.

He forced a smile. "Quite."

"Come now, Jonah. Has the country grown on you?" The bishop scoffed. "Don't tell me you're not desperate to return to city life. Although, I confess, Manchester isn't London."

"What's awl this about London?"

Troy Doland strode into the dining room as if the cretin himself was the master of the manor.

A knife screeched across the bone china.

Faith paled. Christopher sent Jonah a silent demand for an explanation.

But Jonah was distracted by the scowl that darkened the bishop's brow. And the growl-like rumble that erupted from the head of the table.

"Tom Doyle."

The world shook before Jonah, as the table before them trembled. It could have been the result of his fist slamming down upon it. Or the bishop's fist. Possibly Faith's.

The steward gave a phlegmy laugh. "Never 'eard of 'im."

The bishop stared at Jonah for a perilous moment, offering him silent solidarity before rising to his feet in a slow, threatening movement. "Lady Rochford, I regret to inform you that this man is not whoever he claims to be. You are unknowingly harboring one of the most notorious forgers and thieves in Great Britain."

And the man who murdered Jonah's father.

"Quite an accusation, that." Doland sneered. "If it were true. But we know for a fact it ain't, right, Sinclair?"

Slowly, Jonah raised his head and, with every ounce of ice he could muster, he replied, "Tom Doyle died in the Queen's Bench Prison. Shortly after he killed my father."

Faith's strangled gasp filled the silence, but Jonah couldn't look at her to offer assurance; he wouldn't let Doland—*Doyle*—out of his sight.

"Seeing as 'ow I'm not a ghost, but a man of flesh and blood, you're mistaken, Rev." Doland splashed a titanic pour of whisky into a glass on the sideboard, flashed his broken teeth, and took a large sip. "Ghosts aren't real, are they, *milady*?"

Jonah was going to squeeze the life out of Doland with his bare hands. If not for the bishop's presence, he'd have done it already.

Martin rushed into the room. "Pardon the interruption, my lady. Constable Watson is here."

"Show 'im in," Doland replied.

The countess froze, and they all stared in mild shock at Doland taking command of the room as he greeted the constable with a nod.

"Apologies, my lady," Constable Watson stammered. "I'm following up on a complaint of fraud."

"Against whom?" the bishop demanded, eyeing Doland warily.

"An unknown trickster," Doland drawled. "Some brazen young lad is maraudin' over the countryside, claiming 'e's my assistant. Even drew on the earl's accounts to pay for river repairs. Likely, pocketin' it 'imself."

"There's one fraudster in this room," Jonah said. "And he's the only one seated at the table."

His voice was deep and frightening; it echoed off the crystal. The constable had the sense to flinch.

Fists clenched, Jonah stalked toward the steward. "Leave now, Doland. Or I shall make you leave myself."

He detected Christopher at his back, shaking out his cuffs, at the ready to join him, as always.

Doland clucked his tongue. "Believe that constitutes a freat, don't it, Constable?"

"I heard no threat," the bishop insisted.

"You boys do stick togever, dontchya?" Doland taunted. "Guess the only choice left is to take the matter up wiv Lord Rochford 'imself."

The silence was deafening.

Jonah stared at the wall because he did not trust himself to do anything else.

"See here, *Doyle*." The bishop raised his voice. "That's quite enough."

"Didn't let old Archie in on your secret, mouse?" Doland gave Faith a mock expression of shock.

She was gripping her dinner knife, and Jonah hoped she'd do something with it. He tried to calculate how long it would take them to run upstairs and retrieve the pistol.

"I'd say it's past time for a visit wiv Lord Rochford. Come now, Constable Watson." Doland bounded out of the room with surprising speed and coordination, calling out, "Join us, Bishop!"

Alcott shook his head, dumbfounded.

"Jonah." Christopher's voice rose with concern. "What in the world is happening?"

Faith seized her skirts and fled up the stairs. Jonah followed at her footsteps.

She turned over her shoulder and rasped his name in a strangled sort of plea. He didn't care that the bishop and Christopher trailed closely behind them.

Desperately, he reached for her hand, and they both chased Doland and the constable through the tapestry to the third floor.

They paused for a moment of awestruck misery before Christopher and the bishop joined them.

"Good God," Alcott whispered.

Watson backed away from the bed, his head darting between the earl and Doland. "Lady Rochford, is that man in your bed your husband?"

Faith closed her eyes and whispered faintly, "Yes."

"No." The bishop looked frantically at Jonah for an explanation.

"Care to confess the truf, milady?" Doland slurred. "About the night you tried to kill your 'usband? Why else would she hide 'im away?"

Jonah roared and made for Doland's throat, but Christopher and the bishop used their collective strength to restrain him. They were all shouting at each other with enough volume to shake the ancient rafters.

"Do it." Doland grabbed Watson by the collar. "You've got the warrant."

With shaking hands, the constable withdrew a set of iron handcuffs. "Lady Rochford, I am arresting you under suspicion of the attempted murder of your husband, Geoffrey Trenton, Earl of Rochford."

Chapter Twenty-Four

As she stood in the perpetrator's dock, nauseated by her own unwashed stench, Faith barely heard any of the witness's testimony.

"How were you employed at Ravenglass Hall?" the Queen's Counsel asked the burly young man on the stand.

"I was an assistant groom, sir. From summer of 1869 to Christmas of '71."

Faith didn't recognize him, but then again, weeks in solitary confinement in Westminster Prison had eroded much of her ability to think clearly. She suspected *assistant groom* was an exaggeration; given his current age, he couldn't have been more than a stable lad at the time of Geoffrey's accident.

She didn't pontificate on what other embellishments of the truth he might make in his testimony in service of the Crown's case against her.

"And on the day of Lord Rochford's death," the prosecutor drawled, "did the earl instruct you to do anything out of the ordinary?"

"Aye, sir. He ordered his carriage prepared for a long journey and fresh horses brought in. I was to arrange for a second pair for him to change out at Lancaster."

"Did you know his destination?"

"The other staff mentioned he were headed to the Continent."

"Why would the earl need to change out the horses at Lancaster? Wouldn't a team of horses be sufficient to carry him and his luggage to Manchester, where he would then take the train to Southampton for the sea journey across the Channel?"

The man shuffled on the stand.

"Sir, I would remind you that you have sworn an oath to tell the truth."

"His instructions were that the carriage was to carry himself, and Madame Giroux, as well as their luggage."

The courtroom stirred at the mention of Geoffrey's mistress, and the reporters in the gallery scribbled away at their notepads frantically. Thanks to the scandal sheets, half the English-speaking world was following the trial.

"Did anyone at Ravenglass Hall assist you with the preparations?" the Queen's Counsel asked.

"No, sir. Lord Rochford instructed I keep his plans confidential."

"So you told no one what Lord Rochford had ordered."

The man hesitated.

"Please answer the question, sir."

"I was making final preparations on the carriage early that evening, when Lady Rochford returned from the village."

"And she inquired after what you were doing?"

Slowly, the groom nodded.

Faith willed her shoulders not to shake.

"Is that a confirmation?"

"Yes," he said stiffly.

"And you told Lady Rochford what the earl had ordered you to prepare?"

After a beat, he replied, "Aye."

"And what was her reaction?"

The man glanced at Faith and fought off a wince. "The countess told me to carry on with my orders."

Of course she had. They all would have paid for defying Geoffrey. She hadn't wanted to risk the lad being beaten within an inch of his life for something as trifling as packing a carriage.

"To clarify, sir," the barrister persisted. "On the day Lord Rochford suffered his catastrophic injury, Lady Rochford was aware that her husband was set to leave for the Continent with his mistress?"

The groom threw her one sympathetic look before heaving a sigh. "Aye."

"And yet," the prosecutor turned to the jury, "she ordered her husband's staff to proceed with Lord Rochford's orders to conceal what she and Mariah Lawless had planned."

If only, Faith wanted to tell them. *If only we'd had a plan.*

Rumbles took over the courtroom, prompting the judge to bang his gavel and order a recess.

The iron cuffs chafed at Faith's wrists as the bailiff escorted her to a small cloakroom, where her barrister, Henry Eden—the Viscount Wessex—joined her. He carried a small carafe of water and a glass.

"Here, Lady Rochford." He gently pushed the glass into her stiff hands.

Shakily, she lifted it to her mouth. The chains rattled.

Lord Wessex gave her a serene smile, which was surprisingly calming. She reminded herself how fortunate she was that one of the country's most accomplished barristers was representing her.

"Do you remember what I said when this all started?" he asked.

"It's going to be terrible at the start," she murmured.

"That is how the system works. The Crown presents first. We can only pick apart their case after they've rested. And it's weak, I promise you."

It didn't seem weak to Faith. It had felt rather like the impact of an avalanche.

One by one, the testimony added up against her. The court physician concluded that, given the right attention, the earl might have recovered more quickly (although he conceded that the man had been well looked-after). A bank officer testified he'd received an annual missive with Geoffrey's forged signature that matched a sample of Faith's handwriting.

Her tenants had been called to the stand to testify they had no interaction with Doland or the earl over the better part of a decade. They'd directed all of their business to the steward's apprentice.

"It is a circus," Wessex insisted. "But there is promising news. Mr. Kane has convinced the clerk at the East London Bank to testify that Doland withdrew on the earl's account on the day of your arrest."

Which would show Doland had orchestrated the spectacle of a trial to steal what remained in their coffers. Thankfully, Kane had stopped the cretin's attempts to access accounts at two other institutions.

"You must focus on the strength of our case," Wessex reminded her.

After another day of damaging testimony, hope was a hard thing to find.

A soft knock rapped on the cloakroom door.

"My Lord Bishop," Wessex remarked, concealing any surprise with a blank expression.

"Lord Wessex. I was hoping I might have a moment with her ladyship," Alcott said. "I believe that spiritual counsel is within the parameters set by the court."

The barrister arched a brow in silent query. Faith was equally perplexed and tempted to laugh inappropriately, but she mustered a modicum of self-control. "I believe we have a few minutes, Bishop Alcott."

"Indeed." Wessex nodded. "I'll give you privacy and will wait in the hallway."

When he'd withdrawn, the bishop shook his head. "I expect you were hoping I was someone else."

Faith couldn't tamp down the flames that rose on her cheeks. After the first week of the trial, she'd stopped searching the gallery for any sign of Jonah. The continued absence of the one friendly face she'd come to depend on was crushing.

"You know that he'd be here, if I hadn't forbidden it," Alcott added.

"Then we are of a like mind."

Lord Wessex had wanted to include Jonah on the list of defense witnesses, but she wouldn't allow it. He was not proxy to any of her crimes, except keeping her secret for a handful of days. She would not allow him to be punished for it.

"It was my choice to send Jonah to Ravenglass," Alcott said. "Although he brought the letter to my attention, I misinterpreted the request for a tutor as a sign that the earl had truly abandoned you and his estate." His troubled eyes met hers. "I did not know of the extent of Rochford's crimes, or what you and the others who were supposed to be under his protection suffered."

Faith gritted her teeth. "You see, that's the problem with this system that we live under. It presumes that those who inherit wealth and power will spare half a thought for their dependents."

"You did." He caught her with a look that was both tortured and proud. "You've made yourself indispensable. The Rochford estate, its tenants, and Adam depend on you. You cannot allow Tom Doyle to take that away."

The way he drew out the name of Doland's alias with a vicious edge to his voice roused her curiosity. "You recognized Doland—Doyle—at Ravenglass. How did you know him?"

Alcott curled his lip. "Besides forgery, he also was a chief debt collector for the Skinner's Lane Lads."

"Oh, the irony," she mumbled.

"Precisely. I knew of the gang years ago when I was just another London vicar. One of my parishioners owed them money. The man died from the injuries Doyle inflicted on him. I watched Doyle tried and convicted, thinking justice had been served."

"Did you know about his connection to Mr. Sinclair?"

"I knew that Tom Doyle had killed his father in prison. When I learned one of Doyle's victims was a bright lad in need of a leg up, I arranged for Jonah's scholarship to Harrow."

He drew a breath. "Doyle cannot escape justice again. You must allow Jonah to testify on your behalf."

"No." She'd argued it with Wessex and Kane too many times.

"As a respected member of the clergy, he can testify that you did not try to defraud the estate and were acting with its best interests in mind," Alcott argued. "It could counter what the Crown has presented as your motive."

She laughed softly, with genuine amusement. How refreshing to find a man of senior years who was so naïve. She was a little jealous. "But it would do nothing to clear the charges of attempted murder. Why on earth would you suggest risking his reputation over a doomed prospect?"

"Because he cares for you. And we both want you to live."

With every breath, she was fighting for the same thing. But what would that victory cost?

If by some miracle she was found innocent, what were her prospects? As long as Geoffrey lived, she was trapped. And if her husband died tomorrow, she'd have nothing. Despite his foolish, well-placed intentions, the bishop could do little to protect her.

Neither could Jonah.

"Lady Rochford," Alcott pleaded. "Please consider—"

"No, my lord." She raised her voice. "My decision is final."

Jonah's livelihood wasn't something to be risked on some foolish attempt to defend her.

Faith would have to save herself.

Chapter Twenty-Five

As Jonah's train crawled onto the platform in Carlisle, the pelting of the rain against the windows made him sigh with relief. At the very least, the weather was dependably miserable.

Unlike his first visit to Cumbria, he arrived ensconced in a proper mackintosh, his suit of armor for the task ahead. He spared a moment to appreciate how effective the material was at keeping him dry. The cold still penetrated his bones, but that was inevitable. He hadn't felt a moment of warmth since Faith was arrested.

Upon emerging from the station, he turned toward the stables, intent on hiring his own carriage, when two raspy voices called out his name.

Callum Burns and Joe Holland waved to him from a carriage parked at the front of the station.

Jonah blinked a few times. Sleep had not been his companion these last weeks, and the situation was so strange, he could have been dreaming.

Holland removed his pipe and shouted, "Are you planning to stand there all day, man? Or shall we get on with it?"

Jonah grabbed his satchel and ran to the carriage. "This is uncanny timing, gentlemen."

"Not as much." Burns extended a hand for Jonah's valise. "Mr. Kane sent a telegram."

"Aye." Holland opened the door to the carriage and herded Jonah inside. "He's been keeping us informed."

The strained look Holland gave him confirmed the mason's guilt about his testimony for the Crown's case. The men were obligated to tell the truth, but Jonah couldn't help wondering if, had they not been so forthright, the countess's prospects would not be as grim as they were.

Holland cleared his throat. "Kane also mentioned why you were coming."

Jonah doubted that; Kane wasn't privy to the inner workings of his mind. He'd silently swallowed the counsel to stay away from the trial. He'd obeyed his bishop's orders to remain with the Wildes and attend weekly parish services.

All the while, his rage smoldered.

When he'd finally snuck into the Old Bailey's upper gallery, he realized the wisdom of his friends' counsel to stay away. The sight of Faith in the dock, patiently withstanding the vitriol of the Queen's Counsel, nearly ended him.

The carriage lumbered into Rochford village and halted at the Saltcoat, where Jonah was informed that Kane had reserved him a room.

"Welcome back, Mr. Sinclair!" Mrs. Clarence bustled into the taproom, skirts waving. "You should go upstairs and refresh yourself after your journey. You're not due until seven."

Jonah frowned. "Thank you, Mrs. Clarence. Where am I due at seven?"

"The church, of course."

The entire village crowded into the small church.

As he stood on the pulpit, Jonah didn't know what to make of it. While he hoped they were there to lend their support, he expected many wanted to find out how quickly Geoffrey Trenton's wife would hang.

Slowly, he approached the lectern, and drew a ragged breath.

"Genesis, chapter four," he announced, looking out at those gathered, before reciting from memory:

In the course of time Cain brought some of the fruits of the soil as an offering to the Lord.

And Abel also brought an offering—fat portions from some of the firstborn of his flock.

The Lord looked with favor on Abel and his offering, but on Cain and his offering, he did not look with favor. So Cain was very angry and his face was downcast.

Then the Lord said to Cain, Why are you angry? Why is your face downcast?

If you do what is right, will you not be accepted? But if you do not do what is right, sin is crouching at your door; it desires to have you, but you must rule over it."

Now Cain said to his brother Abel, "Let's go out to the field." While they were in the field, Cain attacked his brother Abel and killed him.

Then the Lord said to Cain, "Where is your brother Abel?"

"I don't know," he replied. "Am I my brother's keeper?"

The last words of the passage echoed through the church. No one dared to whisper, although Jonah caught a few sniffles and dabbing of eyes with handkerchiefs, which he welcomed. Shame was something he could leverage.

"You know, it never ceases to amaze me how a well-known, well-studied piece of scripture can reveal something new." He paused before adding, "There's nothing older than Genesis."

Someone in the parish punctuated this with a nervous laugh.

"Today, I find the depiction of jealousy in this passage striking. Cain is distraught by his brother's favor with the Lord because his own offering did not earn God's respect. His work wasn't good enough. Not when compared with that of his brother Abel. But God instructs him that if Cain does well, he will earn God's favor. It is what we, in our modern times, would refer to as constructive criticism."

More soft laughter sounded through the church.

"And rather than take God's advice, Cain sought instead to take the quicker route: eliminate the competition."

His tone turned notably cold. The congregation became noticeably more uncomfortable.

The door to the church slammed open and a chorus of gasps heralded the arrival of Mr. Anders.

The man's timing couldn't have been more perfect if Jonah had scripted it himself.

"As far as we know, this is the first instance in human history of premeditated murder. Cain talks with Abel, takes him out to the field and slays him. And when God asks about Abel's welfare, Cain responds with one of the most notorious lines in the Old Testament: Am I my brother's keeper?

"We summon this quote too often. When we mean to invoke shame for the sin of selfishness. We can sometimes forget that the context is much bigger; it is rooted in envy. But if we dig deeper, where does Cain's jealousy stem from?"

Jonah peered around the room. "Failure and neglect."

Craning his head, he studied the ancient church ceiling before looking back out at the crowd. "When this church was built a century or two ago, there was a defined social contract. A gentleman's agreement of what was expected of the Rochford title and estate, and what it would provide to the tenants and this village."

A few graying heads nodded proudly, some resentfully.

"But over the years, that understanding diminished. For those raised in this system, it is a betrayal of tradition, and expectation.

"Rochford isn't the only place to face these challenges," Jonah continued. "All across England, estates are failing. After decades of landowner mismanagement, their tenants are bearing the brunt of their neglect."

He could see the fear creeping onto their faces. The pump was primed.

"And yet, here in Rochford, we had an advantage. A quiet champion who did everything possible to save this estate from ruin. Who did so at great personal risk. And whose bravery is now being persecuted by those threatened by such actions."

His voice was shaking; it couldn't be helped. He could no more divorce the emotion from his voice than he could cut off his own hand. "I will not mince words. If you have any evidence that would refute the accusations against the countess, anything at all, I am begging you to come forward."

With one final look at the crowd, he proceeded down the aisle, out the door and to the taproom of the Saltcoat.

A pint of bitter was waiting for him at the bar. Jonah sipped it slowly, his hands quivering around the glass. Behind him, scattered footsteps echoed on the ancient wooden floors as people trickled in and gathered at the tables. The barman pulled more pints; quiet conversation filled the room.

Weight sank further in his stomach with every minute he spent alone at the bar. It was laughable to hope that the people betrayed by the Trentons would risk their necks for the countess, but he couldn't have lived with himself without trying to save her.

A sudden hush fell over the room. Jonah turned and saw Anders standing halfway between the fire and the bar, hat in hand.

Holland walked to meet the older man. They exchanged some silent conference and then both proceeded to the bar.

Slowly, Anders sunk down on the stool next to Jonah.

"The talk is you've seen him," Anders said. "Rochford."

"I have," Jonah confirmed.

"And does he suffer, trapped in that bed?"

"Truthfully, I cannot say. He didn't appear distressed. The doctor who attended him has not said that he is. But it is impossible to tell," he added quickly, to appease Anders's scowl.

"Do you think he'll wake up?"

Jonah could hear the implied question the man was asking.

Do you want him to?

"The doctors don't know. Lady Rochford has done everything she could to care for him in his state."

"I'd say she's the one who's suffered, not him," Holland added under his breath.

To Jonah's shock, Anders gave a slow nod.

"Mr. Anders, I am truly sorry for the loss of your daughter, and whatever part Charles and Geoffrey Trenton played," Jonah said gently. "I mourn the fact that she, along with their other victims, is unlikely to ever receive justice for the crimes they have committed. But if you're here to stir up trouble against the countess—"

"I'm here because I've got evidence that might clear her!" the older man shouted.

Jonah teetered on the barstool.

Holland extended a hand to steady him. "At the very least, it should be heard at the trial."

At that precise moment, the tavern door burst open and Emrys Kane marched into the room.

"Bloody hell," the lawyer grumbled as he slumped against the bar. "I thought you were exaggerating about the rain. For God's sake, I'm Scottish and I've never seen anything like it. How have you not all drowned?"

"Well, for starters, we're not Scottish petals," Anders rebuffed.

Jonah's head spun. "Kane, what are you doing here? I thought the defense wasn't scheduled to present until next week?"

"Aye, I'm here on other business." He eyed the two older men. "Might we have a word in private?"

Jonah hesitated, but Holland patted his arm. "It's all right, lad. Anders and I aren't going anywhere, are we?"

"Not if Sinclair is buying the next round."

Kane flung a handful of coins on the bar. "Sorted. Sinclair, now, if you please?"

With a frustrated sigh, Jonah gestured to the stairs and escorted Kane to his rooms. "I was just about to extract evidence from those two that could save Lady Rochford."

"What kind of evidence?"

"Kane!"

"Simmer down, Jonah. This can't be good for your health."

He reached into his satchel and withdrew an envelope. "Your friend Lieutenant Colonel Wilde has uncovered more information, corroborated by our sources."

Jonah snatched the papers and frantically sifted through them. "Is this an arrest warrant?"

"A copy of the one from Madeira. For both Geoffrey and Charles. That's the fraud charge. The second one is where things get interesting."

"This one is for Todd Doran."

"Also known as Troy Doland. Also known as Tom Doyle."

Jonah's head whipped up. "There's proof?"

"A trail of arrest warrants for the same crime: forgery."

Jonah shook his head. "Everything they have against him is circumstantial. They can't link him to the forgeries."

"Look at the last document."

Jonah hastily pulled out the photograph. "Is that—am I looking at a bottle of Madeira?"

"Technically, you're looking at an empty bottle of Madeira. But it's not the bottle that's important."

His hands shook again. "It's the label."

"If it weren't a sin to take you away from your calling, I would highly recommend you consider a career in law enforcement." Kane grinned. "Yes, the label is counterfeit, but that's not all."

"It's the ink," Jonah finished. "It matched the forged notes."

"You really studied your father's trial notes carefully."

An anonymous source had suggested the police search his father's warehouse. They'd found the ink used in the forged notes mixed in with the ink his father used for his importation labels. He'd been set up to take the fall for Doland's crime.

"Can you present this at trial?" Jonah asked.

"We will try. Lord Wessex is asking for a continuance. The possibility that we could help Scotland Yard catch a criminal they've been chasing for decades might persuade them to drop the fraud charges against Lady Rochford. Forgery of currency is a crime of treason."

When they finally found Doland, the man would hang for it.

"Of course, it won't acquit her of the attempted murder charge." Kane crossed his arms. "Hopefully you've found something else, so I don't have to spend one more moment in this godforsaken wilderness."

"It grows on you after a while." As Jonah handed Kane back the photo, his eyes snagged on the intricate seal at the bottom of the note, and he hesitated. "The forged notes were engraved?"

"Yes. Good enough to pass on the street. But any legitimate business or bank would see they're far too simple in design. Doyle must have had an engraver in his pocket."

An odd flutter erupted somewhere in the depths of his belly. "What if we could find the engraver, and he testified that the label was forged by Tom Doyle?"

"And where would we find such a person?"

"Answer my question first."

Kane gave him a level look. "It would be compelling. And the judge might be inclined toward leniency on the other charges."

"And if I tracked down such a person, would you promise to put me on the stand to testify?"

"Sinclair, the relevance to the case versus the damage it would do to your reputation—"

"Hang my reputation. Will you do it?"

"She doesn't want you mixed up in this."

"I've been embroiled in this long before either of us clapped eyes on each other," Jonah bellowed. "There is no extricating *my* circumstances from *hers*. Will you help us?"

A ghost of a smile crossed Kane's lips. "I can be convincing."

"That is what I'm counting on," Jonah quipped. "Now let's see if we can persuade these old codgers to save her."

Chapter Twenty-Six

As early morning fog shrouded the London docks, Jonah thought it a fitting aesthetic for confronting the ghosts of his past.

His limbs vibrated with anticipation. Or possibly, lack of sleep. He and Kane had been awake for the better part of two days, compiling evidence.

They'd taken the sleeper car from Carlisle but had parted ways at the station for Kane to run the traps on what they'd uncovered from Holland and Anders, and for Jonah to pursue his own inquiries.

The stone structure he stood before was at the end of a row of warehouses in various stages of degradation. The three-story building was expansive, but mortar crumbled off the bricks, and the painted sign—once a deep burgundy—was chipped and faded. The only letters of his father's name that remained were *Sin*.

Fighting off a shudder, Jonah reached into his coat pocket and extricated a small ring of keys. He slipped the largest one into the lock on the side door, and it turned with a creak.

His breath stuttered around a rough laugh. The Crown had owned the building for decades. One would have thought they'd had the good sense to change the locks.

He pushed the door back on squeaking hinges and lit the small lantern hanging by the doorway. The vast empty room before him felt as barren as a cavern. Her Majesty's agents had likely pilfered and profited from the valuable stock of wines, spices, silks, and ceramics that had once comprised his father's assets.

How hauntingly quiet it all was. So different from the days he'd spent here as a child, observing the hustle and bustle of shipments coming in and deliveries going out. Once, thirty men had worked here.

Now, there was nothing left, except for the faint scent of tobacco and fortified spirits.

In the years following his father's trial and both his parents' deaths, he'd never returned to the center of his family's enterprise. Despite all of his other efforts to clear his father's name, he'd evaded the warehouse. He'd told himself that there was nothing there to help his search. But truthfully, he'd been avoiding it. The happy memories of his time here with his father were as demoralizing as the pain and frustration of knowing that it was the site of his ruination.

The answers he'd been chasing his entire life could be hidden here. If not for Faith's dire circumstances, he might never have had the courage to confront it all.

A seagull cried, stirring him from his thoughts, and he strode through the vacant storerooms to the back staircase that led to the second and third floors. He jogged all the way to the top floor, which, unlike the first two stories, was closed off by a door.

Fortuitously, the Crown hadn't changed those locks either.

The floor contained suites of rooms his father had leased out to other tradespeople. Small brass plaques, now rusted over, announced the names of the businesses: *Croft Steelworks; Henton's Carpentry.*

At the end of the hallway, he paused at the door belonging to S.W. Engravers.

The only thing in the room was an ancient wooden table composed of planks of rotting boards. While Jonah had expected to find the place empty, disappointment pricked at him, followed by annoyance that he'd allowed himself to hope that he'd find something. The engraver—Stanley Wallace—had vacated the rooms six months before his father's arrest. Kane's sources were scouring the city for leads, but if the man had been Doland's accomplice, he'd know how to hide himself.

Craning his neck, Jonah scanned the room and his eyes landed on the dirty window on the east wall. He walked toward it for one last glimpse of the view of the sun rising over the city before he departed, burying this part of his past for good.

As he crossed the creaking wooden floorboards, his footsteps suddenly echoed deeper and louder.

He stepped back, and they muted.

He danced forward, nearer the table. They reverberated.

Jonah shoved the table aside and crouched down by the floorboards. His fingers traced the floorboard grooves until he found a gap. A bit more prodding, and he pulled the board free.

He pulled the lantern closer and peered at the space between the boards, which had nothing but the rough plywood subfloor.

Flattening himself onto his stomach, he dipped his arm into the hole and frantically grasped around until his fingers brushed against something cold and hard.

Carefully, he withdrew the small metal box and pried it open.

A copper plate winked up at him, and as he lifted it out with his handkerchief, Jonah noted the intricate patterns of a five-pound note.

An unhinged but joyful laugh escaped him. Tears pricked at his eyes, flooding his vision.

He didn't notice the large shadow that had crept into the room before a blinding blow knocked him into darkness.

"I would like to take the stand."

Lord Wessex's face remained motionless. "I would not advise that, my lady."

They'd had this argument civilly three times since the Crown had rested their case. Wessex had aptly taken apart much of the testimony of the witnesses, but the judge and the jury appeared unmoved.

Faith could read an audience. She knew from the curl in their lips to the way they looked down their noses at her that they'd already convicted her.

"I appreciate the counsel, Lord Wessex. However, I must insist."

"And I must insist that you let me finish the defense along the lines we discussed. There is little to be gained by you testifying."

"There is little to be lost," she countered. "And you know it."

An uncharacteristic wrinkle appeared somewhere north of his brows. "Lady Rochford, what is it you hope to accomplish on the stand?"

"I wish to be heard." The wrinkle deepened, and Faith couldn't help laughing. "Forgive me, sir, but I do not believe you can comprehend my motives. For you have not, and never will be, silenced in the manner that most women are."

"That is true, my lady." Wessex nodded. "Neither have any that gaggle of twelve good men who are judging whether you will live or die. That is why we must focus your case on evidence."

"We need them to be sympathetic."

"No. We need them to cultivate reasonable doubt, which does not require sympathy."

The door to the holding room rocked with a sort of half-attempted knock, heralding a breathless Emrys Kane. "My lady, Lord Wessex. We've found something. It could turn the case in Lady Rochford's favor."

Faith sank to the chair in disbelief, while Wessex gave a supportive pat to her arm. "We're listening."

"Two of your tenants—a Mr. Holland and Mr. Anders—have come forward about something they witnessed the day before Lord Rochford's accident. It suggests another person had a premeditated wish for your husband's death."

Wessex looked intrigued. "And they'll testify to that?"

Kane nodded. "The judge is prepared to hear them, if you are willing for us to proceed."

"No," Faith argued reflexively, knowing how deep Anders's anger ran. "The timing of them coming forward now is suspicious. We cannot possibly trust them."

"I interviewed the men myself and found them trustworthy," Kane argued. "They were afraid to come forward before. But Mr. Sinclair was very convincing."

At the mention of Jonah's name, her pulse skittered. "He should never have involved—"

"Sinclair hasn't given up hope or effort in finding something to clear your charges." Kane said.

As Wessex rifled through the folder Kane had provided him, the wrinkle Faith had inflicted upon his handsome brow evaporated. "Lady Rochford, this is the evidence we were hoping to find. It is our best avenue of defense."

The concern—and hope—in his stare told her it was the only line of defense they had left.

"Will you allow us to put what we've found to use in helping you?" Kane asked. In an uncharacteristically gentler voice, he said, "You have friends who will risk their own necks to save yours. More than you realize, my lady."

That caught her breath. She didn't think she was capable of optimism, but she felt it rise, nonetheless.

If Sinclair and Holland and Anders would fight for her, she could hardly refuse them. Since she could not defend herself as she wished to, she supposed they were as good as any as proxies.

She raised her chin. "Let them testify then."

Through the fog of her anxiety, she faintly registered the judge and jury filing in, along with the other court attendants. As she approached the dock hope and dread warring within her, she avoided looking at the gallery.

"My lord." Wessex stood. "The defense recalls Mr. Joseph Holland to the stand."

The mason entered the courtroom wearing his Sunday best coat. He carefully avoided looking at Faith as he took the stand.

"Mr. Holland, where were you on the evening of the twelfth of March 1873? The night before Lord Rochford's accident."

"At the taproom of the Saltcoat," Holland replied. "We'd just finished a roofing job at Owen Randall's barn."

"Who else did you recognize at the public house that night?"

"It was fair crowded, sir. Nearly the entire village were there. Including the master."

"Lord Rochford."

"Aye, sir. The earl and his steward, Mr. Doland."

Wessex had instructed Faith not to react to any of the witness's testimony. It had been easier when the digs and thinly veiled insults of the prosecution had targeted her. That she'd been prepared for.

Holland recounting that Geoffrey had been carousing with his steward the night before his fall was a different challenge altogether.

"Mr. Holland, was it usual for Lord Rochford to frequent the local public house?"

"No, sir."

"Do you know why he might have been there?"

"My lord." The Queen's Counsel stood. "I believe my learned friend is asking a leading question."

"Indeed," the judge agreed. "Get to the point, Lord Wessex."

The barrister smiled tightly. "Mr. Holland, what happened when the earl tried to leave the establishment?"

Holland glanced at the dock but did not meet Faith's eyes. "There was a scuffle, sir,"

"Between Lord Rochford and another patron?"

"Yes sir. Between him and young John Anders."

"And what caused the scuffle?"

Holland's cheeks turned pink. "Both men had been in their cups, sir. Callum's porter can be quite strong."

An appreciative murmur rose among the jury.

"So it was merely a drunken exchange of words?" Wessex asked.

"No, sir. Lord Rochford said something to young John. I was too far away to hear. But everyone in the taproom heard the lad's reply."

"And what did young John Anders say?"

The flush on Holland's cheeks deepened. "Most of it is not fit to repeat with ladies present."

"Indulge us, please, Mr. Holland, with what is fit to repeat."

The mason cleared his throat. "We all John shout, 'I will not!'"

"And what happened after Mr. Anders loudly refused the earl's request?"

"I'm sorry to interrupt, my lord." The prosecutor was no longer smiling as he addressed the judge. "But my learned friend is speculating."

"Let's see where this leads." The judge nodded. "Proceed, Lord Wessex. Swiftly."

Wessex gave a small bow to the judge. "What happened next, Mr. Holland?"

"Lord Rochford struck young John. It was a strong blow. John's head snapped back from the force of it. And then the lad responded with his own fists."

The gallery buzzed. It was a crime to strike a peer, even in self-defense.

"How did the scuffle end, Mr. Holland?"

"We had to pull the two of them apart. They were both banged up. Young Anders had struck Lord Rochford on his ear. There was blood."

Holland glanced at Faith again.

Was she supposed to react with shock? Play the loving wife appalled by an assault on her husband?

Wessex slid a warning look her way. She swallowed her sentiment and merely stared ahead.

"Was the earl able to leave the establishment on his own?"

"Aye." Holland nodded. "But between the drink and the injury to his ear, he was staggering."

"So you noted he had trouble with his balance? Because of the injury to his ear?"

"I'm not a medical man, my lord. But he had trouble walking."

"Thank you, Mr. Holland. Now, what happened after Lord Rochford left the public house?"

"We sat young John down at a table while Callum's boy went for the doctor. That's when Mr. Doland approached him."

"What did the steward want, Mr. Holland?"

"We were nervous that Doland would send for the constable. We all knew what John did. But the steward reached into his pocket and pulled out some banknotes. Started rifling through them, organizing them. We all thought it strange until he selected a five-pound note and put it on the table."

"That was quite a sum. It would have bought a great deal of Saltcoat bitter."

Holland smiled. "Aye, sir, but that's not what Doland wanted."

"What was the money for, Mr. Holland?"

"Doland said, 'That step, the top of the staircase in the main house. See that it's mended. Best of times.'"

"So, he was offering young Mr. Anders work, as a sort of reparations for the incident?"

"I don't believe so, sir."

"Then what was Doland paying Anders for?"

"Not to repair the step, sir."

The jury stirred. Ignoring Wessex's counsel, Faith gripped the rails of the dock for support.

"Why did Mr. Doland—the steward entrusted with the care and upkeep of Lord Rochford's estate—pay someone to do the opposite of what he instructed?"

"The why? I don't know, sir. I only know that he used the phrase 'best of times,' which in certain London circles, is a code word for 'worst of times.' It's what street gangs say to someone when they want them to do the opposite of what they've just said. My son works in London. Doland knew I'd understand what that meant."

"So Doland used these code words to direct young John Anders to tamper with the staircase?"

Everyone in the courtroom drew a collective breath, except for Faith.

She wasn't breathing at all.

Despite knowing the truth of that evening, Holland's evidence was making her believe Doland had caused Geoffrey's accident.

"I believe so, sir, yes," Holland replied.

"Did John Anders accept the money and the job?" Wessex asked.

"No, sir. None of us wanted to be caught up in Doland's scheme, whatever it was. Young John left for the army a few weeks later, for fear of retaliation. The lad's serving the Crown in Ireland, now."

"What did you do with the note Mr. Doland gave you?"

"Left it on the table, sir."

"Which, in a crowded taproom, someone surely must have snatched up."

Holland sighed. "Aye, they did, and more the worse for it. Ellie Jenkins, the barmaid, cleared it off the table and brought it home to her brother. The lad took the train down to Carlisle to deposit it at the bank. And was arrested."

"For what charges, Mr. Holland?"

"Forgery. He's indentured in the Queen's Bench."

The courtroom rumbled, and the judge called for silence before summoning the barristers to the bench.

As Holland stepped down from the stand, the observers in the gallery stirred. Faith had schooled herself not to search for Jonah, but when she could no longer resist looking up at the balcony, she had to grip the rail of the dock again.

Faces she recognized filled the seats. She spotted half a dozen of her tenants with Mrs. Clarence. They sat beside Lady Cora and Miss Hunter, Elyse's friends from the Ladies' Discussion and Improvement Society.

You have far more friends than you realize.

The barristers argued in hushed whispers at the bench for an infinity before the judge finally cleared his throat. "We will recess to allow the court to examine additional evidence Lord Wessex has introduced."

Kane was waiting for Faith and Wessex in the holding room outside the courtroom. "It is good news. The judge will allow further evidence to corroborate Holland's testimony."

"None of this makes sense." Faith shook her head. "Why would Doland attempt to bribe men not to do work at the estate?"

"It was the third such bribe he tried to make that week," Kane said.

"And they all refused?"

He nodded. "Doland approached one man to tamper with the hot water tap in the earl's bathing chamber, and another to compromise the wheel of the gig cart."

"But the only person who used the gig was Clarisse."

"Indeed."

Something cold crept down Faith's neck. "You think Doland meant harm to Clarisse?"

"And so did she. We have a letter she wrote to a friend stating Madame Giroux feared for her life and that is why she insisted on leaving Ravenglass."

Faith shook her head. "It's not enough to prove my innocence."

"But it's enough to demonstrate reasonable doubt by suggesting another suspect was responsible for the circumstances that lead to Rochford's injury. In attempting to set up Madame Giroux, the earl was the unintentional victim of the accident."

"Why would Doland want Clarisse dead?"

"Doland was sinking Rochford deeper and deeper in debt, and Clarisse was worried. She threatened to expose his forgeries. And the location of his accomplice's workshop."

"Are you saying we have proof of Doland's crimes?"

"Documentation of a witness." Kane grinned.

When they returned to the courtroom, they found it as quiet as the grave.

Faith forced herself not to look at the jury. She gave in to the indulgence to scan the upper gallery again, searching and failing to find Jonah. Taking in the familiar faces—taut and pensive as her own must be—she gave a small nod of recognition.

For the first time during the trial, she didn't feel like she was alone.

The judge entered. After a exchanging a flurry of harsh whispers with the Queen's Counsel, he turned to the jury. "Gentlemen, in light of the evidence the defense has introduced, the Crown is dismissing the charges against Lady Rochford."

An uproar arose from the gallery and, despite the judge's protests, it could not be tamed. Faith was only vaguely aware that she was being led from the courtroom, and her shackles removed, as Kane's steady arm supported her.

At the far end of the hall, Holland and the Ravenglass cohort gathered. The cold ice that had lived in her veins for weeks melted as she rushed to greet them.

She was met by a chorus of "My lady," and she fought back tears.

"I'm truly grateful," she choked. "I won't ever find the right words to thank all of you for what you've done."

"Nonsense," Holland argued, his cheeks turning pink. "We were only telling the truth. Had we known it would make a difference, we'd have come forward sooner. Mr. Sinclair convinced us it would, and he was right. Don't want to think what would have happened otherwise."

Kane joined the group, flashing a wide grin. "A fine turnout from Rochford village to celebrate your victory, my lady. Now, where is Mr. Sinclair? Gone to broadcast the good news to the broadsheets?"

"I was going to ask you, Mr. Kane." Holland frowned.

"He hasn't been with you in the gallery today?" Kane asked, his grin fading.

"No, sir. Last we saw him was with you, five days ago at the Saltcoat."

Faith whirled on Kane, not bothering to hide the furious anxiety plastered on her face. The solicitor drew her away from the crowd and down the hallway. When they ducked out of sight, she wriggled her arm out of his grasp.

"Jonah went after Doland, didn't he."

"He's pursuing a lead," Kane countered.

"On his own?" she cried. "How could you let him!"

"How could I stop him?"

A sob caught in her throat. "Tell me everything. Now. I must know."

"That would not be wise. I only just saw you exonerated for attempted murder. I'd rather not have to defend you twice on this charge within the space of a fortnight."

"Mr. Kane!" She gave an exasperated huff. "Where. Is. He."

"He mentioned he had a lead on Doland's accomplice. That is all that I know. I swear to you."

Wherever Doland was hiding, Jonah was with him.

And she was going to move heaven and hell to track them down.

CHAPTER TWENTY-SEVEN

It wasn't the dark that made Jonah especially nervous. Or the throbbing pain at the back of his skull that lingered from Tom Doyle's blow.

Nor did the shackles around his wrists and ankle cause him particular distress. The fact he was wearing them felt more absurd than anything else. It was more like a bad dream than reality.

All of these things combined troubled him far less than the persistent stench of petrol clogging his nose.

God only knew how long he'd been here, shaking, struggling to breathe, his mind taken captive by the memories of the night the Skinner's Lane Lads burned him out of his home.

It had smelled exactly like the scent that hung in the air now, in whatever hole Doyle had deposited him when he'd blacked out. He had to be somewhere inside the warehouse. A thought he was struggling to process around his own choking fear.

Bells rang in the distance, ones that Jonah faintly recognized but couldn't name, and his own panic ebbed enough to fixate on Faith's circumstances. He offered another selfish prayer for her safety, and hope that Holland's testimony had been enough to spare her.

A door creaked open, and lamplight illuminated the edges of the cramped storeroom.

"And 'ow's the seclusion going, Rev?" Doyle rasped. "Figured I'd give ya time to reflect on your sins. What's that they call it—an examination of conscience, innit?"

Jonah forced a laugh. "Go to hell."

Doyle swung. Jonah had enough muscle memory to duck the blow aimed at his head but not enough slack in his shackled limbs to avoid the strike to his stomach.

"Where's Wallace?" Doyle snarled.

"Too lazy to find him yourself?"

The kick to Jonah's abdomen barely registered. "You fink you're clever, findin' that li'il rat and convincin' 'im to tell ya where to find those plates. Don't prove nuffin' to no one."

Jonah grazed the man's chin with enough force to snap back his jaw. "But Wallace's sworn testimony will."

If Kane could track down the engraver and force him to come forward.

Doyle wheezed his wretched laugh again. "Now we bowf know that would require divine intervention."

Jonah dodged the strike aimed at his aching middle; however, Doyle's right hook landed squarely on his jaw, followed quickly by a left jab to his eye.

Disoriented, Jonah staggered to regain his stance and tripped on the shackles. Another blow to his head brought him to his knees.

"No information about Wallace, no use to me," Doyle drawled. "Guess I'll have to off ya."

Jonah forced a smile, swallowing the salty taste of blood, and extended his shackled hands. "At least make it a fair fight."

"You toffs and your egalitarianism. 'oever said life is fair?"

"Afraid I'll take you with my arms and legs shackled?"

The cretin laughed with such force he pounded his chest to regain his breath. "Ah, Rev. You entertain me. What would the bishop say about his precious parson beatin' a man senseless? Those the actions of a kind shepherd of the Church?"

A laugh gurgled out of Jonah's raw throat. As it echoed through the warehouse, it sounded particularly unhinged, which was probably fair, because Doyle was right. After all of this, he could hardly stand up as a man of God before a parish of worshippers and expect them to trust in him as a spiritual leader. He could barely trust himself.

If he survived this, it would be by God's will. And by the gifts God had given him to defend himself.

To protect the woman he loved.

The brute standing before him had terrorized her and stolen her legacy. Jonah's vision tinged with red, and he almost lost himself to the desire to wrap his fingers around Doyle's throat and not let go.

But that wouldn't help Faith. And it wouldn't give any of them what Jonah wanted most.

Justice.

Slowly, he rose to his feet and quelled the shaking in his knees. "Make it a fair fight, Doyle. At least give me that."

"Lady Rochford, are you sure you won't take some refreshment?"

Amelia Hunter gestured to the basket at the foot of the roomy carriage. "I believe Lord Wessex will be some time."

Faith realized she was sagging against the sumptuous leather seats, and forced herself to sit up straight, lest she taint the handsome interior with the filth she'd dragged with her from prison. Grime coated her hair and the hem of her gown. She couldn't understand how her companion could withstand sitting in such close proximity to her.

"You're very kind, Miss Hunter, offering me the comfort and security of waiting in your carriage," Faith murmured. "When I saw you and Lady Cora and the others in the gallery—"

"One of us tried to be here most days. Especially since Lady Blake was detained abroad."

On Kane's insistence, Elyse had fled to the Continent, to avoid an investigation into her treatment of the earl.

"We also wanted to show our support," Miss Hunter added. "The law is rarely applied fairly to women, no matter if they're a countess or a cook."

Their interest likely went far beyond observing the trial. Kane had needed help to piece together the evidence that had cleared her, and Faith suspected he'd received assistance. She never dreamed it would have come from a group of women she barely knew.

"I don't know how I can ever repay you," Faith said.

"Oh, we'll think of something." Miss Hunter winked. "We can start with dispensing with formalities. You must call me Amelia."

Faith nodded shyly and glanced up at the gold-painted ceiling. "This must be one of the finest carriages in London."

"And the fastest. One of my father's new prototypes."

"Perhaps you'd be so kind as to give me a demonstration."

"As soon as Mrs. Lawless arrives, we'll take you wherever you wish to find Mr. Sinclair."

The majority of good society would expect her to be speeding to her husband's bedside. Thankfully, Kane had arranged for nurses to attend to Geoffrey, and she didn't care what it would cost her for them to continue doing so, while she searched for Jonah.

She brushed her cheek with a cold hand to tamp down her blush. "Are my intentions that obvious?"

"Only your affections, dear. Oh, don't cover your lovely face." Amelia reached out to grasp Faith's hand. "The situation is terrible. Truly, truly terrible. But we will find him."

The carriage door swung open, and Lady Cora alighted, followed by a dazed and bedraggled Lawless.

The housekeeper blinked at the luxurious carriage and gave Faith a once-over. "You look a sight."

"Glass houses, Mrs. Lawless."

She huffed in reply. "Wessex says they're searching Ravenglass for Doland—Doyle! Lord, save us. Dat man lied about everything, including his name."

"They won't find Mr. Sinclair in Rochford," Faith murmured.

"You believe he's in London?" Lady Cora asked.

"Easier ta get lost here," Lawless quipped. "The bobbies are out searchin' the gamin' hells. Waste a' time. Dose lads want Doyle dead more than we do."

Faith couldn't imagine anyone wanting that man wiped off the earth more than she desired it. "He must have a hovel tucked away near his old haunts."

"Lady Rochford, you look quite peaked," Lady Cora remarked. "Amelia, have you anything to drink?"

"Will whiskey do?" Amelia pulled open a cupboard in the door, revealing a bottle and two crystal glasses. "Please forgive the informality of the bottle. The glass decanter is too large to fit in the compartment."

She poured the glass and handed it to Faith. Lawless took the whiskey bottle by the neck and took a long pull on it.

Faith's eyes clapped onto the label, and she snagged the bottle.

"Really, my lady, I'd no plans to drain it—"

She silenced the housekeeper with her hand and then glanced at the other women in the carriage, whose worried expressions needed to be put at ease.

"I-I think I know where Doyle might be keeping Mr. Sinclair," she stuttered. "His father had a warehouse in the docklands."

Cora flung open the door and shouted at the driver to head to the docks *tout suite*.

She was still pulling the door closed when the carriage lurched.

"This is thrilling!" Amelia remarked. "Oh, I cannot wait until the police arrest him and drag him away in shackles—why ever do you look so forlorn, Faith?"

Lawless's cackle sounded, and Lady Cora gave her friend a pointed look.

"Oh." Amelia's mouth curved in a perfect O shape. "We're not stopping to tell the police where we're headed."

"No," Faith and Lawless uttered in unison.

"But what will we do if—"

"Not to worry." Lady Cora handed the basket at her feet to Faith. "Before she left, Lady Blake retrieved your personal items from Ravenglass."

Faith plunged her hand inside, searching through the collection of shawls and handkerchiefs until her hand clasped around the familiar grip of a cold steel handle.

The hot release of tears threatened. These women had come through for her, without her having to beg or bargain.

This was what it must be like to have friends. What Jonah insisted was worth sacrificing her self-preservation to gain. The joy and relief and weight of it over-whelmed her.

"No tears, now," Lawless snapped. "There'll be time for dat later."

"Of course, you're right." Faith sniffed as she withdrew a handkerchief from the basket to wipe her nose. "We must focus on what we'll do when we find him."

"This is completely mad. You're going to get hurt, if not killed, and all over a man." Amelia shook her head, before a slow smile spread across her face. "What part do we play?"

Doyle dragged Jonah to his feet and shoved him into the main room of the warehouse. It smelled worse outside: like dead fish and low tide and the moldering hopes of his father.

"A fair fight." Doyle chortled. "Does such a fing exist? Suppose ya fink God treats people fairly, does 'e? What about the poor wretches 'oo sleep in the gutter outside?"

He slapped Jonah across the mouth. "Or those snivelin' kids overrunnin' Covent Garden, scroungin' at rubbish bins to eat. Because their ma drank away all their money for food."

Jonah ducked his next jab, but Doyle's follow-up rammed into his kidneys.

"Makin' this too easy for me, Rev. You'll be mincemeat in short order and where's the fun in that? Maybe I'll allow ya one hand. See what ya do wiv it."

Doyle thrust a rope around Jonah's waist with no mercy for his sore ribs, then tied his right wrist with a biting knot, before unlocking the shackles from his left hand.

After which, he socked Jonah squarely in the jaw. "This fair enough for ya?"

Jonah laughed and returned the blow with more force and better direction, resulting in a satisfying crunching sound from the vicinity of Doyle's nose.

The blackguard roared as red streaks poured down his face and he came at Jonah with a reserve of power, knocking him on his back.

Another kick to Jonah's injured ribs stole his breath.

"Life ain't fair, Rev. If it was, this warehouse would be full to the brim. Not empty and abandoned."

Jonah tried to push himself up, but his arms shook so badly he fell flat on his face.

"Everyone forgot about this place. Looks like they've all forgotten about ya too." A pistol cocked by his ear. "Tell me where Wallace is."

Through gritted teeth, Jonah rasped, "Never."

A shot reverberated through the warehouse.

He found it curious that he heard, rather than felt, the bullet that would take his life, even above the roar of blood in his ears.

More curious was the fact that Doyle's screaming rose above the cacophony.

Flipping himself over on his back, Jonah frantically searched his body, finding sore spots abounding, but no bullet wounds.

"You li'il bitch!" Doyle shouted.

A familiar chortle rang through the warehouse. "Mercy! First time anyone's referred ta me as little in decades, *Tom*."

When Jonah cracked his swollen eye open, Mrs. Lawless wavered in his hazy vision.

Beyond her, Doyle had fallen to the floor and was gripping his bleeding hand, roaring like a wounded grizzly bear.

His gun had fallen to the wayside.

Jonah tried to sit up, but his howling ribs wouldn't allow the movement, nor would they cooperate with his attempt to reach for the discarded pistol.

"Don't ya move now, Sinclair," Lawless ordered. "May rattle what brains ya have left right out of your head."

Deftly, she lifted Doyle's gun with a handkerchief. "Look what we have here."

Doyle pulled himself to his feet as if to charge at them when another shot hit him squarely in the knee.

The voice Jonah believed he might not hear again shouted, "That's quite enough, Tom Doyle. One more move and I'll aim for something that a doctor cannot easily repair."

Jonah forced himself to sit up and pried open his other eye. Faith approached them, one arm extended as she gripped her Weston.

She sank to her knees, keeping the pistol pointed at Doland.

The other arm, she extended to Jonah. He pressed her hand to his lips and indulged in a deep sigh, ignoring every one of his bones and muscles that were screaming in pain.

Faith returned his sigh, equally breathless. "Where does it hurt the most?"

"Nowhere." *Everywhere.* "Are you well? I'm afraid I can barely see you."

She laughed softly. "Count yourself lucky. I'm a disaster. I really shouldn't be standing this close to anyone. The stench of prison may never come off me."

"How fortunate then that my nose is likely broken, and I can't smell at all. Come here."

He tugged on her arm, and she acquiesced, murmuring another sigh.

"Lady Cora and Miss Hunter have a doctor outside. They're waiting for the police to arrive. I could not risk them coming in before."

"But you were happy to risk yourself."

"Seemed a shame for you to have gone through all the trouble to free me without receiving my personal thanks."

"Indeed." His head was spinning badly now, and he had to close his eyes as he murmured, "The pleasure was all mine, my lady."

"Jonah?"

He forced his eyes open, cupped her chin to pull her mouth to his for a gentle kiss. "See? Only thing I can smell is oranges and lemons."

The last thing he saw before blackness descended was the shimmer of tears in her eyes.

Chapter Twenty-Eight

In the fortnight following her release, Faith had bathed twice a day, and still felt she'd never fully clean off the taint from her time in Westminster Prison.

When she returned to Ravenglass and staggered into her bathing chamber for the first time in weeks, the familiar surroundings and the scent of her trusty citrus bath oil didn't take the edge off her discomfort. Perhaps it was fatigue catching up with her; she'd lugged the cans of hot water for her bath upstairs by herself. Not knowing when (or if) she'd return, the servants had taken on other work in her absence and weren't due back until the morning.

She dressed herself in a simple wrapper to peruse the house, checking every room for intruders, before making her way to the third floor of the north wing.

For the better part of an hour, Faith stared at the same passage of her book while her husband lay in his bed, unaware of all the tumult that had occurred around him.

"I wish you'd decide where my fate lies, Geoffrey," she whispered.

A rosy-cheeked nurse entered the bedroom with a tray. The woman had replaced Dolly, who departed for a rather hasty marriage during the trial. "Sorry to disturb, milady. It's time for his lordship's bath."

Faith stood. "I don't believe we've been properly introduced."

"Pardon me, ma'am." She ducked a curtsy. "I'm Edna."

"Thank you for bearing with us in these circumstances. I hope it hasn't been too lonely here for you. The rest of the staff will return tomorrow."

"Oh no, ma'am. Everyone's been very kind at the village. My mother's people were from this area. Near Windermere."

The nurse eyed the towels on the tray pointedly. Faith made to leave, but she hesitated by the door; an unsteady feeling twisted in the pit of her stomach.

Edna looked up and gave her a kind smile. "All's well here, my lady. Go on and rest yourself from your journey."

The way that she drew out the word *journey* implied more than Faith's travels home, as did the knowing look the other woman gave her.

Rest was an unachievable goal at the present moment. The only remedy she could think of to soothe her frazzled, weary temperament was fresh air. She lit a lamp, wrapped a shawl over her shoulders, and wandered over to the orangery.

On the worktable, the potted seedling Elyse had left her was leafing well. She held the light closer to examine it.

"Shall I help with that?"

With a shaking hand, Faith placed the lamp on the table, unsure if she'd imagined Jonah's voice. It was entirely possible that her mind was finally breaking under the strain of propping herself up for such a long time.

But when she turned, he was there, walking straight toward her. The cut on his lip hadn't fully healed and faint bruises still marred his jaw and cheeks.

"Forgive me, I've startled you," he murmured.

She realized she'd said nothing while she gripped the table hard enough to point splinters into her palms. "H-how are you?"

"A little sore," he conceded with an unusually demure smile. "But on the mend."

Dr. Blake had arranged for the best physicians she knew in London to examine Jonah after Doyle's assault. They had all concluded he'd make a full recovery. Mrs. Wilde had informed Faith of his progress regularly, and only when she'd reported he'd been up and about, talking and taking food, had Faith found the courage to remove herself from London.

"And you, my lady? Are you well?"

As he inched closer, she wanted to tell him she was quite ill at the moment.

"On the mend," she settled on, with a small smile.

"Adam and Lawless?"

"They stayed in London. When I went to retrieve him from Mrs. Wilde's care after the trial, he'd sprouted." They both laughed. "He must have grown four inches overnight. Lawless is getting his new clothes made in London. But I couldn't put off my return to Ravenglass any longer."

"No, of course not."

Neither of them looked at the house.

After an eternity, she whispered, "Why have you come, Jonah?"

"I have news that could not be put down in a letter." He exhaled audibly. "Doyle is dead. Another inmate attacked him, and he suffered a knife wound to the belly. Followed by a fever."

Her hand found his. "You saw him?"

"Yes. He—" His voice broke. "He sent for me. To administer Last Rites."

"Jonah."

"I didn't make it in time. But I stayed while the doctors examined him. And to see to it that he was buried properly in the prison graveyard."

Although his voice was calm, his hands shook in hers, and she couldn't stand it. He needed something solid to hold on to.

She folded herself around him. His arms immediately took hold and pressed her closer.

"I thought I would be relieved," he whispered. "But I find myself strangely bereft."

"I know," She felt the same sort of emptiness. "Thank you for coming all this way, to tell me."

"There's more." He withdrew slowly. "I'm not going to Manchester."

Though he remained close, it was so much colder standing outside his embrace. "The parish won't take you now. After your association with me."

He gave her a long look, and she was relieved that her immediate reaction was a familiar anger. "Unacceptable. What gives them the right?"

"Their bishop, I'm afraid," he replied. "And it's for the best, truly. I've decided to go to Madeira. To see for myself if there's anything to my father's connections to Safra."

This stunned her more than the news of Doyle's death. "Do you have another lead, beyond what Kane has found?"

"Mrs. Wallace's files have been very revealing."

Kane had tracked down the engraver's widow. In exchange for passage to America, she'd signed a sworn testimony that Doyle had forced her husband to produce the counterfeit plates. She'd also handed over his business records, which were surprisingly detailed.

"If your father was one of the Safra shareholders, then you can claim the assets," she said. "It's your legacy."

"It is *our* legacy. Yours too."

She shook her head. "Jonah—"

"I couldn't accept it," he insisted. "I'd have to make a substantial donation from it to the Church, as part of my vocation and commitment."

The Church would expect its cut, and in return, he'd finally receive a permanent living somewhere, as a vicar.

"Faith, I want to sign over my share to you."

Her mouth coiled in protest, but he held up a hand. "Twenty thousand pounds. That's what Kane believes the land could be worth. More than enough to live on."

"It won't be mine."

"Yes, it will," he argued. "It is personal property, bequeathed to you by your next of kin prior to your marriage. The Marriage Act stipulates a woman can inherit property and it will remain separate from her husband."

"But once it is sold, it's personal property, and indistinguishable from the estate under couverture."

"Then wait," he whispered, drawing close enough that his arms wound around her waist. "Keep it, Faith. Keep it because I can't."

And because she couldn't keep him.

This was how he wanted to say his farewell, with a parting gift.

How she wished she could give him something half as valuable in return. What he'd given her was immeasurable.

Her arms circled his neck and their lips met softly, slowly.

She tried to pull away. At least, she told herself to, instructed her arms to release him, but only found herself pulling him closer.

Finally, he wrenched his mouth from hers. "Say you'll accept the land, Faith. Please."

The moment she did, he'd leave her.

As she traced the faint bruise on his cheek, he seized her hand and pressed it to his mouth.

"Is that what you truly want?" she whispered.

He nodded fervently. "After you were arrested, throughout the entire trial, I prayed. For you, of course." He smiled wistfully. "But mostly for me."

Taking her hands in his, he brought one, then the other, to his lips. "I made a vow that if I found a way to save you, I'd recommit myself to the promise I made. To devote my life to one of service, to the Church."

Anger bubbled up, hot and pricking, and she couldn't stop herself from wrenching her hands free and seizing his lapels. "Do you truly think God wants you to be this miserable in his service? When you could have a different life, a better—"

He gently folded his fingers over hers. "I know nothing of my father's business, or any other trade. This is all I know. It's what I trained for and what sustained me through the darkest of hours. It's all I have."

She wanted to tell him he had her, at least her heart, but what good would that do? There was no arguing with him when he was set in as he was. She knew this by now. And she loved him for it, despite the frustration it caused her.

There was no possibility of asking him to forsake the Church, since she had nothing to offer him in its place. Nothing but a love she wasn't free to give.

"All right," she conceded. "If it will make you happy, I agree."

He pressed another kiss to her hand. "Thank you."

She withdrew more abruptly than was necessary. One more moment and she'd lose her self-control. It was fraying at the edges as she said in a shaking voice, "Come into the house, and we'll sign whatever it is you brought for me."

They walked out of the orangery, then came to a startled halt.

With a shaky hand, Jonah pointed to the third floor of the north wing, where orange flames lit up the windows.

God only knew how long they stood there, staring dumbly at the fire.

Jonah recovered the ability to move first. He shouted Faith's name several times and had to give her shoulders a gentle shake before she blinked her eyes up at him.

"We've got to do something," she whispered. "I can't quite think of what. At the moment, everything seems rather floaty and cold."

"I believe that's shock, darling. I confess I'm not at my best either."

"We've got to get them out. Geoffrey's nurse is up there, too. Edna."

"Edna?"

"Jonah, are you listening? They could be trapped; we've got to get them out. Please."

The desperation in her voice crushed him. "We'll find a way. What about the water engine?"

"Too large. We'll never manage it."

"I should ring the warning bell."

She frantically shook her head. "No time."

They stared at each other for a long moment before he said, "Once more unto the breach."

Faith buried her face in her hands. "Absolutely not. I can't ask that of you."

He pulled her hands away and gave them a squeeze. "We'll find a way. Together. We do not let go of each other. Do you hear me?"

They ran up the main staircase, pausing at Faith's room to grab an ewer of water and towels, then ran to the hidden staircase. Smoke curled from the door.

"Edna!" Faith shouted. "Edna, can you hear us?"

When no reply came, Jonah dipped his handkerchief in water and handed it to her. "Am I right in thinking you'll just come after me anyway if I ask you to stay?"

"Give me that." She yanked the wet cloth and pressed it to her nose as she climbed the stairs.

He could barely compose enough coordination to follow her lead.

Heat built as they mounted, and when they landed in the first room, black smoke clouded their view. Ignoring the dizzying nausea that assaulted him, Jonah reached for the heavy candlestick and smashed the nearest window, creating an escape path for some of the smoke.

Faith lurched toward the bedroom, but he held her back, squeezing her hand.

"Together," he rasped through the smoke. "Do not let go of me."

Rochford lay peacefully in his bed, oblivious to the fact that the bed skirts were aflame. There was no sign of his nurse.

Pulling Faith with him, Jonah smashed the other windows, which only provided slight relief from the mounting smoke.

"Edna's not here!" Faith shouted, coughing through her kerchief.

"We cannot get this under control ourselves," Jonah shouted, his head bobbing between the broken windows, the rising flames, and Rochford. "What do you want to do?"

It was as if he'd arrived at the very gates of hell, and they were reaching to let him in.

He'd thought of the earl's death countless times. Had wished for it more.

And yet.

He'd made vows.

Faith had made vows too.

She coughed into her kerchief and drew a shaky breath. "We must move him."

Relief washed over him, weakening his knees for the moment, but the terror of the growing flames forced him to release her hand. He threw back the bedclothes and hoisted Rochford over his shoulder.

"The back stairs," Faith choked out. "Go, Jonah. Keep moving."

Every ounce of his energy focused on extending his free hand toward her. For a terrifying moment, it met nothing but air, and he screamed her name.

Finally, her warm skin found his.

As Faith pulled him along, Jonah had no sense of where they were going. The smoke thickened, the heat approached, and his shoulders ached.

But her firm hand in his guided them through the narrow corridor, down the rickety, dark stairs.

Faith halted. "The door won't budge!"

"Can you kick it?"

"I can't see anything!"

Her voice was so hoarse, the sound of it threatened his composure. "Don't suppose you have your pistol handy?"

"What?"

A hysterical laugh came out of him. "We could shoot the door down."

He heard the distinctive click of a hammer arming. "Step back, darling."

When the shot wrang out, the spark of the bullet ricocheting off the latch briefly lit the darkness.

They both pushed their weight forward. The door sprang free, and as they tumbled out into the abandoned ballroom, his knees buckled.

"Jonah?"

"Keep going," he barked. "We must get out of the house."

They scrambled together. His neck and shoulder throbbed as they staggered through the corridor, out the newly painted door, and toward the copse of trees in front of the house.

Jonah's legs wavered, and he clumsily laid the earl on the grass before collapsing onto his hands and knees.

"Faith. Faith!"

She was coughing beside him. "I'm here, I'm fine."

He didn't trust her words and pulled her closer, then struggled with his examination of her due to the darkness and his own faltering breaths.

She eased him with a soft palm. "Be still, love. I'm going to the pump for water. Don't move."

He protested loudly, bellowing nonsense that approximated the rantings of a mindless drunk, until she placed a tin of cool water in his hand.

"Drink, Jonah. And please stop shouting. It's not good for your throat."

Her own voice was raw and husky. In another circumstance, it would have aroused him, but at the present moment, all he wanted was his shoulders to stop shaking long enough for her to rest her head there.

And as if he'd said the wish—the prayer—out loud, she took his empty cup and did exactly that.

Eventually, his breaths eased enough to utter a single word. "Rochford?"

"His pulse is weak. But it's beating." With a sigh, she added, "We did our best, didn't we?"

"The very best," he replied, stroking her hair.

They sat together, entwined, and watched the Earl of Rochford's legacy burn.

CHAPTER TWENTY-NINE

In the sumptuous confines of Amelia Hunter's carriage, Faith fidgeted with her worn kid gloves.

She'd debated wearing them. The third button was loose and with the start of autumn and cooler weather, light-colored adornments were surely pushing the bounds of fashion.

Good society would have demanded she maintain her widow's weeds and her isolation for a full year following her husband's death, but she'd already spent seven years grieving her marriage. And she couldn't stand one more day ensconced in black from head to toe.

The carriage door opened, and Amelia's bright smile greeted her. "Welcome back to Mayfair, dear."

Faith stared up at the grand white columns of the Georgian mansion before her. A small bronze plaque next to the door read *Vota House*.

"It won't bite, I promise you. Neither will we." Amelia's lips twitched. "When Lady Blake said you were here in town with her to finish Adam's school shopping, I was hoping very much that you'd pay us a visit. Mourning can be such a lonely business."

Amelia led her inside, across the plush Persian carpet. The foyer walls were painted a muted blue to match. Faith immediately loved the soothing effect of the color, despite how dingy her clothes appeared in comparison. Her muslin looked more brown than mauve in the bright light that filtered in from the broad windows.

"The Ladies' Discussion and Improvement Society began a few years ago, rather informally," Amelia said. "Now we have a waiting list of young women, eager to receive special tutelage in social graces needed to distinguish themselves."

"Quite the thing," Faith murmured.

"That's the receiving room." Amelia tilted her head toward the flower-laden morning room. "And here is our library, where we provide instruction on correspondence and popular literature. How do you do, Mrs. Ellington."

"Miss Hunter." An older woman wearing a spectacularly large diamond broach nodded. "I'm waiting on our Adelaide to finish her harp lesson. Madame Grenoble is designing her recital costume."

"How charming." Amelia hurried Faith along before the other woman could insist on an introduction. "Music room, ballroom." She puffed and dragged Faith up a carpeted staircase. "And up here, we have the visual arts, painting, and embroidery."

Flying down a twisting hallway, Amelia pointed to more classrooms for language instruction.

"Some mamas find anything beyond French to be superfluous. But we insist if the girls are to gain an appreciation for opera and compete with opera singers for the attention of young bucks, Italian is a must."

As Amelia mounted a third staircase, she said loudly, "And my dear, having run your own household, you'd be quite interested in our service instruction program."

Faith was too breathless to respond in any eloquence, but merely nodded.

Amelia withdrew a key from her pocket, unlocked a narrow door, and gestured for Faith to walk through. It led to a standard servant's corridor.

Which opened onto an extraordinary work room.

A clamor of typewriter keys, punctuated every so often by a high-pitched *ding*, echoed through the room, along with the steady hubbub of a score of female voices.

"No, Sally. The headline needs to read 'Women's Hour Has Struck.' Not 'stuck,' dear."

Lady Cora's voice rose above the racket. She was dressed in a fashionably cut walking dress with the tiniest bustle Faith had ever seen, and envied immensely, since it gave the other woman more freedom to hop between the long tables where the women worked.

Blackboards hung along the back wall of the room, listing a grid of surnames, followed by a series of columns. Some were marked off with Xs.

Faith thought it resembled a bookmaker's shop.

"Amelia!" Lady Cora walked to meet them, pausing three times to gesture to six different women, in a manner that resembled a police officer directing traffic at King's Cross.

Faith was out of breath just watching her.

"Welcome, Lady Rochford. Would you care for tea while we plot the revolution?" Cora scurried over to a small seating area at the far end of the room, where a tea tray had been placed.

"Don't worry, you'll get used to her pace." Amelia smiled. "At least, we hope that you will consider spending enough time with us to get used to it."

Lady Cora poured Faith a cup. "Milk or sugar?"

"Only lemon, please."

As Cora served their tea, she said, "We do need a name for our endeavor. I've been calling us the Clandestine Court, but it's a terrible name."

"Truly," Amelia agreed. "We're not a court at all. More of an underground Parliament."

"Amelia, that makes us sound like insurgents. We're not trying to overthrow the government."

"Well, no, not entirely."

"You're suffragists?" Faith scanned the room. "Campaigning for the vote for women?"

"Much more than that." Cora gave her a conniving smile. "We're working to influence Parliament and move it in the right direction, so to speak."

"Women's enfranchisement is years away," Amelia added. "Shouting at men to pay attention to us hasn't been very effective."

"We need to go brick by brick, starting with the basics," Cora said.

"You mean money," Faith suggested.

There was an admiring gleam in Cora's eye. "Property, to be specific. Men can't vote unless they hold property, which is also something that must change as soon as possible, but as I said, brick by brick. Since most women in Great Britain who have the means to buy or own property are married, it's an impossibility."

"Because of couverture." Faith shook her head. "You think you can persuade a man to not only write a bill that would grant us these rights, but get him to convince other men to support it?"

"We will try," Cora said. "Care to help us?"

Faith looked out at the women bustling around them as they examined voting maps, rifled through newspapers, and clicked away at the typewriters. It was a little like observing exotic animals in the zoological gardens.

She glanced down at her teacup. "I'm not sure I have any skills to support your revolution, Lady Cora. I have barely managed to survive ruination."

"That's a hell of a start."

Elyse greeted Lady Cora and Amelia with swift kisses and sank down next to Faith on the settee. "Do hear us out, dear, before you turn down the offer."

"The war room is only part of our operation," Amelia said. "The Ladies' Discussion and Improvement Society also plays an important role."

"We prepare new money debutantes to ensnare members of the gentry. Amazing how an impoverished aristocrat can suddenly change their minds about a family's provenance, if their money can keep them in the luxury to which they're accustomed." Cora smirked. "It's been very lucrative. Enough to fund our advocacy efforts."

"Thank you for considering me to be a part of it," Faith said. "But no one in good society would come within a mile of my tarnished reputation."

Elyse patted her hand. "You're being too hard on yourself."

"No, she isn't," Cora conceded. "The *ton* doesn't want to associate with you at the present time. But plenty of women in the *beau monde* are the daughters, nieces, and spouses of men whose estates are in far worse circumstances than Ravenglass was."

"We could offer instruction in property management. Knowledge and skills you taught yourself, Faith, that other women would benefit from," Elyse encouraged.

Faith hadn't fully considered that other women might have found themselves faced with similar harrowing burdens of keeping their livelihoods.

She stared at the teacup, so dainty and ordinary, amongst the frenzy of the women working around her, and contemplated the suggestion of these new friends who'd come to her aid when she needed it most. They were inviting her to be a part of something. She could work toward something else besides improving her own circumstances.

Beyond just surviving.

It didn't alter the fact that, sitting among them, she felt more of an imposter than she'd ever been in her entire life. To do what they'd asked, she'd be forced to don another mask.

"You're very kind." She placed the teacup on its saucer and looked each of them in the eye. "I owe you all an immeasurable debt for how you supported me, Adam—" Her voice cut out before she could mention Jonah's name. "But I can't accept."

"There's nothing we can say to persuade you?"

"Lady Cora, I have spent my entire life acting out one masquerade after another, pretending to be something I knew next to nothing about. While I appreciate the underground nature of this work, I no longer wish to act in the shadows."

Rising, she smoothed her dress. "I wish to live authentically. However I'm able to manage it."

"I believe I understand, Lady Rochford." Cora stood and composed her posture with an uncustomary stillness. "We're not going anywhere, and if you change your mind, we'd be grateful for however you wish to be involved."

"I'll walk you out, dear." Elyse rose to join her. "This house is a veritable maze."

As they walked to the carriage, she remarked, "I hope you're not too angry with me for trying to rope you into our operation."

"Hardly." Faith smiled.

"When Antony died, I was in the darkest of places. I couldn't see a crack of light to guide me out. This." Elyse nodded to the house. "Cora and Amelia and their enterprise pulled me out of that hole. And gave me the courage to find a way to practice medicine, despite the hurdles."

"I understand."

"And I know it's different for you. Rochford's death is a relief and another type of burden altogether."

"It's been easier than I imagined," Faith assured her. The bishop was allowing her ample time to find an arrangement outside of Ravenglass. Once the probate was complete, he vowed he would find a way to bestow her with a widow's jointure, however small.

"Did Adam's school robes arrive?" Elyse asked.

"The parcel came this morning," Faith confirmed. "And now nothing will ease his impatience for school to start."

"Will Mr. Sinclair accompany you to take Adam to school?"

Faith blushed and glared at her friend.

Elyse smiled darkly. "You knew I would ask. You promised Adam that you would write to invite him to join you."

After the scandalous trial, Adam had little chance of a Harrow education. But the bishop had helped him secure a place in a school in Edinburgh that they hoped would suit him.

"Judging by your reticence, my dear, I'm guessing you haven't written Sinclair."

Faith hung her head. "I asked him not to write. When we parted, after the fire, it was—"

Too painful to have to live with the expectation he might write and the disappointment if he didn't.

When Geoffrey's heart had finally given out a week after they'd rescued him from those flames, she would not allow herself to kindle the wild hope that she was free to be with Jonah.

It was a stupid sort of torture she'd imposed on herself, for not a day had gone by that she hadn't thought of him a thousand times.

"I don't know when he's due back from Madeira," Faith said.

"How fortunate, then, that he and I have maintained our correspondence." Her friend opened her reticule and withdrew a small collection of letters. "He wrote to me yesterday. He's staying with the Wildes at Hatfield."

Gently, Elyse put the packet in Faith's shaking hands. "Now, aren't you glad to have an interfering friend in your life?"

"We've been staying with you for months! Why didn't you say anything?"

"Because you weren't ready to ask for them. But now, there's no more time for stalling."

Faith stared at the letters with an elated sense of disbelief. "Whatever will I say to him?"

"Whatever is in your heart," Elyse replied. "If you want to live authentically, Faith, here's your chance."

Chapter Thirty

As they stood on the platform for the Edinburgh train, Adam bounced with excitement.

"Can we board now?"

"Merciful God," Lawless muttered. "The answer is the same as it was two minutes ago. No, we cannot board until the conductor blows his whistle."

"But the men are loading all the luggage—"

"And we must allow them space to work." Faith took a firm hold of his hand to prevent his curiosity from drawing him too close to the tracks. "Tell me again what you know about how the train engine works."

"It is a steam locomotive," Adam replied matter-of-factly. "There's a great boiler at the front of the train. Coal fire heats the water, and it expands into gas."

"And then what happens to the gas?"

He scrunched up his face. "Mr. Wilde and I didn't get that far."

"No doubt he was distracted by Mrs. Lowe's fine biscuits," came a deep voice.

Adam's face lit up like a galaxy of stars. "Mr. Sinclair!"

While the boy flung himself at his former tutor, the little fracas gave Faith a moment to drink in the sight of him.

Jonah's skin had turned a golden tan from the months spent outdoors in Madeira's tropical climate, and his hair was longer, nearly skimming the collar of his new suit. Instead of his typical somber black, the fabric was a fine charcoal gray, and his shirt had a subtle blue stripe running through it.

If she was being truthful with herself—as she was committed to being now—Faith hadn't expected him to look so well. She'd half hoped there would be some traceable evidence of him wasting away because of their separation.

"Good morning, Lady Rochford." He extended his hand in friendly greeting, and she was proud of herself that she did not grasp for it desperately. They might have held onto each other a bit longer than propriety dictated, but he was taking his time to peruse her, marking her new plum walking suit and the more fashionable way she was wearing her hair. After so many months as Elyse's guests, she'd fallen victim to the machinations of her maid.

"Good morning, Mr. Sinclair," she replied. "We are most grateful you could join us."

A loud whistle pierced the air, and there was no stopping Adam from bounding onto the train. Lawless took hold of the hamper containing their lunch and the four of them boarded the second-class car.

She settled into her seat next to Lawless, across from Sinclair, and as he lifted his gaze to meet hers, she had a momentary lapse in courage. She wasn't sure she'd be able to withstand four hours near him without falling apart.

When they arrived at Edinburgh's Waverly Station, Lawless took command of the luggage. "I'll take the rest of the trunks, my lady, and settle us at the hotel. You take your time at the school."

The town of Musselburgh was a five-mile drive from the city center, Adam's knee bobbed with anticipation from the moment the left the station until they pulled into the front drive.

"Welcome to Loretto School, Lady Rochford." A young master in black robes greeted them. "I hope you had a pleasant journey. Master Fitzcharles, do you have everything?"

"Yes, sir!" Adam replied.

"Well, let's get you settled in, then." He gave them a harried smile and shouted to two older boys to help with the luggage.

Faith made a move, but Jonah placed a gentle hand on her sleeve. "We'll take a tour of the grounds while Adam unpacks. I trust he'll meet back here for chapel just before five, and he might see us off."

"Yes," the teacher said absently, as he eyed a fight about to break out. "Capital plan. If you'll excuse me."

When he took off across the field at a surprisingly fast pace, Jonah remarked, "At least he's keeping up with the little menaces."

"My word, he is fast," Faith murmured as the man leapt over a low stone wall.

"Shall we follow the trail? At a slower pace, mind you. This suit wasn't designed for jumping fences."

He took her arm—or did she take his? She couldn't distinguish who had moved first, but when he threaded her hand through the crook of his elbow, they both exhaled.

The rhythm of their breath and the whisper of the wind through the falling leaves were the only sounds between them. As the path drew them into a cluster of trees, they paused, the silence all-consuming.

Jonah's hand rested on hers. "If you were to write a postcard about this moment, what would it say?"

He was so very talented at distractions, breaking the tension between them by easing them into each other's company.

Lord, how she'd missed him.

"To whom am I writing?" she asked.

"Yourself."

She surprised herself with a laugh. "It's too much to fit on one postcard."

"Summarize, then. Go on."

They'd resumed walking and rounded the loop of the trail heading back toward the school. The sun was on its downward journey, and she loathed how fast the day was flying by.

"Dear Faith," she began in a shaky voice. "Loretto School is much prettier than you imagined, although the sun sets early here. Thankfully, the teaching staff are the swiftest in Great Britain."

Jonah laughed.

As they arrived back at the chapel, she added, "I believe Adam will be happy here."

"As do I." His smile faded, but he gave her hand a soft squeeze as if to assure her their wish had already come true.

They found Adam in front of the chapel, sporting the new frock coat of his uniform. He wore the biggest, broadest grin she'd ever seen.

As they neared, the smile wobbled, and when Faith bent toward him, she caught an anxious look in his eye.

"It's okay to be nervous and excited at the same time," she whispered. "I know I am. Because I am so proud of you, Adam. And I love you very much."

She pulled him close, and to her surprise, his arm clasped her tightly. "You promise to write every Thursday?"

"Without fail." She bit the inside of her cheek so she wouldn't cry. "Do you promise to reply?"

"Of course." He laughed as he gave her a gentle push before his eyes rose to meet those of his former tutor. "Mr. Sinclair—"

"I need no reminder of my promise, Adam." He tapped his coat pocket, then pulled Adam to his side, using the excuse of straightening his coat as cover for the embrace. "You're the best of this bunch. Never forget it."

Adam beamed and bounded into the chapel on the pealing of the five o'clock bells.

The fading sun broke through the cloud cover with a blinding last burst of light. Between the brightness and the bells and her raw feelings, Faith hardly registered Jonah handing her up into the carriage. It was dark and colder inside, and the sudden change made her shiver.

Jonah reached for the blanket and tucked it around her, before folding himself into the seat across from her. As the carriage pulled away, she forced herself not to look back.

"All will be well," he murmured.

"I hope and pray that's true." Faith lifted her eyes and allowed herself to stare without restraint at his beautiful face. "Jonah, I have little right to ask this, but I must beg your forgiveness."

"Forgiven."

"Won't you let me say what for?"

"Does it matter?"

From her reticule, she withdrew the stack of letters that Elyse had given her.

He regarded them with a quirk of his mouth. "You got my letters then."

"Only after you'd returned. It took me months to tell Elyse I regretted not writing to you." She shook her head. "How stupid and selfish I was to isolate myself from your friendship. I convinced myself it was the best thing for you. I was following the rules of good society, a system I was never a part of from the start, and one I'll never truly belong to."

In a softer voice, she added, "That excuse was an elaborate story I constructed to distract myself from how much I love you."

"Then I suppose it's a good thing I ignored you."

Despite his playful tone, it seemed to be more a question than a declaration, and even in the dark, she could sense his intense attention on her.

"Your last letter said that you'd verified the Safra assets' ownership and arranged the property sale."

"And those profits are being transferred into your name."

Faith's jaw dangled open.

"Kane and I have been working on the transfer to a trust since my return," he went on, ignoring her shock and stupor. "It wasn't the amount we expected, I'm afraid."

"I don't care—"

"It was more." He grinned. "Forty-two thousand, three hundred pounds in the end."

Double what Kane had estimated.

"You must take half," she insisted. "It's your birthright, for God's sake! If you won't take it for yourself, find a way to use it for something charitable."

"Perhaps I could donate it to a cause that helps children like us, who weren't as lucky as we were. Those who have no one to care for or fight for them."

Her breath caught. "Something like that. Anything like that."

"That decision will have to be up to you." He handed her an envelope. "These are the details of the trust, to be administered by you, with Mr. Kane as executor."

His dismissal squelched the little ember of hope rising in her chest. "Do you feel that the money will interfere with your vocation to lead a parish?"

"On the contrary. It would have helped a great deal. Unfortunately, other circumstances have forced me to reconsider those plans."

He leaned forward. "The Crown offered a generous sum for Doyle's capture and the evidence we uncovered. They awarded me ten thousand pounds. And the return of my father's warehouse."

Her jaw dropped for the second time.

"I was equally speechless," he remarked dryly.

With a prime location on the docks, the warehouse could provide him with an excellent living. The sale of it would be easily ten times the sum he'd received. "Will you take up your father's business?"

"No. After everything, I know it is not my calling."

"I see," she said around the lump in her throat. "You'd rather stay with the Church."

The carriage stopped abruptly. Darkness had descended after they left the school, and Faith suddenly realized that while she had no idea where they were, it wasn't the Lothian Edinburgh Hotel.

"Jonah, where are we?"

A strange expression crept over his face. "Before I show you, there's something I'd like to ask you."

He fell to his knees and reached for her hand. "My dearest friend, these past months without you have been dark and empty days. To say I missed you is an affront to the veracity of my feelings. I have not stopped loving you since the minute we fell into each other's arms. Will you do me an honor I don't deserve of becoming my wife?"

"Oh, Jonah." Her throat wrenched with the burn of tears. "I'm glad I was too much of a coward to write, because I would not have been able to conceal what a wreck I was without you. Nor would I have found adequate words to tell you how much I love you."

She gripped his hand. "But the Church would never approve. A vicar cannot be an example of Christian values married to a person like me. You would have to renounce your calling. I refuse to ask that of you."

"My darling, you don't have to."

Rising, he pushed open the door and handed her out of the carriage onto a tidy drive before a quaint brick house.

Squinting in the darkness, Faith saw they were at the top of a hill. The lights of Edinburgh twinkled below them.

"I don't understand."

Turning back, she caught his face in the lamplight. Expectation and fierceness pulled at his brow.

"While I wandered across the ocean, what I missed most of all was you, Faith. And Adam. And also a decent cup of tea."

He took her hand, pressed it to his lips. "But mostly, it was you. I did not miss the Church, or God, for they were always with me. They are the reason I survived all these months without you. But surviving is not thriving. For that, I need you."

"For that, you need more than me." She pressed her palms against his chest. "I cannot ask you to put me before your life's work."

"You can ask whatever you want of me because I love you. And you love me."

"It's not that simple. You'll never be content with the life of an idle gentleman. You need an occupation. And I will not be the thing that divides you from your calling."

"Then it's fortunate I have decided my calling is not with the Church. But rather, with the state."

He gestured to a point in the darkness below them. "Edinburgh School of Law. It's half a mile down that hill somewhere."

She frowned. "I don't follow."

"Well, I should hope not. It's far too dark."

"Jonah!"

"Adam and I are both students starting off at new schools."

"Will the Church allow you to become a solicitor too?"

"No, they won't. I had to choose. Turns out it wasn't much of a choice."

His fingers curled around hers. "In the course of knowing you and uncovering the injustices of our pasts, not to mention the existing gaps in the way the law is applied across our society, I realized where *my* work is."

"You sound like Mr. Kane."

"Who do you think helped me with all of this?"

Her head spun at trying to keep up with everything he'd shared. "You're talking about changing existing laws. A fight with Parliament."

"Oh, it's much bigger than that, love. I'm talking about a battle. One I'll happily wage if it prevents one woman from the harm you've suffered from the current writ of the law."

Jonah walked her to the front of the house. "I'll be staying here. Until I finish my studies, likely a year."

"Then what?" she managed.

"Well, that depends very much on the question I asked you earlier."

When she opened her mouth, and closed it again, her words caught somewhere between her brain and her throat, he smiled.

"This is a bit of an ambush," he confessed. "You'll want time to think it over. But remember, my love, that you think, and think, and rethink yourself into saying no, more often than yes."

He glanced at the carriage. "Wait in the coach, if you must, while you deliberate. You can take it back to the hotel if that is what you want."

"Or?"

"Or you can say yes to my offer and stay with me. Here."

"That wouldn't make me your wife."

"Wouldn't it?" Kissing her languidly on the cheek, he whispered, "This is Scotland, darling. All we need is a witness."

He reached for the coach blanket and wrapped it around her, before walking into the house.

He'd lost his mind entirely.

Only a complete idiot would leave the woman he loved outside, shivering on the doorstep, while she decided their collective fate.

It wasn't as if he was completely thoughtless. He'd done too much thinking since he'd left her. In the last few weeks, his plan had unfolded before him so clearly that it seemed strange that he hadn't always been working toward the goal of creating a space he and Faith would share together.

Of course, she hadn't had the benefit of all that time. He'd sprung it on her because he knew the more time she had, the more excuses she'd make to refuse him.

As he darted inside the house, the composure he'd fought to preserve wavered. Staggering through the front room, he turned up the lamps and stoked the fire, so that it would be warmer when she walked through that door.

If she walked through the door.

And when the sound of an impatient knock finally came, he ran over and flung it open, breathless.

Faith marched inside defiantly and extended one hand to stop him from speaking. "It has been a remarkably long day and I find myself in need of your bathing room."

"Yes, of course." He seized the table lamp. "This way."

He rushed as quickly as he could up the carpeted staircase. He wasn't sure how dire her situation was and didn't want her to think he was dawdling.

There would be no dawdling.

Jonah needed her answer to his question as much as he needed his next breath. He didn't know what he would do if she refused him. Regroup, he supposed. Find another way to wear her down.

Accepting her rejection was not an option.

She followed him at a less frantic pace. "This is a fine house."

"Is it? Yes, I suppose so. There are three bedrooms upstairs, one down for a cook-maid."

They walked into the largest bedroom, where he'd had her steamer trunk delivered, which she acknowledged with a haughty sniff.

Stifling a smile, he opened the door to the en suite bathing room. "There's a tap with hot water, fresh towels, and soap by the sink."

The door closed promptly in his face.

While he waited, he crept around the house, lighting more lamps, unsure of where to settle himself for when she would emerge. He glanced out the front window and spotted the hack carriage waiting outside.

The prospect that she might still plan to leave made him disproportionately angry.

Jonah bounded up the stairs, where he was forced to wait by the bay window of the bedroom, arms crossed.

An eternity later, she opened the door.

She'd removed her hat and coat. The top buttons of her collar were undone. Her face glistened with a faint flush and a stray curl wound its way across her collarbone. As the aroma of citrus clung to the air, he could barely control himself.

"Your soap smells of oranges and lemons," she said softly.

He'd found it at a small shop by the university and bought every bar.

"Yes," was all he could muster. Now that she was here, in this room, making real what had been a fantasy, he wanted to enact every other thing he'd dreamed of. Every touch, every taste, every promise.

But in all of his imaginings, he never pictured her silent fury. She paced the length of the room, as if she was arguing with herself instead of him. He wished he could ease her from the burden of her decision.

Finally, she paused in front of the fire. "I have questions."

More like conditions, he was sure. He'd agree to just about anything at this stage if it meant she would stay. "Fire away."

"You must have some plan for after you finish your studies."

"Loads," he confessed with a smile.

"How do I factor into them? You said they depend on my answer."

"More than that, I'm afraid." He stepped away from the window. "They depend on what you want. If you were interested in trying your hand at managing an estate, then we'll find one. I could become a country solicitor. Keep up with political work by correspondence."

She scoffed, bracing her hands on her hips. "I thought you didn't like the country."

"I've developed an appreciation for it recently."

"And if you didn't become a country solicitor?"

"We could go to London. Kane could sponsor me for a partnership in chambers. We could hold down our own corner of the revolution there."

"Sounds a little extreme."

"No less extreme than fighting off forgers and frauds."

That drew her smile and gave him the courage to inch forward. "Or we could stay here in Edinburgh. For however long it takes to figure out what we both want. And to be close to Adam if he needs us."

Her shoulders sagged as she released a breath. "Adam and I, we're a package. You cannot have one of us without the other."

"I was hoping you might say that." He strode to the desk and reached past her—fighting off his eager response to the heat of her body—and handed her a set of documents. "While Kane set up your trust, I also asked him to prepare these."

She read through them slowly, her hands shaking around the pages.

"When the earl died, Adam became a ward of the Church, officially," he said. "I want him to be ours, officially. Legally too. Kane has put together a petition for us. Of course, we can't do it together unless we're married."

The papers fell onto the desk as she buried her face in her hands. "You want to adopt him."

"Yes." He gently pried away her hands and wiped a stray tear from her cheek.

"Do you want more children?" she asked, searching his face.

"Truthfully? I don't know."

Childbirth was a risky business, child rearing even more of a gamble. The idea of leaving his own children without a father, the way he'd grown up, terrified him.

"Neither do I," Faith whispered. "All I know is that I'm not ready for them now. I don't know if I'll ever be."

He caressed her small fist. "Then aren't we lucky that we have our Adam."

"Please don't placate me."

She was trying to control her voice, but her expression gave away everything. There was hope there, warring with her fear. She'd lost her independence to a man before, and he had to make her see what he was offering wasn't the same.

"Would you prefer a marriage of celibacy, then?"

"What?" She tried to withdraw her hand, but he held fast to it. "Is that what you want?"

"Of course not." He traced a finger along her chin. "I've wanted you practically from the moment you fell off that horse. For weeks, I hungered for your every look, and after I finally touched you, tasted you—"

Her breath hissed, and as she stared at his mouth, his blood stirred with desire and unabashed hope. "I have been haunted for months by those scant hours I held you in my arms. But if the potential consequences of sharing my bed make you feel you're trapped, like you have no independence, I would forsake it."

Shaking his head, he added, "How can I expect you to love me if doing so comes at the expense of feeling free?"

Through her tears, she whispered, "And what right do I have to restrict your freedom to love me as you want?"

"Every right." He wound his arms around her. "It is your choice."

"Then I choose you."

Her mouth met his, sealing her promise, and his entire being surged with bliss as he devoured her lips. He held her so close he had a fleeting sense that between the kissing and his grip, she might be struggling to breathe.

Loosening his hold on her a fraction, he grazed kisses up her neck. "Say it."

"I love you, Jonah."

She pried off his tie, making quick work of his waistcoat, and he broke apart from her lips to turn her around and unfasten her dress bodice. "I love you too, darling. Now say the other part."

As he undid her corset, she gasped with relief. "Other part?"

"You heard me." He slipped his fingers beneath her chemise to stroke her hardened nipple, drawing another hoarse gasp, and the softness of her skin, the warmth of her jagged breath, made his cock rock hard. "I've been a patient man, Faith."

Her skirts unfurled, and he turned her to steal another long, heated kiss, which had the happy effect of making her cling to him for support.

"Hold on to me, love."

Her arms circled his neck. She stroked his shoulders through the fabric of his shirt, creating a delicious friction that spurred his craving for the feel of her bare skin against his. He hauled her legs around his waist, fitting her sweet cleft against his erection.

She moaned his name against his lips and began to move on him. Had he not been hell-bent on composure, he would have soiled his trousers.

Pulling back, he demanded, "Tell me now, Faith. Tell me what you choose. What you want."

As she searched his face, her eyes shined. "I choose you. I want you. And I want to marry you. To become husband and wife."

He surged forward, his mouth seeking hers, and with her body pressed up against him, he had to stagger to the bed to avoid coming apart.

After ripping off his shirt, her hands found his trousers. She pried them from his legs with surprising force. Despite all his fantasizing, he wasn't quite prepared for her taking him in hand. The shock of her touch, her enthusiastic grip on him, made him tremble.

Gasping her name, he tumbled onto the bed. He caressed her legs, tracing his way up her thighs and teasing her sensitive skin as she held him, stroking his shaft with maddening pressure.

His mouth sought hers again; his tongue slipped in to taste her as he slid a finger inside her. When she gasped and tightened her hold on him, he added a second finger, matching his movements with the thrust of his cock against her hand.

She came so fast, they both cried out in surprise. Her hold on him was pulverizing.

"Faith." He gasped.

She blinked down and laughed an apology as she eased her grasp.

"Jonah." Her gaze grew heavy. "Be with me."

He kissed her gently. "I will be careful to withdraw."

"It's all right. I've taken precautions." Her cheeks flushed a deeper shade of pink. "Elyse fitted me for a pessary."

His fingers brushed her hair. "Are you sure? Nothing is guaranteed."

"I know. I still want to."

"And if something happens?"

"You will be beside me to navigate the waters. However smooth or choppy." She traced his lip with her thumb. "Let me love you this way."

Reaching between them, she guided him between her legs, and with one stroke, he entered her.

They gasped, clinging onto each other. Their pace was slow, a beautiful agony, for he wanted it to last. This closeness and softness, her damp skin, her scent of oranges and lemons.

"Jonah." She took his face between her hands. "I'm not going anywhere. I'm yours. You are mine. You don't have to worry. Be with me. Stay with me."

She thrust up onto his cock, and his thin control slipped free as he drove into her with rapid strokes that brought on her climax.

He followed her into oblivion as she murmured words of love and praise and nonsense.

When he recovered his senses and withdrew, she wouldn't let him retreat very far.

"Don't worry," he rasped. "Wild dogs could not tear me from this bed."

"Hmmm," she murmured. "But I suspect your growling stomach will, eventually."

"I've a stash of biscuits in the wardrobe. There's water in the washroom. Could last up here a week if we had to."

"Well, I suppose I already have a scandalous reputation for keeping husbands locked up."

He laughed deeply and held her so tightly her breath caught. "Have I told you how deliriously happy I am becoming your captive?"

"In our previous conversations, I've mentioned that actions speak louder than words."

"Then allow me to demonstrate."

Every kiss, every caress that followed, was a proclamation of his pledge.

To keep and guard her heart as she kept his.

Thank you for reading *Keeping the Countess*, book one of *Damsels in Disguise*.

Ready for more *Damsels*? Ian and Diana's epic story unfolds in *Runaway Rogue*. He's a docklands devil plotting to steal an infamous necklace. She's the heiress it belongs to. And did I mention she's also his brother's bride?

Read on for a sneak peak.

THIS IS THE SECTION, my dear reader, where I hope you'll indulge me in a moment to nerd-out on a few historical tidbits that shaped this book.

My fellow *Jane Eyre* disciples will recognize the myriad allusions to Charlotte Brontë's masterpiece throughout this novel. This story began when I started imagining what would have happened if Jane's uncle had found her early in life and taken her to Madeira.

While on a trip to Portugal a few years ago, I learned about the double-whammy wine blight caused by oidium disease (a vine fungus) and phylloxera, an invasive insect that attacks grapevine roots. It decimated wine production across western Europe in the mid-nineteenth century, and Portugal and Madeira were particularly hard-hit. I'm grateful to our wonderful guides and the fascinating exhibit at Quinta Do Bomfim in Pinhão for inspiring part of Jonah and Faith's story.

For those unfamiliar with the hierarchy within Victorian-era Church of England, curates were traditionally schooled at Oxford and Cambridge. Once ordained, they often did the lion's share of parish work assisting a vicar, or in Jonah's case, the Bishop of London, until they were awarded a parish of their own. By the middle of Victoria's reign in 1878, the Queen's enthusiasm to expand churches in growing cities like Manchester and Liverpool, combined with tithing mandated by the government, meant that clergymen were less dependent on the aristocracy to provide them with a parish and a living. Earning such a position, however, depended heavily on connections, class, race, and other privileges. Anthony Trollope's *Clergymen of The Church of England* and David Yeandle's *A Victorian Curate: A Study of the Life and Career of the Rev. Dr John Hunt* are two references I recommend for those eager to learn more.

Acknowledgements

I'm immensely grateful to:

My emotional support pumpkins and kissing book critique partners Kate Happ, Maggie Eliot, Evie Jacobs, Maureen Ewing, and Caragh Leon. This novel is a better book, and I'm a better writer, because of all of you.

Faith Williams and The Atwater Group, my editing and proofreading gurus. I promise I will learn the difference between toward and towards before the next book.

Sarra Cannon, for giving me the tools and the confidence to get this book to readers. Thank you for helping me make a life-long dream come true.

Jen Prokop and Sarah MacLean. The Fated Mates podcast changed me as a reader and a writer. This book would not exist without them and the amazing community I found among my fellow magnificent firebirds.

And finally, to my spouse, who believed I could do this before I did. Thank you for your unwavering support and encouragement.

ABOUT THE AUTHOR

Lille Moore writes romance with a twist on time-honored tropes and tales. Her first career in public diplomacy and strategic communications took her across five continents and six of the Seven Seas and spurred a lifelong love affair with uncovering new worlds through storytelling. She lives with her spouse in Texas

Sign up for Lille's newsletter to get an exclusive FREE novella at:

www.lillemoore.com

Connect with Lille online at Instagram, Facebook, Threads, and Pinterest:

@lillemoorebooks

WANT MORE DAMSELS IN DISGUISE?

Here's your sneak peak of Runaway Rogue, Book 2 of Damsels in Disguise.

**Protect the family; steal the emeralds; resist the heiress.
And survive when she captures your heart...**

Ian Holt—the Devil of the Docklands—has one job: steal a legendary emerald necklace from his brother's bride before the wedding, and he'll save the family shipping empire. Simple.

Until the groom vanishes.

And the bride, Diana Rives, refuses to be sidelined in the investigation.

Suddenly, Ian's carefully orchestrated theft becomes a high-stakes chase across Europe—from London's criminal underworld to Monte Carlo's glittering casinos. And Diana is matching him move for move, secret for secret.

Kiss for kiss.

As shadowy vigilantes and ruthless rivals close in, Ian realizes Diana is running a con of her own—one far more dangerous than anything he's planned. Loving her could destroy his family, his future, and the carefully built walls around his heart.

But walking away might be the one gamble he can't survive.

CHAPTER ONE

The worst morning of Ian Holt's life was shrouded in flowers.

Blooms covered every inch of the Mayfair home where he'd spent his childhood. It was a veritable sea of white and pink petals and Ian could not—and would not—fathom how much it all cost.

He paced the last bastion of free space in the drawing room like a caged tiger until an enormous arrangement of orange blossoms and birds of paradise arrived and forced him to halt.

He gave the thing a halfhearted shove, to prove he had influence over something in his life.

"Have you resorted to smashing things?" Henry Eden strode across the room and extended his hand to offer a pacifying handshake.

Ian accepted it with a huff. "I recall from our Harrow days that we both became rather good at smashing things."

"As your legal counsel, I'd advise neither of us confirm or deny that statement."

Despite his sour mood, Ian fought off a smile. Their public school prefects had tried to make cowering servants out of them. He and Henry had endured daily humiliations of being pelted with eggs, and nightly beatings, until they'd learned how to throw a punch. Not getting caught was Ian's first lesson in self-preservation.

"I'm not condoning violence, but one thing that could do with a clearing out is that gaggle of reporters outside," Henry remarked.

"They're still there?" Ian ground his teeth. He'd sent some of his men to spook them off hours ago. New vultures must have arrived, eager for a scoop on the biggest society wedding of the season. They were like vermin, nearly impossible to shake without force, which Ian would have enjoyed using immensely if he could have evaded the consequences.

He swatted a wreath of roses instead.

"I don't think destroying the drawing room is going to dispatch them," Henry said. "Or make your brother arrive any sooner."

"Are you sure about that?"

Henry was at a loss for words. Ian couldn't blame him. Few people would have anything courteous to say when a man went missing on the morning of his wedding.

"The groom is always late," Henry finally managed. "Jared is no different."

Ian refrained from asking how many of those grooms never returned home the night before their weddings. He'd sent his most trusted man to search for Jared discreetly, but so far there was no trace of his brother at any of his usual haunts.

"And what about the brides? Do they struggle with punctuality?" Ian deliberately did not turn an eye upstairs, where Jared's intended was finishing her bridal preparations. If he allowed himself the indulgence of turning his thoughts in Diana's direction, he'd lose what little control he was hanging on to.

Henry carefully moved a swan-shaped cascade of lilies out of Ian's striking distance. "This has to be difficult for you. If it were me, I'd hate—"

Ian's glare promised a violent follow-up if Henry violated their long-standing, unspoken agreement never to utter Diana's name in his presence.

"I'd hate being shut out of my family's business," Henry amended.

"On the contrary. My new position as lead clerk in the Bombay office will be most rewarding. I'm looking forward to it."

Both of them knew it was a lie. Neither acknowledged it.

After the wedding, Ian would depart London. But he was leaving the newly aligned family business far behind.

Jared's marriage to Diana Rives would conclude a merger their fathers had dreamed and schemed about for years. Uniting Holt & Company's trading venture with the Rives Shipping empire would grant them many competitive advantages and the lion's share of the market. Ian had successfully manipulated the business papers to report it that way. So they would avoid digging around and uncovering the significant debt Holt & Company had acquired in the years Jared had assumed control of the business.

His brother would have run the company into the ground after their father's death, had it not been for Ian's quiet interference. Practically, it was a matter of his survival. Their father had named Jared as his sole heir, leaving Ian financially dependent on the small salary the company paid him to officially—and unofficially—arrange things.

Ian detested the role. But it was necessary, to keep the promises he'd made to his father.

"You don't have to go through with it," Henry said in a low voice. "I can't believe your father would want you to make this dangerous gamble."

"I never should have told you. The less you know, the better."

Henry regarded Ian's clenched fists—and the grazes on his right knuckles—for a length of time. "Is Jared still in the dark about it all? Or did you tell him last night, and he reacted...badly?"

"Getting physical with the groom would have been poor form the night before his wedding."

Thankfully, an attempted cargo theft at the docks had required Ian's immediate attention, and he was happy to depart Sunderland's Club after the first round of drinks. He rarely handled enforcement himself these days; his men were exceedingly well-trained and needed little oversight. But last night, he'd welcomed the chance to demonstrate what happened to the jackals who had the audacity to come after Holt & Company.

And the Devil of the Docklands, as Ian was known there.

Afterward, when the heat in his blood had cooled, he'd felt hollow. And the emptiness only exacerbated his conflicted emotions about his brother's impending marriage.

Henry's mouth quirked around another probing question, but a sharp knock and muffled shouts from outside prompted them to hurdle over the flowers and dash into the foyer.

The door flung open.

A footman staggered inside with Jared's unconscious body. His brother's coat and waistcoat were missing, as was his tie, and his shirt was half open. A sickeningly sweet scent, peppered with whiskey, wafted off him.

This sight was further complicated by the other man who stood propping up Jared's slumped body.

"Don't worry, he isn't dead," Leo Ashton, the Duke of Sunderland, quipped. "But he's well and truly sozzled. Even a bucket of water wouldn't revive him."

Ian clapped his gaping jaw shut, and Henry had the sense to mutter something that ended in "Your Grace," as they relieved the duke of Jared's weight.

Sunderland's glance darted between Jared and Ian, as was often the case when people found out they were brothers and searched for some physical similarity. The duke wouldn't find much evidence of it. Jared's fair skin and hair were even more washed out with his pallor. In comparison, Ian must have appeared like a dark-haired, dark-eyed fiend.

With the help of the footmen—and the duke himself—they transported Jared upstairs. Mrs. Turner, the housekeeper, gave a small squawk before she harangued a footman to send for a doctor and took command of settling the patient into his bedroom. She tossed a glare at Ian, Henry, and the duke before slamming the door.

In the sudden quiet of the corridor, the three men carefully evaluated each other.

Ian finally said, "Thank you for your...help with my brother, Lord Sunderland. I would be most grateful for your discretion about all of this."

"Where did you find him?" Henry asked.

When the duke replied with an infamous address in Soho, Ian and Henry exchanged a grave look.

"That wasn't where his friends said they were taking him," Ian said tightly.

"No," Sunderland confirmed. "He departed after them in a separate carriage."

"How keen of you to make note of it."

"They were at my club. Everything that happens at my business is my business."

"And to protect Sunderland's reputation, you wouldn't want people to think he left your establishment in the state he's in now," Ian said.

"Precisely. When your man turned up this morning inquiring about your brother's whereabouts, I thought it best to go myself."

"Was there anything else...of note, where you found him?" Ian kept his expression intentionally blank.

"Not that I recall." Sunderland assessed Ian with a chilling air. "My discretion has a price, Holt. It would be in both our interests to talk about it soon."

As the duke barreled down the stairs, Henry murmured, "Should I be worried about that?"

"No more than usual."

"Right, then. Back to our present debacle." Henry clasped his hands together. "Someone must give Miss Rives the disappointing news she won't be getting married today."

"Why?" Ian snapped. "Jared's drunk; he'll revive. When he does, things will proceed."

"Kind of you to consider Miss Rives's feelings. Don't you think she should decide for herself how she wants to handle this?"

If Diana knew the true state Jared was in, she might call off the entire thing, and that brought a host of uncertainties that made Ian's head throb. Their engagement had tormented him for eight years. The wedding had to happen today. So he could move on with his life.

He swallowed the lump that rose in his throat and said, "I'll tell her."

A maid greeted Ian's knock with a stricken expression.

She ducked her head as he walked into the room, and directed her agitation at a vase of flowers that rested on the floor at the edge of the room, as though someone had placed them in a sort of quarantine.

"Good morning, Mr. Holt." Amelia Hunter's soft voice was a contrast to her statuesque height. Diana's friend and bridesmaid wore a subdued frock the color of milky tea. Ian would have sworn it was the same shade as the beige damask wallpaper.

"Mind the flowers," she cautioned.

"What's wrong with them?" Ian asked.

"They're nefarious."

The voice that haunted his dreams and nightmares directed his attention to the window.

Diana sat on a small stool at a dressing table. A stray beam of watery sunlight gilded her from the crown of her chestnut hair to the hem of her multi-tiered white silk gown.

Her hair appeared darker pinned up in its elaborate coiffure. When they'd run along the shore together as children, it used to tumble down her back, glittering gold and copper. Like pennies in a fountain.

Ian silently pleaded to a pantheon of divinities that she would remain seated. The moment she stood and he took in the full depth of her in her wedding costume, she'd steal his last remaining breath.

Then again, she could wear a sackcloth, and she'd stun the hell out of him.

"Nefarious...flowers," Ian intoned. His tongue dragged as if it were moored to the bottom of his mouth with treacle.

The maid wrung her hands. "White oleander with yellow roses!"

"You think someone tried to poison Miss Rives?"

"Only if they expected me to eat them." In the mirror, Diana raised an elegant eyebrow, which Ian knew rationally was not a gesture of seduction.

His body didn't understand the difference. A familiar tightness gathered south of his waist, and heat rose along his neck.

"In the language of flowers, this arrangement relays a message to beware of betrayal," Miss Hunter offered rationally. "The card was addressed to Diana, but there was no signature."

"It must be from some seedy journalist," Diana said. "They love to manufacture a scandal."

Ian swallowed a growl.

"We'll get rid of them." Miss Hunter nodded to the maid to retrieve the vase. "Be back in a moment."

When the door had closed behind them, and Diana turned to him, a small frisson hit the room.

Neither of them acted surprised. It often happened in the rare circumstances they found themselves alone together. And being alone with Diana was something of a terror, because unlike the rest of their mutual acquaintances, Ian knew the danger she could render.

She radiated with a restrained feminine power, but when he regarded her sitting there alone, a slight pain bloomed beneath his ribs. She'd no sisters, no aunts or female cousins to help with her preparations for the day that would transform her life. Even her dearest childhood friend had been lost to a watery grave a week after the announcement of Diana's engagement to Jared.

As she rose from the stool, Ian couldn't resist staring at the way the silk folds of her dress hugged the curves of her body. The journalists they despised would pay a fortune to see it; she was the most drawn woman in London. She'd spent the last year in mourning for her father, but the scandal sheets couldn't resist sketching her on the few occasions she'd ventured out in society. They never quite captured the color of her eyes—green like a Chinese jade statue—nor could they depict the precise way her bow-shaped mouth dipped with her true smile.

His eyes clapped on the fortune of emeralds and diamonds resting on her collarbone and he was grateful for the sharp and necessary reminder of what was at stake if the wedding didn't take place.

"Now that the threatening petals are gone, are you going to tell me why you're here?" she asked.

"Jared is ill," he said bluntly. "He overindulged last evening."

"Given it was his stag party, I expected him to."

"As did I. But I've never seen him so foxed."

"That explains why it took so long to find him." In a softer voice, she added, "You don't have to hedge. I know he didn't come home last night."

Ian made specific plans to hunt down and fire every one of his brother's traitorous, gossiping servants before the day was through. "Jared wasn't where his friends said they were going."

"You didn't join them?" She seemed surprised he'd refrained from carousing with his brother.

He couldn't decide if this flattered or insulted him. "No. I left early to attend to business."

"Do you think he was...interfered with?"

She brushed her fingers against the necklace in a casual motion that agitated him. If she had an inkling about what they truly were, she wouldn't handle them with such little care.

His father's will had included an eccentric instruction to gift the necklace to "his son's intended" to wear on their wedding day. Diana wore it now out of respect for him, and the deathbed promise she'd made him to wed Jared. If she had disliked the look of the thing, she could have bought a hundred other jeweled collars without putting a dent in her fortune.

It made Ian feel slightly guilty about his plans to steal it from her.

"We should come up with a plan. The guests will arrive in less than an hour," Ian said. "Perhaps we'll ask people to attend the breakfast first, until Jared recovers, and then do the ceremony?"

"You didn't answer my question." A small furrow surfaced between her lovely brows. Most of Diana's admirers would have interpreted it as an adorable look of puzzlement, but Ian knew her face too well.

She was angry with him.

The trouble was, he liked her angry. She behaved unpleasantly when she was infuriated, and it was one of the few honest things he knew about her. It made him want to forget about all the lies between them.

"Was Jared interfered with?" Diana repeated.

The edge in her voice could have been the result of her frustration with him for withholding his answer. Or she was truly worried about her fiancé.

He hoped it was the former. "I don't know."

Her nod assuaged him.

Briefly.

"We must find out what happened."

As she gathered her skirts and crossed the room, Ian was so distracted by the hypnotizing sway of her bustle that he was slow to process her words.

He scrambled to block her path. "You don't need to do anything. I'll take care of it." Like he always did.

"Don't be daft. We both know it will be hours before Jared wakes, and I can't sit here." She deftly dodged around his larger frame and headed toward the back of the room, where a small shade concealed the dumbwaiter.

Horror washed over him, along with a chilling sense of déjà vu. "Don't try it."

"That's what you said last time I dared you to beat me down to the kitchen." She lifted up the shade with a devious grin. "How old were we?"

He'd been twelve; she ten. "It was a foolish idea then. It's a mad one now. The draw rope will snap and—" He couldn't threaten that she'd plummet to her death out loud because his superstitious constitution would not allow him to speak the words he dreaded coming true.

"Nonsense. Do you know how much a silver service weighs?"

With characteristic grace, she tucked herself into the dumbwaiter.

And then, in a diabolically sweet voice, she asked, "Are you coming after me or not?"

Thank you for reading this preview of *Runaway Rogue!* To find out what happens, get your copy at your favorite bookseller, or check out my website for a list of retailers: **www.lillemoore.com .**

www.ingramcontent.com/pod-product-compliance
Lightning Source LLC
Chambersburg PA
CBHW010608310726
48969CB00010B/2618